Praise for earlier Cra
myst(

"A fun read with humour throug
Crime Thriller Hound

"An excellent novel, full of twists and turns, plenty of action scenes, crackling dialogue - and a great sense of fun."
Fully Booked 2016

"A highly enjoyable and well-crafted read, with a host of engaging characters."
Mrs Peabody Investigates

"An amiable romp through the shady back streets of 1960s Brighton."
Simon Brett

"A highly entertaining, involving mystery, narrated in a charming voice, with winning characters. Highly recommended."
In Search of the Classic Mystery Novel

"A romp of a read! Very funny and very British."
The Book Trail

"Superbly crafted and breezy as a stroll along the pier, this Brighton-based murder mystery is a delight."
Peter Lovesey

"It read like a breath of fresh air and I can't wait for the next one."
Little Bookness Lane

"By the end of page one, I knew I liked Colin Crampton and

author Peter Bartram's breezy writing style."
Over My Dead Body

"A little reminiscent of [Raymond] Chandler."
Bookwitch

"A rather fun and well-written cozy mystery set in 1960s Brighton."
Northern Crime

"The story is a real whodunit in the classic mould."
M J Trow

"A fast-paced mystery, superbly plotted, and kept me guessing right until the end."
Don't Tell Me the Moon Is Shining

"Very highly recommended."
Midwest Book Review

"One night I stayed up until nearly 2.00am thinking 'I'll just read one more chapter'. This is a huge recommendation from me."
Life of a Nerdish Mum

The Tango School Mystery
A Crampton of the Chronicle adventure

The Tango School Mystery

A Crampton of the Chronicle adventure

Peter Bartram

Deadline Murder Series Book 1

THE BARTRAM PARTNERSHIP

First published by The Bartram Partnership, 2018

ISBN: 9781980567158

For contact details see website:
www.colincrampton.com
www.peterbartram.co.uk

Text copyright: Peter Bartram 2018
Cover copyright: Barney Skinner 2018

All characters and events in this book, other than those clearly in the public domain, are entirely fictitious and any resemblance to any persons living or dead is purely coincidental.

All rights reserved. Except for brief quotations in critical articles or reviews, no part of this book may be reproduced in any manner without prior written permission from the publishers.
The rights of Peter Bartram as author have been asserted in accordance with the Copyright, Designs and Patents Act 1988.

Book layout and cover design: Barney Skinner

Also by Peter Bartram

Crampton of the Chronicle Mystery novels
Headline Murder
Stop Press Murder
Front Page Murder

Deadline Murder Series novels
The Tango School Mystery
The Mother's Day Mystery

Novella
Murder in Capital Letters

Morning, Noon & Night Trilogy
Murder in the Morning Edition
Murder in the Afternoon Extra
Murder in the Night Final
The Morning, Noon and Night Omnibus Edition
(All four Morning, Noon & Night books are also available as audiobooks)

Short stories
Murder from the Newsdesk

Chapter 1

My Australian girlfriend Shirley looked at her porterhouse steak and said: "That's a real beaut, Colin."

The lump of meat which overlapped Shirl's huge dinner plate was the same shape as South America - broad at the top, narrowing down to a tip. It was cooked so rare I half expected to see the thing twitch. It had a kind of fierce red which made it look as though it had been out in the sun too long rather than under a grill.

A rivulet of blood oozed from one side - roughly where Sao Paulo would be - and merged with a slice of grilled tomato. As though the steak had been served with a blood clot on the side.

I said: "Don't you Aussies believe in cooking your food?"

Shirley seized her knife and fork and made an incision in the steak close to Venezuela. "If I were back in Adelaide, I'd have slapped this on the barbie so quick it would barely have had time to brown its bum." She forked a lump of the meat into her mouth and chewed contentedly.

We were sitting at a corner table in Antoine's Sussex Grill in Brighton's Ship Street. The place had oak-panelled walls, a green carpet, and dusty chandeliers. It was like being in a baronial hall on the baron's night off. In this case, on everyone's night off. Shirl and I were the only diners.

But that suited me just fine after the day I'd had in the *Evening Chronicle*'s newsroom. Twenty minutes before the afternoon edition deadline, the Press Association ticker spewed out the news that the Prime Minister, Sir Alec Douglas-Home, had announced that the long-awaited 1964 general election would take place on the fifteenth of October. That meant a tasty little front-page splash I'd conjured up about a jewel heist in Lewes got bounced to an inside page.

And with politics dominating the news, my byline - Colin

Crampton, crime correspondent - wasn't going to appear on the front page much before polling day in just over three weeks' time.

Not that I'd have much time for proper journalism. Not with the special assignment my news editor Frank Figgis had handed me. But I wasn't going to trouble Shirley about that.

Not just yet.

Shirl wiped a dribble of blood from her chin with a napkin. She cut a slice off Ecuador and stuffed it into her mouth. She pointed at my own plate and said: "What's that? It looks like bits of a dead rat."

I said: "It's jugged hare."

"I'd rather eat a juicy steak than a mouthful of hair."

"It's not hair with an A I R. It's hare with an A R E," I said. "You must have heard the story about the creature that got beaten by the tortoise."

"Guess the bludger should have spent less time snoozing by the road. Then he wouldn't have ended up in the pot with all those vegetables."

I reached for the bottle of Burgundy we'd ordered and refilled our glasses.

Shirley hoisted her glass and had a generous slurp.

"Still, this is ace tucker. I'll hand you that," she said.

I cut some of the hare's tender stewed flesh from a leg bone.

"It should be," I said. "This place is owned by a bloke who used to be head waiter at the Ritz hotel in London before the war. Made a name for himself by cooking crêpe Suzette at the table for Winston Churchill."

Shirl made a long cut in her steak somewhere near the Atacama Desert.

"I bet the old boy's never eaten here, though," she said.

"Not likely to now. He's retiring from Parliament at this election. But he may have eaten near here when he was a kid."

"How come?" Shirley asked.

"He was at a school in Hove for two years. Sent there by his mum and dad after they'd discovered he'd been savagely beaten by a sadistic headmaster at his previous school. Never happened to him here, though. The Hove school was run by two maiden ladies - they were sisters. I think someone told me their name was Thompson. According to the stories, Winston loved it here. I suppose anywhere would seem good after your bum had been whipped until the blood ran down your thighs. Anyway, he later went on to Harrow, the posh public school, so I guess the Misses Thompson must have done him some good."

"Guess so," Shirley said.

"Anyway, speaking of blood, I don't remember seeing that blob before." I pointed at Shirley's steak. A little red lake had formed in the Amazonian rain forest.

Shirl brushed it to one side with her knife. "Probably released from inside as the meat cools," she said.

Plop.

A fresh drop of blood landed in the Argentinian Pampas.

"But that wasn't," I said.

"Jeez," Shirley said. "I've never seen that before."

We looked at each other for a couple of seconds. Together, our necks swivelled back. Our gaze travelled up to the ceiling.

A round crimson patch, like a carnation in bloom, flowered on the plaster. Our eyes widened and our jaws dropped. We watched blood ooze through the ceiling. It formed into the shape of a teardrop. For a moment it swayed gently from side to side. Then it detached itself, slowly as though reluctant to leave its resting place.

It fell like a solitary raindrop. A scarlet raindrop.

Plop.

It landed on the tablecloth and splattered like a gunshot wound.

"Antoine's not going to be thrilled by the laundry bill," Shirl said.

I switched my attention back to her. "It may be a laundry bill down here, but what's the damage upstairs?"

Shirley dropped her knife and her hand flew to her mouth. "I must be as dumb as a box of rocks. What's up there?"

"It's an apartment over the restaurant. Nothing to do with Antoine. I don't know who lives there."

"And I guess he hasn't just dropped a raw steak on the floor. Not for that amount of blood."

"No. I'm going up there to find out what's happened."

I pushed my chair back from the table and stood up.

I looked at Shirley. Her eyes had glazed with concern.

"What a way to end the day," she said. "It couldn't be worse."

"Not worse?" I said. "I'm not so sure. Not after what happened earlier today at the *Chronicle*."

Chapter 2

The worst thing had happened that morning.

I was sitting at my desk in the newsroom at the *Evening Chronicle*. I was eating a bacon sandwich and a blob of brown sauce had dripped on my tie. My wardrobe held seven ties with brown sauce stains and I was pondering whether it might prove cheaper to buy a tie with a brown blob pattern. Or give up bacon sandwiches with HP sauce.

My telephone rang. I lifted the receiver.

A voice like compressed air escaping from a busted piston said: "I need to see you now."

Frank Figgis sounded unusually tense.

I said: "This need to see me - is it merely a whim or part of a deep-seated addiction?"

"I'm in no mood for your cracks."

The line went dead. I put down the telephone, stood up, and headed for Figgis's office.

I opened his door without knocking and barged in. Figgis was sitting behind his desk fumbling with the silver wrapping paper on a tube of Trebor extra strong mints.

I said: "You do know you can't smoke those?"

He looked up with defeated eyes. "Unless I can get this paper off, I won't even be able to eat them."

"Give them here," I said.

He handed over the tube. I inserted a fingernail under the paper and ripped it away. A couple of the mints tumbled onto Figgis's blotter. He picked them up, popped them in his mouth, and sucked like his life depended on it. His cheeks moved in and out like a set of bellows.

He said: "Keep the rest of the packet. I've got plenty more."

I shoved it into my jacket pocket, pulled up the guest chair, and sat down.

"What happened to the Woodbines?" I asked.
"Apparently, I've given up smoking."
"Who says?"
"Mrs Figgis. And my doctor. They said I was wheezing."
"Were you?"
"Only when I breathed."
"So the condition was well under control."
"I thought so, but Mrs Figgis has still hidden my ciggies."
"I hope you haven't asked me in here because you want me to find them," I said.

Figgis's teeth crunched on one of the mints. "It's worse than that," he said. "It's the worst thing since I joined the paper. Do you know when that was?"

"Thirty years ago, wasn't it? You told me you joined just before the Trunk Murders up at Brighton Station. That was in 1934."

"And do you know how many editors I've served under in that time?"

"Let me see. There was old Charlie Unsworth when you joined. But he died in a bombing raid in the war. Then there was Victor Granger, but he slipped down the stairs to the print room and broke his neck. And, finally, Gerald Pope - His Holiness to you and me - pitched up around eight years ago."

"Do you know how many of them have asked me for personal favours?"

I said: "What is this? *Twenty Questions?*"

Figgis's lips twisted into a moue of annoyance. He reached for a paper on the top of his in-tray. Removed his hand like the paper was infected with smallpox.

He said: "His Holiness has a problem."

"Just the one? Life must be looking up for him."

"This is a big problem. Big with a capital B. And he's dumped it on me."

I shifted in my chair. Sat up a bit straighter. I didn't like the sound of this. If Pope had a problem and landed it on Figgis, there could be only one reason why I was now sitting in his office.

I said: "Has the problem got anything to do with that sheet of paper in your in-tray? The one you're treating like a leper's bandage."

I craned my neck to get a better look. The paper was packed with tight typing. It was too far on Figgis's side of the desk for me to read.

Figgis glanced at the paper again. "Everything," he said. "Did you know that His Holiness has a brother? Gervase."

"A name like that is a problem," I said.

"If only. The real problem is that he's vanished."

"Like a magician's bunny rabbit in a top hat?"

"I might have known you'd treat this as a joke."

"As it's about vanishing, I'd prefer to treat it as an example. For Pope himself. Besides, what's this got to do with me? The Salvation Army deals with missing persons."

The wrinkles on Figgis's forehead scrunched up like an old sponge being squeezed. He took another packet of mints out of his desk drawer and began to fumble them open.

He said: "It's why Gervase has vanished that makes it so bad. His Holiness thinks his brother is planning to kill someone."

My body jolted like I'd just been touched up with the business end of a cattle prod.

I said: "Now that has to be a joke. A bad joke."

Figgis shook his head. Popped another mint into his mouth and sucked. "Afraid not. Pope is deadly serious."

"No pun intended, I suppose."

Figgis's lips twisted into a rueful grimace.

I said: "Is Gervase planning to kill anyone at random or has he got someone special in mind?"

"That's where we come to the difficult bit," Figgis said.

My eyebrows lifted at that - like they'd just been launched in a rocket from Cape Canaveral.

I said: "I thought we'd already had the difficult bit. There's something worse?"

"Yes. It's who he's planning to kill that's the really difficult bit. Or should that be whom?"

I said: "I don't suppose it will matter to the bloke by the time he's lying in his coffin."

Figgis shuffled in his seat. Harrumphed a couple of times. Looked out the window and back at me.

"According to Pope, Gervase's intended victim is Sir Oscar Maundsley," Figgis said.

"Not the old fascist leader from the nineteen-thirties? 'Hurrah for Hitler' and all that. The one that was interned by Churchill at the start of the Second World War. I thought he was dead."

"No, not dead. Only shortly about to be if Gervase gets his way."

"So if Maundsley's not dead, where is he?" I asked.

"After the war, Maundsley realised he wasn't welcome in Britain any more, and shipped himself off to Spain," Figgis said. "Plenty of old fascist mates over there to keep him company. Not least the Generalissimo himself."

"You mean Franco?"

"Yes, Franco had been a big help to Hitler during the war so Maundsley probably felt at home over there. And Franco was easily seduced by Maundsley's upper-crust charm. He even loaned him a villa outside Marbella. Maundsley has lived there since the nineteen-forties."

"But no longer?" I asked.

"Apparently, Maundsley came back to Britain earlier in the summer. According to Pope, Maundsley reckons enough time has passed for people to forgive his previous indiscretions. I can't see it. But then public school toffs like Maundsley - he went to Harrow School, you know - always have a high opinion of themselves."

"So supporting a man who launched a world war that killed tens of millions is an indiscretion to Maundsley, like forgetting to tip a waiter?"

"The man trades on his upper-class blarney, but underneath he's a monster," Figgis said. "In any event, the main reason he's returned to Britain is that he knows there has to be a general election soon. He always had an inflated opinion of his own right to lead. You're too young to remember all that 'man of the moment' nonsense. He thought he should have been in charge during the war instead of Churchill. He wanted to negotiate a peace settlement with Hitler. Never got the chance, of course, but there were plenty in the upper reaches of the establishment who would've backed him. Now he's planning one last attempt at getting into parliament. He's set up a new political group. They call themselves the British Patriot Party. He's going to be a candidate in the election when it comes."

"Where?"

"Here. In Brighton."

"So an old fascist is going to scratch together a handful of votes. Why's that got Gervase all riled?"

Figgis reached for the paper in the in-tray. Picked it up between thumb and forefinger. Beetled his brow as he focused on the words.

"That's where this comes in," he said. "Pope gave it to me. It summarises the relationship between Gervase and Maundsley. It seems Gervase was a strong supporter of Maundsley in the 'thirties. But he kept himself out of the spotlight. He avoided the rallies in the Albert Hall and the punch-ups with communists during marches in London's east end. So when war came, and the leading fascists were rounded up for internment, Gervase slipped through the net.

"At least, he thought he had. But Maundsley hadn't. He was fuming somewhere inside Pentonville prison scheming for a way out. Then a supporter handed him a cache of letters Gervase had written to a fascist friend years earlier. Apparently, they contained indiscretions about a number of people. Anyway, the long and short of it was that Maundsley swapped the letters for a lighter spell inside."

"He grassed up his supporters?" I said.

"Some of them," Figgis said. "The powers that be decided that because he'd helped to lock up others, he didn't represent such a serious threat to the realm. They let him out. But, on the evidence in the letters, they put Gervase inside. And he stayed there until after Hitler had shot himself in his bunker. According to Pope, Gervase has hated Maundsley with a passion ever since."

"And I assume it's Maundsley's decision to fight a Brighton seat at the election that has pushed Gervase over the edge?"

"Correct," Figgis said. He swallowed the last of his mint.

I leaned back in my chair. Studied my fingernails. Tried to feign insouciance. Never my strong suit.

"I can't see how all this affects me," I said.

"It's simple," Figgis said. "Pope wants you to use your legendary powers as an investigative journalist to find Gervase before he croaks Maundsley."

Chapter 3

In Antoine's Sussex Grill, Shirley slammed down her knife and fork.

She'd lost interest in the South American-shaped steak. The blood-stained remnants lay on her plate. The steak's T-bone stuck up like the Andes.

Another droplet of blood formed on the ceiling. It shone like a ruby.

I glanced up at it and sighed in a resigned sort of way. I knew I wasn't going to enjoy what I had to do next.

"I'm going upstairs," I said.

"How?" Shirley asked.

"There's a separate front door to the apartment in the street."

"I'm coming with you."

"No, it's best you wait here. If we both rush out Antoine will think we're doing a runner to avoid paying the bill."

Shirley grinned. "Would be great exercise, cobber."

"Not now. There are more important things to deal with."

I crossed the room and stepped into the street. Across the road, a couple of drunks lurched out of The Smugglers. A young woman with blonde hair in a beehive, tight skirt and killer stilettos, staggered by. A taxi cruised down the street looking for a fare. The driver eyed me briefly then focused on the blonde.

I stared up at the first-floor apartment window. The light was on and the curtains - tired brown numbers that hung like a beggar's rags - were half drawn. They let out a shard of light.

The front door to the apartment was at the end of the building. It was recessed into the wall in a kind of porch arrangement. I stepped into the porch and rapped firmly on the door.

Twice.

On the second rap, the door moved. It hadn't been shut

properly.

I pushed gently and it swung open. Its hinges creaked like a pensioner's kneecaps. I stepped into a small hallway which led to a flight of stairs.

The place was lit by a dusty bulb hanging from a short flex cable. The walls were covered with embossed wallpaper painted a muddy cream. A picture of a yacht sailing in a stormy sea had slipped sideways in its frame. An umbrella was propped in the corner. There was a threadbare grey carpet on the stairs. The hallway had the fusty smell that comes from wet clothes drying in front of gas fires.

I moved to the foot of the stairs wondering whether this had been a good idea.

I shouted up: "Hello! Is anyone at home? I've just come round to see if you're all right."

Somewhere in the house something creaked. But that would be the result of the cooler air flooding in after I'd opened the front door. Natural in an old building like this.

At least, that's what I told myself.

I shouted again. "Nothing to worry about. I'll just come up to make sure you're all right."

I listened. Something else creaked.

Softly.

But twice.

I shouted: "I'll come up now unless you say not to."

Nobody shouted: "Clear off and leave me alone."

But then a dead body wouldn't.

Nor would an intruder. Especially one whose soft-shoe shuffle made the old floorboards creak twice.

I looked over my shoulder at the door. Wondered whether I should leave quietly and shut it behind me. Call the cops. Let them take the glory. Or a bullet in the forehead.

The safety-first option.

But safety-first leaves you standing on the outside. Forever wondering what it must be like to be the guy who gets the action. Never the guy who wins the medal. Or, in my case, lands the front-page story. Safety-first leaves you growing old wondering what life could have been like.

Besides, what would I tell Shirley if I scurried back with nothing to show for my original bravado? And, anyway, I knew I had to find out who was upstairs.

Or what was upstairs.

I slunk up the stairs with all the enthusiasm of a Tommy going over the top at the Battle of the Somme.

The stairs led into a landing with three doors. Two of them - one in front of me, one to the left - were closed. The door to the right was open. A light was on inside.

I stood in the landing and listened for a sound. Any sound.

Like a moan. Or a whispered plea for help. Or a rasp of breath from an intruder.

But I only heard silence.

And then a creak. Not once or twice this time. Three times. And it came from behind the closed door to the left.

I stepped silently over and put my ear to the door. Like a nosey-parker listening in on the neighbours.

The floorboards creaked again. But softly. As though they didn't mean to.

I took hold of the door knob and turned it. I pushed the door gently. Nobody pushed back.

So I flung open the door and stood back.

A tabby cat shot out of the room with a piercing screech. It raced across the landing and stopped at the entrance to the lighted room. It turned round and stared at me. Bared its teeth and snarled. The moggie equivalent of: "Don't try anything if you know what's good for you".

I bared my teeth back, but its eyes radiated withering contempt. Besides, I was in no mood for a staring competition with a cat.

I stepped into the darkened room where the little beast had been imprisoned and switched on the light. It was a bedroom. There was an iron bedstead with bedclothes in the kind of tangle that comes from restless sleep rather than passionate love making. (Believe me, there are ways to tell.) There was a dressing table with a hair brush, a couple of combs and a half-used jar of Brylcreem. Across the room, the door of a wardrobe hung half open. I walked over and looked inside. The wardrobe held a couple of shabby jackets, a pair of grey flannel trousers, three shirts with crumpled collars, and a cardigan with frayed sleeves.

Evidently, Beau Brummell didn't live here.

There was a bedside table. A glass of water, a bottle of pills, and a book rested on it. I moved across the room and looked at the book. It was called *Hitler's Permanent Wave: How the Führer Escaped Berlin and Began a New Life as a Ladies' Hairdresser in South America*.

Its three hundred pages of nonsense had been penned by someone called Titus Scrivener. I flipped open the cover to see whether the inside flap held any further information on Scrivener. Instead I found an inscription on the title page: *To Derek Clapham - time for the truth - best wishes, Titus.*

So, presumably, this was Clapham's apartment.

He'd used an old letter as a bookmark. I opened the book at the page and studied the letter. It was from his bank. Dated five days earlier. The bank manager would like Mr Clapham to call and discuss his overdraft which now stood at two hundred and thirty-two pounds, three shillings and four pence ha'penny. At the foot of the letter Clapham had scribbled a note: "Have asked UBH for £200 loan."

I replaced the letter and put the book back on the bedside table.

But I'd forgotten why I was flipping through Clapham's bedtime reading. Downstairs in the restaurant, there had been blood on the ceiling.

Up here, in the apartment, there should be a corresponding pool of blood on the floor. I'd been too diverted by a creaking floorboard and a cat to focus on the main purpose of my mission.

If the blood had been leaking on to our table below, which room of the apartment would it be in?

I glanced out of the window into the street to help me get my bearings. The Smugglers was slightly to my left. When we were sitting in the restaurant, Shirley and I had been exactly opposite the pub.

So that must mean the blood was in the lighted room. The room that had been to my right when I'd come up the stairs.

I hurried out of the bedroom, thoughtfully turning off the light after me.

I crossed the landing and entered what was obviously a sitting room. In the middle of the room, there was an ancient settee upholstered in brown leather. The leather had long ago faded and started to crack. A small Indian rug covered the bare floorboards in front of the settee. There was an easy chair piled high with an eclectic collection of old newspapers and magazines. I spotted the *Daily Telegraph*, the *New York Herald-Tribune* (European edition), the *Spectator*, the *New Daily*, *Paris Match* and *La Stampa*.

On the far wall, a glass cabinet held a half-empty bottle of scotch and a few glasses. I resisted the temptation to help myself.

To my left, another door was ajar. By the half-light from the sitting room, I could see a sink piled with dirty crocks and the edge of a cooker. My brilliant deductive powers were on top of that straight away: the kitchen.

But the kitchen was at the back of the building. And Shirley and I had been sitting at the front. So any blood must be in the sitting room, where I was standing.

I looked around the room. Couldn't see any blood on the floor.

Then the cat stepped out from behind the settee. It looked a lot less cocky than when we'd eyeballed one another on the landing. It slunk across the room leaving a trail of red paw-prints on bare boards.

I took a deep breath and crossed the room. I looked behind the settee knowing I wasn't going to like what I would find.

A man's body was lying there. He was middle-aged, had thinning brown hair, and was dressed in a pair of blue slacks and a grey pullover.

His throat had been cut so deeply I could see neck bone showing. It was as though his neck had opened in a scream. Death must have been quick but not instant, because a pool of blood had flowed from his wound. The floor wasn't level - common in older buildings in central Brighton - and blood had drained into a crack between the floorboards. That would've been how it formed the stain on the ceiling below.

My heart pounded hard. A troupe of acrobats turned somersaults in my stomach. The jugged hare churned like it was still alive and eager to compete in the Waterloo Cup.

I belched and tasted the rich flavour of the hare's sauce. It wasn't as tasty coming up as it had been going down.

I reached for the edge of the settee to steady myself. Closed my eyes and took a couple of deep breaths. Felt a little better.

Knew that my next step must be to call the cops.

Then a crash like a dozen tin cans rattling in a bin shattered the silence in the kitchen. Something metal and heavy landed on the floor making a racket like scrap metal falling off the back of a lorry.

And then glass smashed like a window had just been punched out.

I swerved around the edge of the settee and dashed towards the kitchen.

But the moggie had been scared witless by the racket. It fled across the room. In front of me. I tripped over the animal and took off like the first man trying to fly without wings. I landed full on my front, like I'd been dumped without a 'chute twenty thousand feet from an aeroplane.

I crashed onto the floor and felt the wind rush out of me.

The moggie hissed and disappeared under the drift of newspapers in the easy chair.

I lay there feeling more foolish than injured while I gasped for air to re-inflate my lungs. Then I pushed myself onto my hands and knees. I stood up and made my way gingerly towards the kitchen keeping an eye out for stray cats.

The floor of the kitchen was littered with half a dozen pots and pans. They'd been pushed hastily from a draining board. The window behind the board was smashed so all the glass had gone. Outside the window, there was a metal fire escape leading down to an alleyway which ran behind the buildings. I climbed onto the board, avoiding shards of broken glass, and peered out of the window.

There was no-one on the fire escape. The alley wasn't lit, but towards the far end I could make out the shape of a man. He was moving at the determined pace of someone who knew that his night's work was done.

And that he was going to get away.

Chapter 4

Detective Inspector Ted Wilson took a sip from his cup.

He said: "That coffee tastes better than anything we get back at the station."

I said: "That's because there's a double shot of five-star French cognac in it. This is the first time ever I've seen you smiling on a murder enquiry."

Shirley, Ted and I were sitting round a table in Antoine's restaurant. Not the one under the dripping blood stain. It was an hour after I'd witnessed the man I presumed was the killer flee the scene of the crime.

Antoine was fretting in the background with a bucket of soap suds and a long-handled mop.

I said: "You won't be able to reach the stain with that and the soap suds would only turn into red bubbles anyway. Best let it dry and then get it painted over. No-one will ever know."

Antoine muttered something in Greek using words that probably weren't in Socrates's vocabulary. Although come to think of it, he'd spent a spell in prison so he could have picked up some salty language from fellow inmates.

I said: "When you've got rid of the mop, you can bring Shirley and me another coffee with a strengthener. You'd better make Inspector Wilson's straight from the pot - or he'll be blowing up red balloons to match his nose and holding a party."

Ted cleared his throat noisily and gave his beard a busy stroke. It was his way of trying to regain his dignity. I'd ribbed him, but I had a soft spot for Ted. He was a country boy who'd made it good in the big bad town of Brighton. He'd not picked up the naughty habits of his fellow 'tecs. His clear-up rate was better than theirs. But they were the ones who flew to holidays on a Spanish costa each year - best hotel and all the trimmings, like soap in the bathroom. They paid with the kind of greasy pound notes that get passed under the counter and stuffed surreptitiously into back pockets. Meanwhile, Ted struggled to pay for a week at a guest house in Bognor.

I'd been pleased when he'd appeared on the scene, minutes after I'd called the cops. He'd spent the best part of an hour in the apartment before coming down to the restaurant.

He drained his coffee and looked at Shirley and me with happy eyes.

He said: "I've got a team upstairs going through the apartment searching for evidence. Now let's go through what you saw again."

I said: "We've already been through it twice. Blood dripped through the ceiling. I went upstairs. Found a dead body. Tripped over a cat. Watched a killer disappear down the back alley."

"Description?"

"Long and thin between two stone walls and littered with chip papers."

"The man, not the alley."

"It was dark, he was fifty yards away, had his back to me, and was wearing a heavy coat with the collar turned up."

"It's a warmish night. It might have stood out when he came out of the alley. There'll be a witness somewhere who remembers a man like that."

"Not if he took the coat off before he stepped out of the alley. You'll probably find it tossed over someone's back wall."

Ted frowned and scribbled something in his notebook.

I said: "I didn't have time to poke around in the flat."

Ted grinned. "That must have annoyed you."

I sniffed. But not so that Ted would think he'd got to me.

I said: "The main clue as far as I'm concerned is the fact there was no forced entry and the front door was still open."

Ted stroked his beard again. "Yes, I've been thinking about that. Your conclusion?"

"I'll tell you my conclusion if you tell me yours first."

"No, you go first."

"I want to hear the official view."

"You're a witness and should answer my questions."

Shirley clunked down her coffee cup and said: "Come on, boys, this sounds like those willie-waving contests I used to watch behind the bike shed when I was at school in Oz."

My eyes widened at that. "You watched willie-waving contests at school?"

Shirley grinned. "There wasn't much to watch apart from cricket. And I could never get the hang of those long legs and short third mans. Besides, you got to see the long and the short of it behind the bike shed."

I shook my head, not without a little wonder. Turned back to Ted.

"My conclusion is that whoever killed Clapham was expected," I said. "Clapham knew who he was. The poor sap let him in never knowing what would happen."

"And the fact the front door was unlocked?"

"I imagine Clapham was expecting a short visit. No point in relocking the door if he was leaving after just a few minutes."

Ted nodded. "Sounds reasonable."

"There's another point," I said.

"Which is?"

"There was no sign of a struggle in the flat. The killer took Clapham by surprise. Add that to the fact that Clapham knew him and wasn't expecting him to stay for long and my guess is that the killer called expressly to croak him."

"But why? What's the motive?"

"The clue to that must lie somewhere in that flat," I said.

"The fact the killer lingered after the killing suggests he was looking for something."

"I agree," I said. "If we knew what it was, we'd understand the motive for the killing. But I suspect he didn't find it. The killer would never have expected Clapham's blood to seep through the floorboards the way it did. He'd think he had time for a good search and then to leave quietly, closing the front door politely behind him."

"Instead, you blundered onto the scene," Ted said.

"Appeared presciently is the way I'd put it. In any event, it meant he had to make an unscheduled exit through the kitchen window."

"You might have tried to stop him."

"Would have done, if I hadn't tripped over that damned tabby. Is it still up there?"

"Probably. Seems to be hiding somewhere."

"Safest way with your finest on the scene. One thing, though, no matter where this story leads, that's the last I want to hear about cats."

Shirley said: "So what's the big secret?"

I tried to look all innocent. "What big secret?"

We'd left the Sussex Grill and were strolling along the seafront. There was a freshening breeze coming in from the south-west. A high-tide was pounding on the shingle. It set up a rumbling roar as millions of pebbles shifted with the waves. The lights from Palace Pier cast a kaleidoscope of colour onto the sea.

It was good to get some salty air into my lungs after the hot fusty fug of Clapham's apartment.

Shirley reached for my hand and squeezed it. "Before you raced upstairs to Clapham's place, you told me something had happened earlier today at the *Chronicle*. What was it?"

"I've been given a job to find a man."

Shirley shot me a sideways glance. "Like a missing person type of guy?"

"Yes."

I told Shirley about my morning meeting with Figgis. About how Figgis passed on an order from Pope to trace Gervase. And about how His Holiness was worried that Gervase was going to kill Sir Oscar Maundsley.

"You're being asked to sweep their doo-doos under the carpet," Shirley said.

"It feels like it - and that's why I think it's bad. It's not part of a reporter's job to run personal errands for his editor. Especially not this kind of errand. But now that I've been in Clapham's flat, it's not as bad as that."

"Tell Pope to shove his job where the kookaburra parks his bum."

"I'd like to, but he'd make my life a misery."

"He'd fire you?"

"It would be worse than that. He'd change my job. Suddenly, I'd discover I wasn't reporting on crime. I'd find myself covering parish councils or writing the gardening notes. No thank you."

"So leave the paper. You've often said you want to work for a national."

"One day. But not yet. There are more stories I want to cover in Brighton. Besides, there are other reasons for staying here."

I put my arm around Shirley's shoulder and she rested her head on me. We sat on a bench and looked out to sea.

"You know my modelling work needn't keep me in Brighton," Shirley said. "I could just as easily move to London."

"But you've made a name for yourself here," I said.

"True, and a lot of magazines choose Brighton for fashion shoots. So that's great for me."

We fell silent for a moment and listened to the sea. The churning shingle sound reminded me of Matthew Arnold's poem about Dover Beach: "…the grating roar, of pebbles which the waves draw back, and fling, at their return, up the high strand". Just as well he hadn't chosen Brighton beach. He'd have had to throw in the sound of kids screaming on Palace Pier's roller-coaster and drunks singing sea shanties in the Fortune of War pub on the Esplanade.

Dover Beach was no poem to think about when you needed

cheering up. Like after discovering a dead body or being given a job you didn't want. But it was a poem to bring you closer to someone you loved.

So I leant towards Shirley and kissed her. She kissed me back and for a few moments the sound of the sea didn't seem so raucous.

An old boy walking a basset hound said: "Ain't young love wonderful?"

I didn't reply. I think he was talking to the dog.

But Shirley and I turned and smiled at him.

We stood up and strolled on towards West Street.

She said: "How are you going to find this Gervase? Missing people aren't easy to track down."

"That's what I've been thinking about. The thing about missing people is that they're only missing to people who want to know where they are."

"What do you mean?"

"I mean that lots of people could know where Gervase is but don't think anything is amiss because, as far as they know, he's not missing."

"So Gervase might not be missing at all - perhaps he's just gone on holiday without telling anyone."

"Normally, I'd buy an explanation like that. But it doesn't account for Pope's belief that Gervase is going to kill Maundsley. And, from what His Holiness told Figgis, Gervase certainly has a motive."

We turned into Clarence Square where Shirley rented a garden flat. The "garden" consisted of a dead begonia in a flowerpot in the small back yard. But, in estate agent-speak, call a basement a garden flat and you add an extra thirty bob a week to the rent.

"So where are you going to start?" Shirley asked.

"I think I have to search Gervase's flat. He may have left something behind which gives a clue to where he is now."

We reached the steps leading down to Shirley's front door.

"Do you want to come in?" she said.

"Yes, but I can't. I've got to drop by the office and bat out something about Clapham's murder for tomorrow's paper before I head for my own bed."

"Good luck with that," Shirley said.

She kissed me, turned and hurried down the steps.

I trudged off towards the *Chronicle* thinking of the intro I'd write for the piece that would splash on the front page tomorrow.

I imagined the headline Figgis might put on the story:

MURDERED MAN'S NECK SLASHED BY KNIFE

The knife! The killer would have needed a fearsome blade to inflict the wound I saw. But there was no such knife in the apartment. Not one that I saw.

I wondered where it was now.

It gave me something other than Gervase to think about.

It was nearly midnight before I reached my own lodgings in Regency Square.

I had rooms on the top floor of a Victorian town house that seemed to have gone into decline about the same time as the good Queen.

Still, it suited me. Beatrice Gribble, my landlady - the Widow as she was known to her tenants, but never in her hearing - had her parlour and bedroom on the ground floor. I always tried to keep out of her way.

I inserted my key in the front door, opened it, and stepped silently into the hall. I was surprised to see a light under the Widow's parlour door. I'd expected her to be in bed by this time. One of her wise old saws was the chestnut about "early to bed, early to rise, makes a woman healthy, wealthy and wise". As far as I could see, it hadn't worked in her case.

I crept towards the stairs hoping that she'd fallen asleep in a chair and wouldn't hear me.

But before I could put my foot onto the first tread, the

parlour door swung open. The widow stood in the doorway dramatically lit by her reading lamp. She was wearing a long red silk dress slit to the thigh. The dress was cut low and her bosom was pushed together so her cleavage looked like a split in the skin on a rice pudding. The slit in the skirt revealed legs clad in fishnet stockings. The stockings were held by suspenders that had a cheeky scarlet bow fixed above the fastening button. She tottered forward in six-inch killer stilettos in two-tone black and white leather.

Her hair was waved in severe Marcel curls and held in place by a headband. The headband included a single bird's feather. Probably from some long extinct species. Like a dodo. The Widow's face had been whitened with face powder. She had blue eye shadow and carmine lipstick. When she opened her mouth it looked like a traffic light winking at me.

She had a long-stemmed rose clenched between her teeth.

I said: "You normally eat Welsh rarebit for a late supper. If you're going to scoff that rose, you'd better have your indigestion tablets handy."

The Widow grabbed the rose out of her mouth. Her lips twisted into an irritated pout.

"I wasn't eating the rose. It was for dramatic effect."

"What effect? To prove your dentures can hold a flower in place without coming loose? Why don't you give yourself a tougher test and try it with a vegetable marrow?"

The Widow crossed her arms under her bosom in an angry gesture. She didn't like anyone knowing she had false teeth. But I'd spotted an empty tin of denture cleaning powder in the dustbin one day.

She said: "Surely you can see what I'm dressed for."

"A French knocking shop?"

"Mr Crampton, kindly moderate your language in my house. Remember that the photo of my late husband Hector resides on my mantelpiece. What would he say to such a suggestion?"

I'd seen the photo. It showed a bald-headed bloke with the beaten expression of someone who knows he will always be on the wrong end of unreasonable demands.

"I'd say that if he'd seen you dressed like that his spirits wouldn't have been the only thing perking up."

"If you must know, I've decided that enough time has now passed since Hector passed on…"

The Widow made it sound as though the old boy had just slipped next door.

"Enough time has elapsed, Mr Crampton, for me to find another husband. So I've joined a tango class. It's a way to meet the right type of gentleman."

"And where do these right types hang out?"

"I have already met several refined gentlemen at the Dolores Esteban Tango Academy in Kemp Town. In fact, this evening I had the privilege of dancing with Miss Esteban's partner Conrad Montez. He is an Argentinian gentleman and he complimented me on my chassé."

"Are you sure it was a compliment? I thought it was buses and railway carriages that had chassis."

The Widow stamped her foot so hard a button pinged off her suspender and one of her stockings fell down.

"Really, Mr Crampton, that is a disgraceful remark. Besides, I can't let you see my bare leg. It could give you the wrong idea."

She stomped back into her parlour and slammed the door.

I'd had a basinful of wrong ideas during the day so I didn't see that one more would make much difference.

I climbed the steps to my room suspecting I hadn't heard the last of the Widow's encounters with the tango.

Chapter 5

There's nothing like a good night's sleep for clearing the mind.

I only wished I'd had one. But the Widow had been playing her tango music on the gramophone until the early hours. I'd been kept awake by the whine of soulful violins and the incessant beat of the four-four time.

So by the time I reached the *Chronicle* newsroom the following morning, I still wasn't any clearer in my mind about how I was going to find Gervase. And now I had an important running story - the Clapham murder - to cover.

I sat down in my old captain's chair and looked around. The newsroom was ramping up for the first deadline of the day. Phil Bailey rolled copy paper into his typewriter and pounded the keys like he wanted them to die. Sally Martin whispered seductively into the telephone. She was teasing indiscretions out of some poor sap of an interviewee. When he saw his quotes in the paper he'd vow never to speak to a journalist again. But he would. Susan Wheatcroft hurried in from the tea room carrying a plate with two giant buns and a mug of coffee. She gave me one of her saucy winks as she sashayed across the room to her desk.

I'd already filed copy on the Clapham story the previous evening, but I needed to check whether there'd been any developments overnight. So I lifted my telephone and dialled a number at Brighton police station.

Ted Wilson's rustic voice answered the phone.

I said: "I suppose it's too much to hope that you've made an arrest."

He said: "It's too much to hope that we even know who to collar. But if you quote me on that, I'll find a way to throw you in the cell with the rats and cockroaches."

I ignored Ted's empty threat and said: "Anything interesting from the search of Clapham's flat?"

Ted paused. Then said stiffly: "It's too early to say."

"It usually is," I said.

Ted would have seen Clapham's Hitler book and drawn his own conclusions.

I replaced the receiver. A frustrating call, but at least there was no new information to add to the story I'd already written.

Which meant I could turn my attention to the hunt for Gervase.

I stood up and headed for the *Chronicle's* morgue, where the press cuttings were filed.

When I walked into the morgue, Henrietta Houndstooth was sitting at her desk.

She had a sheaf of press clippings in front of her and was sorting them into three piles.

Henrietta ran the morgue with the aid of three women known around the paper as the Clipping Cousins. They weren't blood related, but they shared a love of gossip and cream cakes. But the table in the centre of the room where they sat clipping newspapers was empty.

I walked up to Henrietta and asked: "Where are the Cousins?"

Henrietta looked up from the cuttings piles and said: "Mabel is being fitted with a new surgical stocking, Elsie has a day off - she's taking her niece and nephew to Chessington Zoo - and Freda is at the dentist. She dislodged her crown yesterday while eating a toffee."

I said: "Perhaps it's just as well they're not here. I've got a confidential enquiry which I'd like you to keep to yourself."

Henrietta brushed a stray strand of auburn hair away from her eyes and grinned. That grin always transformed Henrietta's middle-aged schoolmarm look. Instead, she looked more like an impish schoolgirl about to ping an ink pellet from the end of her ruler. At least, she would if you overlooked her tweed skirt, the delicate embroidery on her cream blouse, and her sturdy brown walking shoes.

"They don't call me Old Button Lips for nothing," she said.

Henrietta had been on the paper for years and knew where the bodies were hidden. But she had a reputation for discretion.

I said: "You'll need zip-fastened lips for this one. I need to know whether we've got a clippings file on one Gervase Pope."

Henrietta's eyes widened but only a little. Anyone who didn't know her as well as I did would have missed it.

She said: "Do you mean our esteemed editor's brother?"

"You know about him, then?"

"Yes. Despite the fact His Holiness would rather I didn't. In fact, when he was appointed editor he went to great lengths to try and prevent me finding out."

This was new. When Figgis had briefed me the previous day, there'd been nothing about Pope keeping information about his brother under wraps.

I pulled up Henrietta's guest chair and sat down.

I said: "Tell me more."

Henrietta pushed the piles of cuttings to one side and leaned back in her chair.

"I expect you know that Pope was made editor eight years ago," she said.

I nodded. "Long before I joined the paper."

"He'd been a surprise choice for the job. There'd been some talk of Frank Figgis being promoted, but Pope's appointment came out of nowhere. He'd had little experience of newspapers and nobody thought he'd been given the job on merit."

"But he knew the right people?" I said.

"Yes, the rumour was that his father had known our proprietor's father. And the proprietor's father owed Pope's father a favour."

"You scratch my back, and I'll tickle your tummy."

"Or something like that. Anyway, I was intrigued, as you can imagine. As soon as I heard about the appointment, I went into the filing stacks to see whether we had any clippings on this Gerald Pope who was now going to be our boss."

"And did you?"

"No. But we did have one clipping about a Gervase Pope. It wasn't clear immediately from the clipping whether Gervase was Gerald's brother, but there were clues to follow up. The clipping mentioned that Gervase had lived at a manor house near Mayfield, up in the Sussex Weald. I contacted an old friend of mine who worked at County Hall in Lewes. I asked her to check old electoral registers for Mayfield."

"And discovered that Gerald was Gervase's brother."

"Yes."

"So what was in the file?"

"It was a news report of an appeal committee hearing in 1942. The committee was considering an appeal from Gervase Pope against his internment under Defence Regulation 18B."

"That's the regulation the government used during the Second World War to intern people they thought might pose a threat to the security of the country," I said. "About a thousand fascists and suspected fifth columnists were detained."

"That's right. They were mostly prominent Britons who'd campaigned with the fascists in the nineteen-thirties. The cutting revealed that Gervase had been one of them."

"But this committee took place in 1942, three years after the war started. Why wasn't Gervase interned at the start, like many of the other fascists?"

"The appeal committee hearing threw some interesting light on that. The assessors heard that during the 'thirties Gervase had written some letters to a fascist friend. The letters made it clear that Gervase was a zealot - a true believer. He yearned to do more than march through the streets and wave banners. He wanted to attack those people he thought were the enemies of fascism. In one of the letters, he set out plans to assassinate leading anti-fascist politicians. The plans were pure pie-in-the-sky stuff, but nobody was prepared to excuse that in 1942. The very survival of the country was under threat. The committee had no qualms about turning down his appeal."

"And these letters had only just been discovered?" I asked.

"In unusual circumstances, too. It seems that Sir Oscar Maundsley, the fascist leader in the 'thirties, who'd been interned in 1940, had used them as part of his appeal for release. They persuaded the authorities that he was prepared to co-operate in naming people who posed a genuine threat. And they released Maundsley under tight conditions. He had to report to a police station every day."

"If Maundsley had the Gervase letters, why did he wait two years before using them to spring himself from jail? Why not use them when he was first detained?"

"That's the point," Henrietta said. "Maundsley had only been handed the letters a few weeks earlier. They were the letters Gervase had written to a fascist fellow traveller called Derek Clapham."

It was one of those moments when my hair literally did stand on end. It was a weird experience. Like being entombed in a fur coat.

Henrietta gave me a worried look. "You know Derek Clapham?" she asked.

"Let's just say we met last night in unfortunate circumstances."

I told Henrietta about Clapham's murder and its aftermath.

My mind was racing like a Formula One car. When Figgis had briefed me the day before, he'd mentioned Gervase blamed Maundsley for his internment. He'd said Maundsley had used Gervase's own letters to shop him to the authorities. But he hadn't said the letters had been provided by Clapham. Perhaps he didn't know. But the news certainly put the hunt for Gervase in a new light.

I said: "Why should Clapham give Maundsley letters which he must've known would land his old friend Gervase in trouble?"

"From what I hear Clapham was one of those dreamers always thinking up new schemes but always short of the readies. He hoped for a hand-out from Maundsley. Do you think Gervase could have killed Clapham?"

I shook my head. "I don't know. He would have known about Clapham's role in his downfall from the moment the police had detained him back in 1942. He's had years since the war to track down Clapham and do him harm if he wanted to. Why wait until now?"

Besides, I thought to myself, according to Figgis, Pope had said he thought Gervase was planning to kill Maundsley, not Clapham.

I said: "Do you still have the original cutting about the tribunal hearing?"

Henrietta pulled a rueful smile. "No."

"Where is it?"

"Gone."

"Gone where?"

"I don't know. It vanished two days after Gerald Pope became editor of the paper."

"And you think he took it?"

"Who else?" Henrietta said. "I can't imagine there was anybody else who would suspect it might be there. Certainly nobody else on the paper who'd have access to the morgue and the opportunity to take it."

"Presumably Pope took it because if anyone discovered it, he'd be embarrassed."

"I reckon that must be the case."

"Was His Holiness a secret supporter of the fascists in the nineteen-thirties?"

"I don't know," Henrietta said. "Do political opinions run in families?"

I didn't answer that. Instead I said: "I suppose if the cutting had been discovered, questions would have been asked. Even if

Gerald Pope had been a war hero with a Victoria Cross, there's still the odium of guilt by association. Perhaps Pope would have been asked to resign. Still, he must be confident that won't happen as the cutting has been destroyed."

"The original cutting has been," Henrietta said. "But the day Pope joined, I took a copy of it."

"You thought he might be after it?"

"It did occur to me. Let's just say I was being cautious."

"Where is it now?"

"Locked in my private drawer. Want to see it?"

"Does the roué want to glimpse the showgirl's garter?"

Henrietta produced a handbag from underneath her desk, reached inside it, and pulled out a bunch of keys. She unlocked the bottom drawer of her desk, pulled it open, and rummaged among a stack of files.

She pulled out a slim buff folder, blew some dust off the top, and handed it to me.

Inside was a single sheet of paper - the copied cutting. I read through it. It was a short report that had appeared in the *Chronicle* in October 1942. In no more than one hundred and fifty words it told me nothing that Henrietta hadn't already mentioned.

I handed the cutting back to her. "You better keep this safe. There could come a time when it will be important."

"To Gervase?" Henrietta asked.

"No. To you and me."

Chapter 6

I stepped out of the morgue feeling a bit like one of those poor blokes being stretched on the rack in mediaeval times.

I was being pulled in two opposite directions. Looking one way, my mission from Pope was to find Gervase before he could harm Maundsley. Looking the other way, it was my duty as an upright citizen - well, a not-far-off vertical citizen - to report suspicion of crime to the police. If I believed Gervase wielded the knife that slashed Clapham's throat I should speak up.

But the question was: did I believe it?

At the moment, I could feel my mind being stretched like someone was making a twisty cat's cradle inside my head. This needed a bit of thinking about.

And the newsroom was the wrong place to do it. Not least, because if I sat at my desk, Figgis would find some reason to question me about my progress.

So instead, I slipped down the *Chronicle's* backstairs into the machine room. The mighty rotary presses had just started to print the midday edition. Normally, I'd pause to watch the magic as a huge roll of newsprint raced through the rollers, sliced through the cutters, was clamped by the folders, and came out the other end as newspapers. But not today. I flitted past the rumbling presses and through the door which led into the publishing yard. The first papers were being loaded into vans and driven off to newsagents and street-corner sellers.

I nodded at a couple of guys doing the hefting, slipped out of the back gate, and walked round to Marcello's.

It was a late September morning. The town had its rough edges blurred by an autumnal haze. Brighton looked like a painting in which the colours had run together. After all, this was the season of mists. But, as far as I was concerned, not much mellow fruitfulness.

The Tango School Mystery

Marcello's had worked up its early morning fug. Equal parts of bacon fumes, cigarette smoke and tea urn steam. The place was crowded with the breakfast rush. A group of bus conductors swigged tea at the back and swopped stories about life on the number thirty-one to Worthing. An office type in grey suit and striped tie ate his scrambled egg like a mouse chewing a nut. A couple of secretaries at the window table slurped coffee from glass cups and chattered over the knitting patterns in *Woman's Realm*.

I stepped up to the counter, ordered a coffee and took it to a free table at the back.

I took a sip, sat back, and tried to think about the predicament Pope had landed me in.

Damn the man!

Who did he think I was? Philip Marlowe?

But there wasn't much point in getting angry about it. I needed to think logically. Pope clearly believed that his brother posed a real threat to Maundsley. His Holiness would have regarded it as an act of self-humiliation to parade his personal problems to Figgis - knowing they'd be passed on to me. But if Gervase was planning to kill Maundsley, why had he vanished in advance of the act? Surely that would only draw attention to himself. It had raised his brother's suspicions. And if Maundsley was killed, it meant Gervase could have to account for his movements while he was missing.

On the other hand, perhaps Gervase was playing a subtler game. Maybe the vanishing act was designed to provide him with a false alibi. So when Maundsley was murdered, Gervase could supposedly prove he was somewhere else. As far as his vanishing act was concerned, it was impossible to reach the truth of the matter.

I drank some more of my coffee and considered the other puzzle. The question of Clapham's killing.

There wasn't a shred of hard evidence as far as I knew that

Gervase had killed Clapham. At least, no evidence yet. But if Gervase were planning to attack Maundsley, killing Clapham first would be a stupid thing to do. It would warn Maundsley that he might be in danger. Yet when the red mist of murder enters their mind, killers don't act with cool logic. And, perhaps, Gervase was intent on a killing spree.

I drained the last of my coffee and clunked the cup back in the saucer.

Thinking through the matter had led me to a clear conclusion. If I stood any chance of finding Gervase, I needed to know more about him.

And the best place to start would be inside his apartment.

Three hours later I was standing outside Gervase's apartment overlooking Brighton seafront.

I had permission to enter. But getting it hadn't been easy. You'd have thought I was asking to sneak into the jewel house at the Tower of London and help myself to the royal sceptre and orb. I'd phoned Figgis from Marcello's to tell him what I wanted to do. He'd spluttered a bit but finally agreed to ask Pope. When Figgis called me back, he'd said he'd seen Pope and had the most uncomfortable ten minutes of his life. But His Holiness had reluctantly agreed. He would call Gervase's housekeeper, one Estelle Daventry, who would let me into the apartment and oversee my visit.

I didn't like the sound of that. I was hoping to have a quiet nose about. I didn't want a fussy housekeeper flicking her feather duster around me. But I didn't have much choice.

So I opened the door and entered a small vestibule which served all the apartments in the building.

The place was painted a pale green colour. The walls were hung with a couple of seascapes. To my right, some stairs led to the upper floors. The place had a damp feel with the kind of whiff you get in swimming baths.

In front of me was a lift door. Beside the door was a telephone. A typed note next to the telephone read: "Lift for Penthouse Suite only. To gain admittance, raise receiver and dial 1."

I carried out the instructions to the letter.

The phone was answered after three rings by a woman with a reedy voice.

She said: "If you're that journalist personage I've been told to expect, enter the lift and press the button for the penthouse. You should be able to manage that. There's only one."

I'd have liked to ask whether she meant one button or one penthouse, just to rile her. But she'd already slammed down the receiver.

I stepped into the lift and pressed the button wondering how much trouble I was going to get from the sarcastic number upstairs.

The lift opened on a room furnished like the lounge of a luxury hotel. There were chintzy over-stuffed armchairs and chunky sofas you could have kipped on all night. There was a glass-fronted cabinet packed with figurines and a gilded occasional table. (If it's a table occasionally, what is it the rest of the time, I wondered?) A lot of the furniture looked like the stuff that's named after one of those French Kings Louis. I can't remember which one - there were too many of them.

Estelle Daventry was standing beside the lift with her arms folded like I was Old Lucifer who'd just rode the elevator up from Hades. She was a slight woman with an unusually long neck, nothing like a giraffe's, but not far off a turkey's. She had a narrow face with thin lips and deep-set eyes. Her brown hair had started to grey and was tied back in a severe bun. She was wearing a tailored grey skirt and blouse with black court shoes.

I extended my hand and said: "That lift must be a boon when you've got heavy shopping to lug up here."

Estelle looked at my hand like it was covered with boils. She said: "Our provisions are delivered by the grocer's boy."

I resisted the temptation to wring her long neck. Instead, I stepped firmly into the room to make it clear I intended to stay. I walked over to the window and looked out. The apartment commanded a grandstand view of the Sussex coast. The early morning mist had lifted. To the east, I could see as far along the coast as the white cliff of Seaford Head. To the west, smoke from Southwick power station drifted in the air. Through the smoke, I could pick out the outline of Worthing Pier.

I turned to Estelle. "Gervase must have had pressing business elsewhere to want to give up a view like this."

Estelle sniffed. "I don't enquire into his business. And it's Mr Pope to you."

I said: "At the moment, there are more Popes in my life than in the Vatican. So for the purpose of this investigation the Pope who lives here is Gervase."

Estelle sniffed again.

I asked: "When did you last see Gervase?"

"It was three days ago. I served him his dinner - liver and bacon, boiled potatoes and cabbage - and left him to eat it in the dining room. When I returned to clear his dinner plate and give him his pudding - treacle tart and custard - he was gone."

"Had he left in the middle of a meal before?"

Estelle crossed to one of the armchairs and sat down. "No. But I thought he may have gone out to a meeting he'd forgotten to mention to me."

I perched on a chunky sofa without being invited.

Beside the sofa was a table with some pictures in silver frames. Gervase with his mum and dad. Gervase with a dog. Gervase dressed in a Harrow School uniform - blue jacket, light grey trousers and a Harrow Hat, a straw boater effort with a blue band which used to make the lads look like juvenile 1930s FBI agents.

I switched my attention back to Estelle. "Was Gervase a forgetful man?"

"No."

"What was he like that evening? Did he seem worried about anything?"

"I wasn't privy to the thoughts going through his mind," Estelle said stiffly.

"But you've known him for a good many years?"

"We first met nearly thirty years ago. I've been his housekeeper for eighteen."

And only his housekeeper, I wondered. But I wasn't planning to open that box of trouble just yet.

Instead, I said: "I've been told that Gervase had developed a strong dislike of Sir Oscar Maundsley. In fact, he hated the man. Did you know about that?"

I watched as Estelle's body stiffened. "Yes," she said.

"Presumably, you know why. About how Gervase was interned during the war on the evidence of letters he'd written. Letters which Maundsley gave to the authorities to secure his own release."

"I am well aware of that. I was also interned. I was mentioned in the same letters."

That had my attention. "So you both hate Maundsley?" I asked.

"We see him for what he is. He uses the cause for his own purposes. But the cause is bigger than one man - certainly bigger than Maundsley."

I've never been much taken with people who espouse causes. They usually make a bloody nuisance of themselves. And I decided I could get to dislike Estelle a lot. But I had a job to do. So I put my views to one side and tried out my winning smile.

I said: "Gerald Pope thinks that his brother is planning to kill Maundsley. Do you believe that, too?"

"Maundsley will meet his fate in good time, with or without the help of Mr Gervase Pope."

"Do you want to kill Maundsley?"

Estelle sat up defiantly. "I would like to. But how could I?"

Well, wanting to kill someone isn't a crime. If it were, I'd have been hanged years ago.

But I wasn't sure where this was getting me. I needed a moment to think. I turned and looked out of the window. Took in the view for a moment. Close to the horizon, a tramp steamer was chugging down the English Channel.

I refocused on Estelle and decided to try shock tactics.

I said: "Do you love Gervase?"

Estelle's eyes flashed like warning beacons. She stood up and strode across to the window. Stared out to sea.

Without turning to face me, she said quietly: "I serve him as best I can."

"That's what I hoped. You can serve him best by telling me anything unusual that happened in the days leading up to Gervase's disappearance."

Now Estelle turned towards me. Her cheeks were flushed and her eyes were moist. Estelle didn't strike me as the type who shed many tears.

"Have there been any unexpected callers at the apartment in the last few days?"

"No, we live quietly."

"Did Gervase receive any letters he wasn't expecting?"

"He receives post regularly, perhaps half a dozen letters a day."

"But nothing unusual?"

"There was one letter, the day before he disappeared. Normally, Mr Pope asks me to deal with his regular post - bills, invitations and so on. But he took this one into his study and locked it in his desk drawer. That was unusual."

"Did you happen to notice from the envelope's postmark where it had been posted?"

"I didn't get the opportunity. Mr Pope collected the letters from downstairs that morning."

"Did you notice what the envelope was like?"

"I could see it was good quality, made out of thick textured paper. Later, Mr Pope went out and I noticed he was taking a letter of his own to the post. Often he asked me to post his letters for him."

"And you think that could have been a reply to the letter he'd received?"

Estelle shook her head. "I don't know, but I suppose it could've been."

"And he posted that letter the day before he left?"

"Yes."

I thought about that for a moment, then said: "Let's go back to the evening when he left. You mentioned you'd served his dinner - liver and bacon, I think."

"Yes."

"And he left after eating it but before you served his pudding?"

"Yes."

"And nothing unusual happened between serving the first course and the second?"

"No. Wait. There was a telephone call."

"You answered the phone?"

"No. I was in the kitchen. Mr Pope must've picked up the extension in the dining room."

"So you don't know who made the call?"

"No."

"Or what was said?"

"No."

"But Gervase left after taking the call without saying anything to you?"

"Yes."

"Did he take anything with him?"

"I noticed a small bag had been taken from a cupboard in his bedroom. It was the bag he used if he was going away for a couple of days."

"He left the apartment without telling you?"

"Yes."

"And you didn't hear him go?"

"No. I was busy washing saucepans."

I stood up and looked around the room. There were some good pictures on the wall - Gervase seemed to favour landscapes. There was nothing that looked unusual. But, then, what is a fascist's sitting room supposed to look like? Beaming portraits of *Il Duce* and paintings of polished jackboots?

I said: "I'd like to look in Gervase's bedroom and study."

Estelle stood up. "I'll come with you."

"No. I want you to stay here."

Estelle sat down again and gave me a rocket-fuelled hate glare. I ignored it. Sticks and stones may break my bones, but names will never hurt me. And dirty looks don't even come close.

I strode across the room to a door which I assumed led into the rest of the apartment. There was a short corridor with three doors on each side. The first I opened proved to be a bathroom. I went in and gave it a quick shufti. The place was spotlessly clean - full marks, Estelle - and had all the usual stuff. The white towels were so plumped up and fluffy they looked like baby polar bears.

I opened the bathroom cabinet and looked inside. There was a stand for a razor and shaving brush, but both had gone. Gervase may have left in a hurry, but he knew how to grab the essentials. I briefly wondered whether he'd had to perform a fast disappearing act before.

The second door I opened was a laundry room with a washing machine and an ironing board.

But the third was clearly Gervase's bedroom. I stepped inside. The man enjoyed his comforts. The bed was a large item with a thick mattress, padded headboard, and big blowsy pillows. I stepped over to the wardrobe and looked inside. Gervase had a collection of clobber that shamed mine. I hefted out one hanger to take a closer look. It was a double-breasted suit that looked like the kind of thing you'd see Humphrey Bogart wearing in a nineteen-forties gangster movie. The wardrobe was full, but a couple of hangers were empty. Maybe for the jacket and trousers Gervase was wearing when he scarpered. I checked a couple of chests of drawers but they contained only the kind of stuff - socks, underwear, handkerchiefs - I'd expect to find.

I reached the last door in the corridor and stepped inside. A large framed photograph of Benito Mussolini smirked at me from the far wall. It was behind a handsome mahogany desk with inlaid green leather and gold-tooled decoration. It made my desk at the *Chronicle* look like an orange box. There were two wooden trays, one on each side of the desk. In- and out-trays, I assumed. Both were empty.

I walked round the desk and tried the drawers. Locked. Estelle had said that Gervase locked the letter he'd received in his desk drawer. That implied Estelle didn't have a key. I certainly wasn't going to rack up a hefty repair bill for the *Chronicle* by trying to force any of the drawers. Besides, if the letter was that important to Gervase, he would've taken it with him.

To the right of the desk, part of the wall was covered by a pair of curtains. I crossed the room and drew the curtains.

If eyes could stand out on stalks, mine would've been hanging off the end of nine-foot bamboo. Behind the curtain there was a glass-fronted cabinet recessed into the wall. The thing was like a private museum. Of Nazi memorabilia. Each item with a neatly lettered description card. Each card had the initials B&H in the top right-hand corner.

There was the swastika-embroidered truss worn by Hermann Goering at a Nuremburg rally. It split when he stood up to cheer the *Führer*, the description card informed me. There was a framed photo of Eva Braun wearing lederhosen and a cheeky grin signed *Heute Nacht ist die Nacht, Eva.* (Tonight's the night, Eva). There was a box containing a dozen stick-on Charlie Chaplin moustaches with a note from Adolph Hitler to his supplier: *Nur für den Notfall. Die Welt darf die Wahrheit nie kennen.* (For emergency use only. The world must never know the truth.)

My bamboo-stalk eyes weren't staring at any of these.

In the right-hand corner of the cabinet, there was a display stand for holding an SS officer's dress dagger. "Very sharp," warned the display card.

But the dagger had gone.

Chapter 7

"Do you think I should tell His Holiness about the missing dagger?" Frank Figgis said.

"Not yet," I said. "We don't know for certain that Gervase has it with him."

We were in Figgis's office early that afternoon. His desk was piled with proofs for later editions of the paper. Normally he'd be scribbling corrections and tut-tutting over wordy headlines. But he'd lost interest in them. He was sucking on a peppermint like it was the elixir of life.

"But you said the museum cabinet was locked," he said.

"Yes, and Estelle Daventry, his housekeeper, confirmed he had the only key."

"So he must have the dagger - and Derek Clapham had his throat cut."

"We don't yet know what cut Clapham's throat. Ted Wilson says he's still waiting on forensics for that."

"It won't have been a lawnmower."

"Or a combine harvester," I said. "But to get serious, forensics may tell us what kind of knife was used from the length of the individual slashes and the depth of the wound."

Figgis wrinkled his forehead. He always did when he wanted to show scepticism.

I said: "Let's leave the Clapham killing to one side for a moment. We do now have an idea what caused Gervase to scarper."

"The letter and the phone call during dinner?" Figgis said.

I nodded. "As His Holiness thinks Gervase is out to kill Sir Oscar Maundsley, let's work on the theory that Maundsley sent the letter."

"Why should he write to a man he knew hated him?" Figgis asked.

"Perhaps he's heard a rumour that Gervase is out to kill him. Perhaps Maundsley's letter was an apology and a peace offering. Perhaps he was trying to make amends for the past."

Figgis tore the paper off another packet of mints and stuffed a couple into his mouth.

"Maundsley doesn't strike me as the kind who makes amends for anything," he said.

"But he might if he was planning to stand for election in Brighton and knew that Gervase could damage his campaign."

Figgis stroked his chin. "I suppose that makes some kind of sense."

I said: "Remember that Estelle saw Gervase posting a letter that was clearly private the following day. Suppose that letter was to Maundsley - a reply to the one Gervase had received. Perhaps Gervase was suggesting a further discussion to clear the air. Then after Maundsley had read and considered the letter, he phones Gervase the following evening and suggests they should meet. Perhaps straightaway. Gervase ups and leaves for talks with Maundsley - and misses out on treacle tart and custard."

"And you think he left to see Maundsley with the dagger?" Figgis said. "Now that doesn't make sense."

"I'll admit it's just a theory," I said. "But it does fit some of the known facts."

"It doesn't explain why he hasn't returned to his apartment," Figgis said.

"Unless he went to see Clapham - and used the dagger on him," I said. "Now Gervase could be in hiding. Or on the run from the police."

It was pure speculation and we both knew it. An uneasy silence hung in the air.

Then Figgis asked: "So what's your next move?"

I shrugged. "If the dagger proves to be important, it might help to know where Gervase got it. That kind of sinister memento can't be easy to come by. It's not the sort of junk you pick up in those seafront souvenir shops."

"People who sell that kind of Nazi crap aren't going to shout about it," Figgis said.

"Except to other Nazis," I said.

"Or their fellow travellers."

"Each of the cards in Gervase's museum case had the initials B&H in the top right-hand corner. Mean anything to you?"

"Could be Brighton and Hove," Figgis said.

"Doesn't make any sense," I said. "Why would Nazi mementoes be advertised as coming from Brighton and Hove? Hitler never got closer to the place than Dieppe. And nobody liked him there. I think it's more likely to be the initials of the supplier - but it means nothing to me."

"So you're at a dead end," Figgis said with a rueful shrug. "I won't fancy telling His Holiness that when he asks me for a progress report."

"You won't have to. I've drawn a blank with Gervase, so I'm going to approach the problem from the other end."

"What other end?"

"If Gervase really plans to kill Maundsley, it would be good to discover what he knows about it. Perhaps Maundsley knows where Gervase is hiding out."

"If he does, Gervase won't be there for long. The Grey Shirts, Maundsley's private army, will see to that. Nasty bunch of thugs by all accounts. Stamp on your face as easily as a woodlouse. You'll never get within a hundred yards of Maundsley."

"A bottle of gin says I will. He's speaking at a rally this evening at the Dome."

Figgis nodded. "I know. But those fascist rallies usually end with punch-ups between the Grey Shirts and hecklers. It's not good publicity for a man who claims he's the only one who can bring peace and prosperity to the country. That's why he bans journalists from attending. He posts Grey Shirts on the door to make sure they can't get in."

"I think I'll be able to winkle my way inside."

"How? Are you going to pop up through the floor, like the demon king in a pantomime?"

"Something like that," I said.

Back in the newsroom, there was a message on my desk to call Ted Wilson.

I lifted the telephone and dialled his direct line.

Ted sounded chipper when he answered. He said: "I've got a little something for you."

I said: "What kind of little something? A little something that will cost me a single whisky? Or a double something? Or will it be worth the whole bottle?"

"Let's just say this one's on the house."

"Tell me."

"The pathologist in the Clapham killing has come back with one early finding. It seems the knife used to cut Clapham's throat had a double-sided blade."

"So not one used to butter his bread. How did the pathologist know?"

"By the direction of the cut. The assailant thrust the knife into Clapham's neck with his right-hand, then tried to lever it up to make a cut - like slitting open an envelope. But flesh and skin's a bit tougher than paper. So it looks like the killer switched to his left hand and levered the knife over and pulled it down - like slicing a loaf of bread."

"And I'm guessing there's no indication that Clapham owned a knife like that."

"No. So the killer brought the knife with him."

"And the killing was premeditated."

"Just like my decision to give you this extra lead on the story," Ted said.

The line went dead.

Ted was right. News about the knife would give my story for

the next edition an edge over rival papers. But it wasn't good news for Figgis to pass on to Pope. When Ted was talking about the knife, he could've been describing how to wield a dagger in anger. An SS dagger.

I rolled copy paper into my Remington, typed "add Clapham" in the catchline, and batted out a couple of pars. Then I called over to Cedric, the copy boy, and asked him to take them up to the subs. They'd weave them into the story I'd written last night.

As Cedric bounced off across the newsroom - he got a fillip from a good murder story as much as anyone else - my phone rang.

I lifted the receiver and a voice as unctuous as a courtier whispering in a king's ear said: "Do I have the pleasure of speaking to Mr Colin Crampton?"

"You do have that pleasure," I whispered back like a monarch dispensing a favour to a crony. "And to whom do I have the pleasure of speaking?"

"Titus Scrivener."

That had my attention. I sat up straighter. I recognised the name. It had been on the cover of the book Derek Clapham had on his bedside table. There'd been a letter used as a bookmark half way through. He wouldn't finish the book now. He'd never know who did it.

Or perhaps he already did. I remembered the book had been called *Hitler's Permanent Wave: How the Führer Escaped Berlin and Began a New Life as a Ladies' Hairdresser in South America*. It was one of those conspiracy theory books which appeal to the gullible. And, as a result, sell well. Gullible is a big market.

I remembered that Scrivener had dedicated and signed the book to Clapham. Perhaps he and Clapham had been fellow fascists in the 'thirties. Or perhaps he was a conspiracy theorist who just happened to know Clapham. Either way, Scrivener could be a useful contact on this story.

So I said: "It's good of you to call, Mr Scrivener. How can I help?"

"I just wanted to thank you for mentioning my book in your article."

In my piece in the Midday Edition, I'd introduced some colour about Clapham's flat - and described how the book had been lying on his bedside table. It was the kind of detail that would let readers form their own conclusions about the man.

Scrivener burbled on: "It's so difficult to draw one's books to the attention of the reading public. So this was a real bonus. Publicity is the life-blood for a writer."

Old Clapham could've done with a little more of the real life-blood himself, I mused. But I kept that to myself.

Instead, I said: "Did you know Derek Clapham well?"

"I met him a few times when I was researching *Hitler's Permanent Wave*. He had some interesting information relating to the *Führer's* experiments with a shampoo and set. Not successful, I'm afraid. It could account for the fact that Eva Braun was so rarely seen in public. After the book came out, Derek and I met for a drink occasionally."

"So you live in Brighton, too?"

"Hove, actually."

Scrivener was clearly living on another planet, but if he'd known Clapham, he might be able to provide important background on the man. Perhaps he knew Gervase, too.

So I said: "I wonder whether you could spare a few minutes to see me. I'd like to talk about Mr Clapham. And, of course, your books."

"That would be most agreeable. I'll be able to tell you about my latest project. I'm calling it *Windsor Knot: Why the Royal Family Keeps the Secret that Mrs Simpson is a Man*."

"Can't wait to hear about it," I said.

Titus Scrivener lived in a ground floor flat in a street not far from Hove Lagoon.

I drew my car into the kerb, climbed out, and gave the house the once-over.

The building was a solid two-storey job in the middle of a smart terrace. The place had a privet hedge round a pocket handkerchief garden laid to lawn.

I opened a metal gate and walked up a short path.

There was a pair of camellias in pots on either side of the front door. The door was a solid oak number with a hefty brass knocker in the shape of an elf. I applied the creature's backside smartly to the wood twice and waited.

Scrivener opened the door wearing a red cardigan and the cheesy grin of a man hoping for a favour.

He was a dumpy little man with a chubby face and protruding upper teeth that made him look a bit like a chipmunk. He wore his cardigan over a blue shirt with a frayed collar. He had a pair of grey corduroy trousers, baggy at the knee.

He extended a pudgy hand and I shook it. He had one of those sweaty handshakes that left me wondering what he'd been doing before he answered the door.

Scrivener leaned forward and in his whispering voice said: "So good of you to come so soon."

"Don't mention it. I'm always pleased to meet a fellow writer." I didn't mention that if Scrivener had important information about Clapham, I couldn't get round to the place fast enough.

Scrivener ushered me into a sitting room which doubled up as his workplace. A small desk in one corner held an ancient sit-up-and-beg typewriter similar to the Remington I had in the newsroom. There was a half-typed sheet in the carriage. There were a couple of easy chairs covered in faded fabric on either side of the fireplace. One wall was taken up with a loaded bookcase. There were overflow piles of books around the room. I glanced at a couple of Scrivener's titles as I made my way to one of the chairs. *Charlie Chaplin: Stalin's Secret Agent* was one. Another was titled *Doris by Day, Vampire by Night*.

I sat down in one of the easy chairs, looked around the room, and said: "Where do you get the information for all these books?"

Scrivener took the other chair. "I'm an inveterate gossip. And an avid picker-up of unconsidered trifles. A listener-in on any grapevine. I have my ear to the ground and my eye to the keyhole."

"You must be quite a contortionist to manage that," I said.

Scrivener giggled in a high-pitched feminine kind of way.

I decided to trade a little gossip in the hope that Scrivener would pay me back handsomely. Give a little to get a lot is my motto. So I gave him an edited version of the events last night at Antoine's Sussex Grill.

I said: "Can you think of anyone who would want to kill Derek Clapham?"

Scrivener rubbed his chin thoughtfully. "Of course, he'd made enemies over the years. Many enemies, given the cause he espoused. But killers?" He shook his head. "I mean to say, Derek wasn't to everybody's taste but he wasn't all bad. After all, he kept a cat."

I said: "Hitler kept a dog, but it didn't stop him launching a war that killed eighty million people."

"But he's making up for it now by providing half prices for old age pensioners on Saturdays."

"At his hairdressing salon in South America?" I asked incredulously.

"In a remote town in Paraguay. I'm sworn to secrecy and not permitted to say where."

"But you've visited this town and met the hairdressing Hitler?"

"Not exactly. But my information is reliable. It comes from a man who'd heard the rumour from a woman who'd been told about it by a guest at a party who'd had her hair styled by Hitler. Naturally, I've verified the accuracy of the information."

"By the woman with the hair style?"

"No, the man who heard the rumour."

"But the idea that Hitler is a hairdresser beggars belief."

"You'd think so. But my reliable sources tell me he got the idea when he was fleeing the *Führer* Bunker. Just before he left, the lights fused. In the dark, he grabbed Eva's curling tongs thinking they were a machine pistol. It was only when he was escaping in the back of a circus wagon disguised as Crusty the Clown, he realised his mistake. But he believed in fate - and decided to put the tongs to good use."

Scrivener was clearly a fantasist who wouldn't be tolerated within a million miles of a serious newspaper. But I was determined to drain him for any real information he had.

"When you were researching your Hitler book, did you meet Gervase Pope?"

Scrivener nodded. "I certainly did. Mr Pope was a keen student of Hitler's life and philosophy. We discussed them at length in his comfortable apartment."

"Did you also discuss how Pope had been interned during the war as a security risk? Put there on the evidence of letters Clapham supplied to Oscar Maundsley."

"Of course, I knew about that but I thought it politic not to mention the matter. Especially as Mr Pope was showing me his excellent collection of memorabilia."

"In the glass cabinet?"

"You've seen it yourself?" Scrivener seemed surprised.

"I gave it a quick shufti. There was no sign of any curling tongs. But an SS dagger was missing. Could Pope have killed Clapham with that dagger?"

"Why ask me? I wasn't privy to the personal relationship between the two - although I imagine it could not have been warm."

"When you were researching your book, did you only meet Gervase Pope at his apartment?"

"Yes. Twice, I recall."

"Not anywhere else?"

"No."

"So you wouldn't know whether he had any favourite hidey-holes?"

"Hidey-holes?"

"A country cottage, maybe. A favourite hotel. A distant relative whom he occasionally visited."

"We never discussed his private life." Scrivener shot me a sly look. "But why ask these questions?"

"Just general background. You know the type you pick up from your contacts who've heard rumours from people who thought they might be true."

Scrivener nodded as though I'd just explained Einstein's General Theory of Relativity.

He said: "So can we talk about my new book?"

"The one you're still writing?"

"Yes. I will prove beyond doubt that Mrs Simpson is a man."

"Sounds like a cock and balls story to me," I said.

Scrivener frowned. "If you can only make cheap jokes…"

"I can make quite expensive ones when I have to."

I stood up and moved towards the door. Scrivener heaved himself out of his chair and followed me.

I turned. "One last question about Gervase Pope's memorabilia collection. Did he say where he got all that stuff?"

"Dealers, I believe."

"Which dealers?"

"Specialists in that kind of material."

"Any of them local?"

Scrivener's gaze flicked left. A sure sign there was something he didn't want to tell me.

"Could be," he said.

I said: "Some of the description cards in the cabinet had a little B&H in the corner. Did that mean anything to you?"

"Brighton and Hove," Scrivener said, unconvincingly.

"You know as well as I do that it couldn't be that."

Scrivener shrugged. "I wasn't going to mention it because I've promised to be discreet. You understand the sellers don't like it known to the general populace that they deal in important historic memorabilia."

"Especially members of the populace who were being bombed and threatened with invasion only a few years ago by people who originally owned it."

Scrivener cleared his throat. "The B&H stands for Box and Hartley. They deal in reproduction antique furniture, their main business. But they have a confidential side-line in memorabilia from the Third Reich."

"And where would I find Box and Hartley."

"The shop is in The Lanes. But there's only one Box-Hartley these days. With a hyphen. Unity Box-Hartley."

"Unusual given name."

"Yes, she gave it to herself. Her name was originally Dorothy although everyone called her Dotty - Dotty Box. It became Box-Hartley after she married Crispin Hartley who originally owned the reproduction furniture shop. But he died just two months after the marriage. Following the funeral, Dotty changed her name to Unity in memory of Unity Mitford."

I recalled the story. "She was one of the Mitford sisters."

"Yes. There were six of them. They first made their name as socialites - bright young things, as they used to be known in the 'twenties and 'thirties," Scrivener said.

"But Unity was a bad penny," I said. "She was a Nazi who hero-worshipped Hitler. He attended her wedding in Berlin. She shot herself when Britain declared war on Germany but made a mess of the job and lived - at least until after the war ended."

Scrivener grinned like a man with a secret. "At least, that's the official version."

"But no doubt one day you'll be telling the story you heard

from the rumours that might have been true."
"Someone has to," he said.

Chapter 8

I stepped out of Scrivener's house of fantasy feeling I needed to wash my hands.

Or perhaps it was my brain that needed cleansing. Of the rubbish he'd been spouting. He could give Alice in Wonderland's White Queen a run for her money. She could only believe six impossible things before breakfast. Scrivener could do it before lunch, tea and dinner. And not limit himself to six.

But, "oh my ears and whiskers", I was in danger of being as late for the action as the White Rabbit. I was haring about - these puns just slip out - trying to cover a murder and find a missing man. I wasn't making much progress at either. I needed some focus.

I climbed into my MGB, fired up the engine, and drove towards Brighton. Traffic was heavy along the coast road. I tucked in behind a green Southdown double-decker bus and chugged along. The poster on the back of the bus carried the slogan: Keep Britain Tidy. It showed a blue cartoon man picking up a piece of litter. Or perhaps he'd dropped it. He looked shifty enough.

Anyway, there was nothing tidy about my predicament.

The more I thought about Clapham's murder and Gervase's disappearing act, the more I wondered whether they could be connected. Gervase certainly had the motive to kill Clapham. The SS dagger provided a means, too. But did he have the opportunity?

I wondered, too, about how well Scrivener had known either Clapham or Gervase. He'd admitted speaking to them for his Hitler book, but that didn't make either of them his bosom buddy. The journo who wants to uncover big stories needs the knack of making his interviewee feel like a firm friend. Then the interview becomes like a cosy chat between good mates.

Confidences are shared. Secrets are whispered. Skeletons are released from cupboards. But the old pals act only lasts for as long as the interview. And I should know.

Besides, Scrivener lived in the land of make-believe. The man was obsessed with conspiracies. His mind was like a corkscrew. He couldn't think straight. Which made me wary of almost everything he'd told me.

But there was one fact I felt I could rely on. That Gervase had bought many of his Nazi knick-knacks from Unity Box-Hartley. Perhaps she'd known Gervase better than Scrivener. Perhaps she'd have a clearer idea where he'd hide out.

At the moment, I couldn't think of a more promising lead.

I parked the MGB in East Street and hoofed it into The Lanes.

Even though summer was in its dog days, the narrow streets were crowded with tourists. A pair of schoolgirls sniggered over engagement rings in a jeweller's window. An old bloke cricked his neck sideways to read the titles on some ancient volumes in a second-hand bookseller's. A blowsy woman with a henpecked husband in tow barged down the alley. He lumbered along with a huge copper kettle looped over one arm.

I shouldered my way through the throng.

I was thinking about how I should handle Unity Box-Hartley. If she was anything like her namesake, Unity Mitford, she'd be a handful. The Mitford woman had been a fanatic who made the Gestapo seem like the Band of Hope. No wonder she'd been Hitler's poster girl. She was rumoured to have borne the *Führer* a child. What did Eva Braun have to say about that? But the rumour could have been another hoax.

If Box-Hartley was cut from the same uncompromising cloth as Unity Mitford, she wouldn't take kindly to an intrusive journalist asking awkward questions. She sounded like the type who'd be on to you with a pair of red-hot pliers before you could say goodbye to your toenails.

Box-Hartley's shop turned out to be a single-fronted building in a courtyard off Meeting House Lane. The place was in a position most browsers would miss unless they'd been tipped off to look out for it. But I guessed that was Box-Hartley's idea. If most of her trade was in Nazi relics, she wouldn't want a neon sign flashing the fact to passers-by. Her relic hunters would be a furtive crowd well-practised in sneaking up narrow passages and lurking in dark corners.

But Box-Hartley's premises were smart enough. The fascia board above the window read: "Box-Hartley. Quality reproduction antique furniture." It featured the B&H logo I'd seen on the cards in Gervase's display case. The main item in the window was a small dark wooden table with a lot of fancy gilt work. It had those curvy legs which made the thing look as though it wanted to dance. Its price tag read: "£395". That was another clever ploy. If you lacked the kind of boodle to fork out for a table that'd barely hold your dinner plate, you weren't going to step into the shop.

Unless of course you were on a personal blitzkrieg to Brighton for the special merchandise inside.

I strode up to the door feeling a bit like Monty about to take on Rommel at El Alamein.

But there's nothing like a surprise attack. So I flung open the door and hustled inside.

A bell clanged noisily behind me and I jumped.

Nerves.

I don't normally suffer from them. But this was the first time I'd met a fully paid-up Nazi.

I shouldn't have jumped. It was only a bell. What was I expecting? An air-raid siren?

And, anyway, I scanned the shop and the place was deserted.

I say shop, but the place was rather like stepping into someone's house. I was in a room about twenty feet square. It had a parquet floor - polished with a tub-load of elbow grease

– and regency-stripe paper on the walls. The centre of the ceiling had one of those plaster rose arrangements that snooty Victorians liked to show off their new electric light.

A selection of the repro antique furniture was arranged tastefully around the room. There was a Georgian commode made out of walnut. I'd have happily sat on it of a morning with my trousers around my ankles and leafed through the newspapers while I waited for nature to take its course. There was a regency whatnot with three shelves and a lot of fancy work on the legs. There was an Edwardian hat stand with enough hooks to hang a houseful of titfers. There was a chaise-longue upholstered in plush red velvet. It had a curved back at one end and a kind of scrolled arrangement carved in the wood at the other.

There wasn't a Third Reich memento in sight. Not so much as an Iron Cross. But the Nazi rubbish would all be out the back.

On the other side of the room, there was a business-like desk which obviously wasn't part of the goods for sale. It held a drift of papers. Behind the desk was an archway with a curtain drawn over it. Next to the archway was a corkboard. A couple of dozen business cards had been pinned to the board.

I briefly wondered why the shop had been left unattended. But perhaps Box-Hartley was in the back fitting one of her special regulars with a pair of Waffen SS dress jackboots. Besides, there was no cash-register and a chance shoplifter was hardly likely to make off with a Georgian commode stuffed under his arm. Not through the crowds in the Lanes.

I stepped smartly over to the desk to take a quick shufti. The papers on the desk seemed to be mostly invoices from suppliers. But Box-Hartley had fixed a "To Do Today" list to a clipboard which rested on the other papers.

I leant over and read the list:

Confirm order for Victorian bookcase.

Phone accountant re tax.

Hairdresser at 4.30.
Delivery Cucking St.
Check printer for new brochure.
None of it seemed out of the ordinary. So I glanced at the corkboard. There were a couple of business cards for French polishers, another for an upholsterer, three for cabinet makers, one for a stationery supplier and a dozen more for various firms Box-Hartley evidently did business with.

I was about to turn away, when my eye caught a card pinned in the bottom left-hand corner of the board. A card for the Dolores Esteban Tango Academy.

It was the dance school where the Widow was hunting for a new husband. Was Box-Hartley learning to trip the light fantastic? Or was she also on the hunt for a terpsichorean hubbie?

But before I had time to think about that, somewhere behind the archway curtain a lavatory flushed.

I hurried to the other side of the room and admired the chaise-longue.

Ten seconds later, I heard the curtain rustle as it was pulled aside.

I turned from the chaise-longue.

A tall slim woman was standing behind the desk. She had fair hair that fell to her shoulders in a row of carefully combed curls. She had a straight nose, thin lips and eyebrows which had been plucked within an inch of extinction. Her eyes were grey and hard like they'd been cast out of molten lead. She wore a dark blue pinstripe suit over a cream blouse. The suit had a tight-fitting jacket fastened with three buttons and a pencil skirt cut just below the knee.

She looked at me with suspicious eyes and said: "The chaise-longue is a faithful reproduction of the one owned by the Edwardian actress Mrs Patrick Campbell."

"The actress who was first to play the part of Eliza Doolittle in *Pygmalion*," I said.

Box-Hartley said: "You're very well informed." She made it sound like a criminal offence.

So I pointed at the item and said: "No wonder she preferred the 'deep, deep peace of the double bed after the hurly-burly of the chaise-longue'."

Unity frowned and stepped around the desk towards me. I half expected her to whip out the pliers. But I held my ground.

Captain Courage!

In a voice as warm as a penguin's tail, she said: "You don't look to me like a typical collector of reproduction antique furniture."

I said: "I've never been much of a one for reproductions. I'm more interested in the real stuff."

"We have no real stuff here."

"That's not what I've heard."

"Heard? From whom?"

"Gervase Pope."

That brought the Rhine maiden up sharp in her tracks. So I'd never met Gervase. But I knew his brother Gerald. His Holiness. Damn the man. I even worked for him. I was doing so now.

And felt perfectly entitled to lie.

Box-Hartley's eyebrows lifted. At least, I think that's what happened. As there wasn't much left of them, it looked a bit like a shadow moving over her forehead.

She said: "You know Gervase Pope?"

I said: "I've seen his collection." And that was the truth. "I know he bought most of it from you."

"Who are you?"

"I'm someone who has a few questions about Gervase Pope to ask," I said.

Her shoulders snapped back, like General Von Rundstedt had just walked into the room. "I never answer questions about my customers. Our business is strictly confidential."

"I can understand that. You wouldn't want ordinary decent people - especially people who'd lost loved ones in the war - knowing too much about the stuff I expect you keep out the back. No doubt the reproduction chaises-longues and commodes are a useful front."

"My business is private and there is no reason why people should want to know about it."

"Unless I choose to write a piece about it."

"You're a newspaperman?" Unity hissed.

"You're quick. Let's hope you're as quick with this one. I need some information about Gervase Pope. If you answer my questions - and I'm satisfied you've answered them honestly - I'll go away and you won't hear from me again. But if you want to play the high and mighty, I'm going back to write a full-page feature for the *Evening Chronicle* about this place. It will carry the headline: Nazi Fan's Bargain Bazaar."

If the look Unity shot me had been an artillery shell, I'd have vaporised. Her eyes glowed with hatred.

She said: "There was a time when there were strong men who knew how to deal with people like you."

"And look what happened to them," I said.

Unity turned, walked back to her desk and sat down behind it.

"I have your word that if I answer your questions, you'll keep my business out of your newspaper?"

"Cub's honour," I said with my hands in my pocket. And my fingers crossed.

"Very well, what do you want to know?" she asked.

"How long have you known Gervase Pope?"

"About three years."

"That would be about the time you came to work at this shop?"

"Yes."

"And shortly before you married Clive Hartley, your late

husband?"

"You know about that?" Unity said. She had a shifty look. Shuffled the papers on her desk nervously. Decided she was giving herself away. Sat back and folded her arms.

I said: "We journalists have our sources. Did you know Gervase well?"

"Not well. He was a customer."

"How often did you meet him?"

"Perhaps a dozen times over three or so years. He came to the shop to see what I had in stock. Other times, he ordered from a catalogue I sent him."

I said: "Did Gervase Pope collect Nazi memorabilia because he had sympathy for the fascist cause?"

"There are many reasons why people collect. Some have an academic interest in the history of the period."

"And some have sympathy for the movement. Gervase Pope was one of them. Are you another?"

Unity's eyes glared. She looked down at her desk. Tidied her papers into a neat pile.

There was a silence.

Then she said: "Yes."

I said: "Sharing the same views as Gervase must have brought you closer?"

"That is a naïve view. Trotsky and Stalin were both communists but they hated one another."

She was right, of course. Members of the same political party often spend their time fighting like rats in a sack. But the answer didn't suggest she and Gervase were close comrades in arms.

"Presumably, you knew that Gervase spent time in prison during the war?"

"Yes."

"And that didn't bother you?"

"No."

"Did you know that he was in prison because of letters he'd

written? Letters which were passed to the security services by Oscar Maundsley."

"Yes."

"And Maundsley secured his release as a result."

Unity's eyes shone with passion. "Sir Oscar was - is - a great man. He is the lost leader we should've had in the wartime years. The leader who would've ended the conflict with Germany. He is the leader we need now."

"So he'll have your vote when he stands for Brighton in the general election."

"I will be proud to be at his side."

And from the flush that had come to Unity's cheeks, not necessarily in a vertical position, I thought.

I wondered whether Unity was having an affair with Maundsley. Or wanted an affair with him. Perhaps she longed to emulate her namesake and have a child with one of those strong men-of-action types.

At least that ruled me out.

Unity looked like one of those strong women-of-action types. The kind that do a hundred press-ups before breakfast and crack walnuts between their thighs.

If I told her Gervase was on his way to croak her beloved Maundsley, she might take it personally. So I decided to keep that little secret to myself for the time being.

Instead I said: "When was the last time you saw Gervase Pope?"

"I don't recall," she said. "Must have been three or four months ago."

"So you wouldn't have seen him recently?"

"No. But why this interest in Gervase Pope?"

"Just a general enquiry," I said. "Shall I give him your regards next time I see him?"

"No," she said.

There didn't seem much else to say. I headed towards the

door. A final thought occurred to me. I turned back.

I said: "Do you dance the tango?"

"No," she said.

The bell rang again as I opened the door and stepped into the street.

Chapter 9

"This doesn't look good," Frank Figgis said. "What am I going to tell His Holiness?"

"Give him the good news. His brother isn't yet wanted for murder." I said.

We were in Figgis's office late in the afternoon. I'd just briefed him on my meetings with Titus Scrivener and Unity Box-Hartley.

"But we still don't know where Gervase is hiding." Figgis said.

"We don't know that he is hiding," I said. "For all we know he could be on holiday. Even now, he could be frolicking on the sands at Margate with his bucket and spade."

I don't know whether that did much for Figgis's morale. It didn't convince me.

"Pope seemed adamant that Gervase was missing," Figgis said. "He should know - after all, he's his brother."

"Brothers don't always know as much about each other as they like to think. I bet Gervase hides many of his Nazi secrets from His Holiness."

"But not enough of them," Figgis said.

"Maybe, but I'm not his brother's keeper."

"Clever arguments won't get you out of this one. If His Holiness is forced to resign because of something Gervase does, he could drag us all down with him."

"Pope's family troubles don't have anything to do with us."

Figgis ran a hand over his forehead as though it was hurting. Perhaps it was. He was sucking another peppermint, but looked like a man who missed his ciggies.

"Nothing to do with us," he said. "I wish that were true."

"Why shouldn't it be?"

"Ever heard of guilt by association?"

"That idea was debunked years ago when that American Senator Joseph McCarthy was exposed as a charlatan. 'Are you or have you ever been a member of the Communist Party?' It was a witch hunt. And, as a result, witch hunts are now out of fashion. Nobody would ever believe we're a bunch of Nazis stomping around the office."

"Not believe it? I wish that were true. If Gervase is exposed, there are plenty who will ask questions. The witch hunts will start again. This time looking for fascist sympathisers."

"With good reason?" I asked.

Figgis shrugged. "Who knows? You're too young to remember, but back in the 'thirties, there were a lot of mugs attracted by those strong-man fascist types. The witch-hunters will start with His Holiness and when they discover he's not squeaky clean, they'll turn on the rest of us."

"What? And discover you're a member of the British Legion? You only go down there for the snooker."

"That won't matter to people who want to bring us down," Figgis said. "They rely on the whiff of suspicion."

"Like the stench of a rotting haddock," I said.

"It will pervade the whole place," Figgis said.

"So finding Gervase before he finishes Maundsley isn't just about saving Pope?"

"Not entirely," Figgis said.

"It's about saving us," I said.

"Yes."

"So no pressure," I said.

I was standing on the corner but not, like Bobby Darin, watching all the girls go by.

It was just before seven o'clock and there were plenty of them. They were dressed in their evening togs and off for a night on the town. Some wore A-line skirts in primary colours like red and yellow with woolly jumpers. Studious ones with listen-to-me spectacles wore pencil skirts and sensible heels. Sporty ones wore Capri pantsuits and flat shoes - all the better to run fast and catch the boys.

As I say, not watching the girls at all. Observing. There is a difference. And it's drummed into journalists from the first day we pick up a notebook and pencil.

But nobody ever said you can't get pleasure out of observation. The only trouble was I had some dark thoughts in my mind.

I lurked in the doorway of the National Provincial bank to consider them. Until my meeting in Figgis's office an hour earlier, I'd felt easy about finding Gervase. Perhaps I would. Perhaps I wouldn't. Perhaps he'd pot Maundsley. Perhaps he wouldn't. It mattered a lot to His Holiness. But it didn't matter a lot to me. To me, every life is sacred, except the ones that aren't. There are very few in that last category, but Maundsley might just be one of them. He'd cheered as the forces of darkness had unleashed a tide of death and destruction across Europe. And still, apparently, didn't regret the fact.

I didn't bother one jot whether His Holiness found himself making excuses for Gervase at smart cocktail parties. ("Yes, the killer was my brother, the fascist - always been a bit of a scamp!") But if the contagion spread to the paper as a whole, that was different. It would affect dozens of my colleagues. People who wrote the paper, who printed it, who sold the advertising which paid our salaries. And I couldn't have that.

Which was why I was standing on the corner of North Road and Pavilion Buildings.

I was waiting for Freddie Barkworth, the *Chronicle's* chief photographer. Maundsley had barred reporters and photographers from his rally. They'd got rough in the past. And punch-ups are bad publicity for politicians. But Freddie and I were going to attend anyway.

I glanced at my watch, then looked up.

Freddie stepped round the corner. He was a short man, not

more than five foot six. He had an impish kind of face and sticky-out ears. It made him look at bit strange which meant a lot of people didn't take him seriously. Which was just what he wanted. While they were ignoring him, Freddie would insinuate himself just where he wanted to be. He'd snap the shutter on his camera and capture a legendary newspaper picture.

But today Freddie looked as though he may have overdone the freaky style. He was wearing a hacking jacket which bulged out around his stomach. He had a pair of baggy grey flannel trousers held at the waist by a sturdy belt. He looked as though he'd put on about three stone in weight since I'd seen him that morning.

I said: "You look like a badly made Guy Fawkes left over from bonfire night."

He said: "I'll take that as compliment. I've got a neat little Zeiss camera strapped round my middle. I operate it from a shutter release cord in my right-hand trouser pocket. The lens is sticking through a hole in my shirt but hidden under my tie. When I want to take a shot, I just undo these two buttons on my jacket, lift up the tie with my left hand, click the shutter with my right - and we have a front page picture for tomorrow's paper."

I grinned. "Sneaky," I said.

"The only problem, as I see it, is how we get in there in the first place."

I nodded. "Maundsley will have both the public doors to the Dome auditorium and the stage door round the side guarded by his Grey Shirts. But there's a route inside he may not know about.

"I'll tell you about it on the way."

Almost a year earlier, I'd been in Prinny's Pleasure, a kind of drinkers' doss house which I use when I want to meet a contact on the sly.

I was arguing with an informant called Reg. He claimed to

have uncovered a plot to kidnap the mayor and hold him to ransom.

Reg was the kind of bloke who plagues crime correspondents. He knew that newspapers had budgets for tip-off money. He thought that all he had to do was to convince me he had a good tale, and he'd walk away with a fistful of fivers.

But on newspapers, it doesn't work like that. Before we hand over the cash, we demand evidence. And Reg's evidence boiled down to an over-heard conversation between a couple of drunks in a pub.

So I'd told Reg that he could whistle for the fifty quid he wanted. But as a reward for the most outrageous scam of the week, I'd buy him half of bitter and a packet of crisps. Like a lot of people whose dreams are shattered when they crash into reality, Reg got angry. We argued. He shouted a bit and then stormed out.

I was about to finish my own gin and tonic (one ice cube, two slices of lemon) when the door opened and a drunk lurched in. He staggered across the room.

He leaned on the bar and said: "Gimme a pint of bitter."

Jeff Purkiss, who runs the place, looked at him like he was a slug that'd just left a trail of slime on the carpet. But he reached for a glass and poured the beer.

He put the beer on the bar and said: "Sixpence."

The drunk scattered a handful of coins on the bar.

Jeff sneered at the coins and said: "That's only four pence. You need another tuppence."

The drunk rummaged in his pockets and pulled out the linings. A few bits of black lint fell on the floor. The drunk said: "All I got on me."

Jeff whipped the glass away and said. "No cash, no beer."

The drunk said: "Do you know who I am?"

Jeff said: "You're Marty the Mole. And you're drunk."

Marty said: "And you look like a compost heap on two legs."

At which point he tried to throw a punch at Jeff. But he couldn't reach across the bar. And he was off-balance. So collapsed on the floor.

Jeff said: "I'm calling the cops."

But, by now, I was up at the bar and helping Marty back to his feet.

I winked at Jeff and said: "Don't do that. I'll take him outside."

I'd heard rumours about Marty the Mole, but never met him. Wasn't even sure he existed. It seemed an opportunity too good to miss.

I took Marty to a late-night café and plied him with black coffee and bread pudding. As he sobered up, he told me about his work at the Royal Pavilion, the ornate palace originally built as a seaside pad for the Prince Regent, later King George the Fourth.

Every year the place attracted thousands of visitors who admired the extravagant oriental decoration and over-the-top architecture. What they never saw was the part of the building Marty looked after. Under the Pavilion, there was a network of tunnels. In its heyday, servants scurried around the tunnels as they went about their work.

But there'd been a rumour there was also a tunnel used by the Prince when he went a-courting. He had an affair with a Mrs Maria Fitzherbert and, it was said, a tunnel linked the Pavilion to the naughty lady's home nearby in The Steine. But Marty told me that wasn't true. There was a secret tunnel. But it linked the Pavilion to the building which had originally been used as the King's stables and riding school. The stables had long ago been converted into the Dome theatre.

Where Maundsley was holding his rally.

"So that tunnel is going to get us into the rally?" Freddie asked.

"We'll come up inside the Dome and Maundsley and his Grey Shirts will never be any the wiser," I said. "I've arranged for Marty to meet us inside the Royal Pavilion. He'll take us through the tunnel."

We turned into Pavilion Buildings and stopped. Ahead of us a crowd of protestors surged through the Pavilion's gardens. They raced across the lawns. They trampled through flower beds. They waved homemade posters with slogans like "No Fascists in Brighton", "Go home Maundsley" and "Hitler is dead. Hurrah!" They yelled and they screamed and they blew whistles.

A row of uniformed police with arms linked tried to keep the protestors away from the Dome. But the crowd was pushing hard and the police line wavered. Behind the police, groups of Grey Shirts loomed menacingly on the Dome steps. They bristled with aggression. They scowled at the police and protestors. They made angry gestures at the crowd.

I said: "Let's get into the Pavilion and away from this lot."

We hurried under the *porte-cochère* at the Pavilion entrance and through the main door. Marty was lurking inside behind a large red-padded porter's chair.

He was twitching from foot to foot and his eyes darted from side-to-side. He was sober.

We hurried up to him.

He said: "You're late. I've been hanging around here for five minutes. Any longer and the above-ground staff would have started asking awkward questions."

"Then let's go."

Marty led us at quick-march pace through a fancy saloon and some smaller rooms. The place was quiet. It had closed a couple of hours earlier. The only person we passed was a cleaner.

We hurried down a corridor and stopped outside an anonymous-looking door. Marty fumbled in his pocket and brought out a bunch of keys. He unlocked the door and we hurried into a kind of landing. On the far side, a circular staircase descended into the Pavilion's basement.

Marty turned and said: "Follow me."

The metal staircase creaked and clanged as we whirled down. Round and round we went, like we were on a merry-go-round, until we reached the bottom. We came out into a small chamber with an arched roof. The roof had been painted green, but a long time ago. The place was lit by a bulb behind a metal grille.

The chamber acted as a junction of corridors - a subterranean cross-roads - running off in four different directions. The corridors were narrow but had vaulted ceilings like the chamber. Two of the corridors were lined with blue-glazed tiles. The other two had brick walls.

I sniffed the air. The place had a heavy damp smell, like someone had been boiling old rags.

"Imagine when this was lit by candles," I said.

"I'd rather not," Freddie said. "It's spooky enough as it is."

Marty pointed down one of the tile-lined corridors. "This leads to the Dome," he said.

We started along it. Marty led the way. The clump of our footsteps on the stone floor echoed off the walls. We didn't speak. We were too keyed up by the experience - and by what we might encounter when we came out at the other end.

At last, we turned a corner and Marty led us to another circular staircase. It was made from wrought-iron and clanged as we stepped on it.

"Be quiet as we get near the top," Marty whispered. "People outside can sometimes feel the vibrations through the floor."

We picked our way up the last few steps like a posse of ballerinas on pointe.

We reached a heavy wooden door. We clustered round in a group.

Marty whispered: "I'm going to unlock the door. You must slip out quickly in case there's anybody about. I'll lock the door after you - so you'll be on your own."

I nodded. I pulled a fiver out of my pocket and handed it to

Marty.

He unlocked the door. We waited a second. Strained our ears to hear whether there was anyone on the other side. All we heard were chants and screams from the protestors in Pavilion Gardens.

I turned the door knob, opened the door an inch, and looked out. There was a small foyer outside the door. It was lit by red wall lamps and had a stained carpet. It was empty.

"Now," I said.

I flung open the door and Freddie and I shot through. Marty yanked the door closed behind us. It shut with a loud clunk. There was a moment's silence and then a key turned in the lock.

There was no way back.

We turned around.

And came face-to-face with a gorilla of a man. He had broad shoulders and a fleshy face creased by the sour lines of a permanent scowl. He had thick arms and a bulging stomach. He was dressed in a grey shirt with fancy epaulettes on the shoulders. His grey trousers sagged below his belly and were fastened by a broad leather belt. The belt had a skull-and-crossbones buckle. He wore a peaked cap. Not quite like an army officer's. Not quite like a bus conductor's. Somewhere in between. Perhaps something like a park keeper's. Of a royal park. The cap had a fancy badge on the front. Circular with a zig-zag through the centre like it had just been struck by lightning.

He stood in front of us with his large fists resting comfortably on his hips.

He said: "I am Captain Wellington Blunt, the British Patriot Party's head of security. Who are you and what are you doing in this private part of the building?"

Chapter 10

I glanced at Freddie whose mouth had fallen open in a gormless gape.

He tried to say something but it came out as a high-pitched squeak.

I turned to Blunt and said: "I am the leader of the West Chiltington battalion of the British Patriot Party."

The tiny village near Storrington was one of the few places in Sussex hardly anyone had heard of. There was more chance of me being struck by a thunderbolt personally lobbed down by Zeus than Blunt ever having visited it.

He said: "I know it well. But this is the first time I've heard West Chiltington has its own battalion."

I said: "Oh, yes, sir. In *East* Chiltington, we're right behind the party."

The other Chiltington was near Lewes and even tinier than its West namesake.

Blunt scowled. "You said West Chiltington."

"I'm sure I said East." I turned to Freddie: "I said East, didn't I?"

Freddie squeaked. It could have been "yes". It could have been "no". It could have been "get me out of here".

Blunt scowled some more and balled his fists. Looked like he was ready for a rumble.

I said: "'East is east and west is west and never the twain shall meet.'"

Blunt grunted. "Rudyard Kipling - only decent poet this country's ever produced." He relaxed a little. His hands hung limp at his sides. They looked like a couple of flounders hanging off a fisherman's hooks.

I said: "Couldn't agree more about Kipling." I turned to Freddie. "Couldn't we?"

Freddie squeaked twice. Possibly in a rhyming couplet.

Blunt flexed his shoulders and looked hard at us.

He barked: "Stand to attention when you're addressing a superior officer."

We shuffled our feet together and straightened our backs. Tried to look like a couple of guardsmen on parade. It wasn't easy for Freddie with the camera strapped round his stomach.

Blunt strode slowly around us, like he was inspecting his troops before a big battle. The man fancied himself as the brave commander. Probably modelled himself on Marlborough or Montgomery or one of the famous generals of the past. He had the given name for it. Wellington, victor of the battle of Waterloo. The most famous general of them all. But under the cod-uniform and the officer's epaulettes there was just a street bullyboy. He was a thug living a fantasy. But that made him dangerous.

He circled us twice. Came to a stop in front of me. Leaned closer. I could smell the rancid reek of his breath. You could have bottled the stink and used it to frighten off rats.

He said: "What's your name?"

I said: "Ponsonby Crampton." I thumbed at Freddie. "And this is Bert Buckle, my deputy."

Blunt's eyebrows parted like a theatre curtain.

He said: "Ponsonby. That's an unusual name. A familiar name."

"Naturally, to an officer such as yourself. Wellington led British forces at Waterloo. Ponsonby commanded the Second Union Cavalry Brigade at the battle."

Silently, I congratulated myself on staying awake in the school history lesson when we'd covered the Napoleonic wars.

I said: "My father was a fan of the general who died a hero's death and named me after him. So we have something in common."

Blunt looked unconvinced. He moved back and stood further

off. Brushed an imaginary fleck of dust from his shirt. Gloated a bit. He was named after the top man. My moniker came from an under-strapper. Just as he liked it. He allowed himself a small smile. Fleshy lips parted to reveal grey teeth.

Blunt turned an evil eye on Freddie.

Freddie's shirt was bulging around his midriff from the camera. The buttons on his jacket strained. If he wasn't careful, the lens of the camera would pop out from behind his tie.

"What's wrong with your deputy?" Blunt asked.

"Heavy bandaging," I said. "Just recovering from an appendix operation."

"Grumbling?" Blunt said.

"The appendix was - but Bert doesn't complain," I said. "Do you Bert?"

Freddie looked at me with desperate eyes. "No, er, Ponsonby."

"We still haven't cleared up why you're in this restricted area," Blunt said.

"Security check," I said.

"What security?"

"Checking the lavatories for hidden communists before the rally starts."

Blunt's brow furrowed. He'd never thought of that.

"Find any?" Blunt asked.

"No, Captain."

"Carry on, then."

Freddie and I turned and marched away like a couple of troopers heading into battle.

I could feel the heat from Blunt's eyes burning my back as we went through the door.

"That was close," Freddie said as we took our seats in the main auditorium.

"It could get worse," I said.

We looked around the place. It was half full but crowds

streamed through the doors. They had tight lips, angry eyes, flushed cheeks. Mean faces. They'd come to hear their hero. They'd expected to feel the power of his words. But they hadn't expected to meet opposition outside. After all, wasn't Sir Oscar Maundsley the fount of all truth? A saviour for the nation?

Not if the hundreds of protestors had their way. They hated Maundsley. And everything he stood for.

And the people who stood by his side.

That's why Maundsley's supporters looked sour and angry. Because when you believe you know the one unquestionable truth, you can't understand why other people hate you for it.

Inside the auditorium we could hear the shouts and whistles of the protestors.

Maundsley out! Maundsley out!

I said: "Have your camera ready, Freddie. This is heading the way of other Maundsley rallies. To a punch-up."

Freddie grinned: "Great," he said. He'd recovered from the shock of meeting Blunt. "Is that why we're sitting at the back?"

"If you're in the front row, you don't see what's happening behind you. You miss stuff that might make good copy - or pictures."

Freddie said: "What did you mean just now when you said it could get worse?"

I said: "I interviewed one of Maundsley's fan club this afternoon. A Rhine maiden by the name of Unity Box-Hartley. She wouldn't miss this. I just hope she doesn't spot me. She'd give me away faster than you could say '*Sieg heil*'. If Blunt realises we're journos and not Maundsley fans I wouldn't fancy our chances."

We kept our heads down but risked occasional peeks around.

Freddie said: "Will Maundsley have his wife with him this evening? I'd like to get a picture of them together."

"I wouldn't think so. She divorced him three years ago. There's no Lady Maundsley on the scene at the moment."

The lights dimmed and the crowded auditorium fell silent. The air was electric with anticipation. You could have powered the seafront illuminations with it.

From the back of the auditorium drums began beating.

Dum-di-dum, dum-di-dum.

Then they appeared. Four drummers marched down the central aisle two abreast. They beat their drums in a steady rhythm. One drummer was old and bald. One drummer was young and walked with a limp. One drummer was tall and thin. The drummer next to him was short and fat. They were dressed in grey shirts and grey shorts. Their knees were knobbly. They marched out of step.

They looked like a bunch of guys who needed a uniform to make them feel good. And a drum to beat made them feel better. They could pretend the instrument was someone they didn't like. As a way of raising their self-esteem it looked like it wasn't working. They'd have felt better going to the pub and getting drunk.

I whispered to Freddie: "This raggle-taggle army wouldn't frighten the brownies."

Freddie pointed to the back of the hall.

"What about them?"

Two Grey Shirts marched in holding flaming torches.

"They're either holding a barbecue or planning to burn the place down," I said.

But Freddie didn't have time to reply to that. Because Oscar Maundsley marched in behind the torch-carriers. The crowd were on their feet cheering as Maundsley stomped down the aisle.

He passed as close as if we'd shoved past one another in a corridor at the *Chronicle*. I caught the astringent whiff of pricey cologne as he strode by. He was old enough to own a pension book, but he walked ramrod straight. He'd maintained the slim figure I'd seen in old newspaper cuttings. There were wrinkles around his neck and the beginning of crow's feet around his eyes, but otherwise his skin was smooth. His black hair receded a little from his forehead but it was still thick. His moustache was pencil thin. He was dressed in tailored grey slacks designed to show off the line of his leg. He had a grey shirt and wore a Sam Browne belt over it. He didn't need any fancy epaulettes on his shirt. He strode with an easy confidence which made it clear who was in charge around here.

The drummers fanned out at the front of the auditorium. The torch bearers mounted the stage and disappeared into the wings.

Maundsley took the steps to the stage slowly. I sensed he wanted to savour the moment. Wanted to hear the cheers ringing in his ears a little longer. Wanted to lap up the adulation.

He reached the stage and turned to the audience. The shouts rose louder. They drowned out the cries of the demonstrators outside. And then Maundsley turned to face his faithful.

He moved forward and his arm shot into the air as if he was hailing a taxi. But I'd seen that salute on *Pathé* newsreels too often. By a little man with a Charlie Chaplin moustache. And I didn't like it.

Freddie undid his jacket and fumbled with his hand under his tie. It looked like he was playing with his belly button. I hoped Blunt or one of his goons didn't notice. He'd have us slung out for indecency.

Freddie lifted up his tie and I heard a faint click as the shutter on the camera snapped. It snapped twice more before Freddie replaced his tie.

The crowd had been on their feet delirious with joy. Goodness knows what they'd have done if something really good had happened. Now they sat down. Slowly, as if they were trying to understand what they'd just done. They shot little sheepish looks at their neighbours as if to say: "I may have been foolish but you were doing it too."

On the stage, Maundsley moved to the lectern. He stood silent for a moment, then threw back his head and spoke.

"My friends, we come together in this great meeting at a critical moment in our nation's history." He had a rich baritone voice. "I come to you tonight with a profound sense of that history and with a bold vision for our future. We have been a great imperial nation in the past - and we can be great in the future. We can be even greater."

The audience cheered. Maundsley let the cheers run, then quietened them with a dismissive flip of his right hand.

"It is some forty years since I first offered my services to our nation in a general election. Forty years during which we have seen an economic depression that impoverished our people, a war that shattered our great country, and a cowardly government that has given away much of our great Empire. There are guilty men and I shall name them. And they shall pay the price. Now, forty years on from the first of my election campaigns, I bring fresh hope to our nation."

He lifted a thick document from the lectern. Held it up so that all could see it.

"This is my legacy. My plan for Britain. It is a plan for making our country great again. We shall triumph once more over the inferior races of the world. We shall be strong again so that all may fear us. We shall conquer where we have an inalienable right to go. We shall taste - as is our nation's birth right - the fruits of our conquest. And now let me tell you, like the real friends I know you all to be, about my plan."

But it looked as though we weren't going to hear the plan.

A delicate hand with red painted fingernails landed on my shoulder. I looked up. Unity Box-Hartley grinned at me. Like a lioness about to eat a gazelle. Behind her, Blunt's scowl was working overtime.

Unity said to Blunt: "If he's leader of the East Chiltington Patriots, I'm Queen of the May. He was a journalist with the

Evening Chronicle when he interviewed me this afternoon."

Blunt said: "We have ways of dealing with journalists."

I said: "I hope it doesn't involve thumbscrews. I have enough trouble opening sardine tins with those fiddly keys as it is."

Behind Blunt the two torch-bearers moved menacingly forward.

Beside me, Freddie squeaked.

On the stage, Maundsley had launched into his plan to subjugate the world.

The audience had fallen silent. They were enraptured.

The shouts of the demonstrators outside grew louder.

And then the doors at the side of the auditorium burst open, and protestors flooded in. There were young ones dressed in jeans and tee-shirts. There were old ones in corduroy trousers and cardigans. There were men in rat-catcher caps. There were women with scarves knotted under their chins. Some waved placards. Some blew whistles. Some charged forward looking for a rumble.

Maundsley stared at them with a disdain that would have been impressive had it not also been stupid.

Blunt roared: "Grey Shirts, to action stations."

Around the hall, men rose to their feet and scrambled towards the protestors.

But the demonstrators were already swarming up the aisles.

Blunt yelled: "Drummers - attack beat."

The drums started up in a pounding staccato rhythm.

Dum, dum, dum-ti-dum.

And then the fighting started.

Blunt rushed towards the thick of the battle.

Fists flew and feet kicked. But the protestors and the Grey Shirts had crushed together and there was little room to launch a haymaker punch or deliver a swinging kick. Instead they pushed and shoved like angry commuters in an overcrowded rush-hour train. They shouted and yelled insults at one another.

I looked around. In the melee, Unity had vanished. On the stage, Maundsley gathered up his papers and walked slowly towards the wings. Like an ageing actor who couldn't be bothered to take a curtain call.

I grabbed Freddie, who let out another squeak.

I said: "We should follow Maundsley."

We pushed our way into the aisle. Maundsley disappeared into the wings.

The first casualties were crawling away holding red handkerchiefs to busted noses, bleeding lips, black eyes. Men shouted, women yelled. Crowds pushed towards the emergency exits. More demonstrators piled in. They wielded placards mounted on staves. Shouts and cries and screams rent the air.

Freddie and I elbowed our way through the crowd towards the stage.

The fight was moving closer. The demonstrators were outnumbered by the Grey Shirts. But the demonstrators had the momentum.

Blunt emerged from the melee and scrambled up the steps to the stage. He hurried after Maundsley into the wings.

Freddie and I pushed forward faster. We reached the stage and climbed up the steps. The Grey Shirts had mounted a counter-attack and started to push the demonstrators back. But now more demonstrators poured through a second door.

We hurried towards the wings. There was no sign of Maundsley or Blunt.

I turned to Freddie: "They'll make for the stage door."

"Which way?" Freddie said.

I pointed ahead. We hurried through a corridor. Ahead I heard a door open and slam shut.

We reached the door and flung it open. We stepped out into Pavilion Gardens. Most of the demonstrators were over to our left. They were trying to force their way in through an emergency exit, but the crowd from inside was pouring out.

In the distance, a police car bell was ringing. The plods would circle the building a few times and hope the trouble would pass so they wouldn't have to wade in and sort it out.

Freddie and I raced into New Road.

I nudged Freddie and pointed. "Over there, outside the Theatre Royal."

A smart Bentley was parked by the kerb. A chauffeur in a peaked cap sat behind the steering wheel.

Blunt opened the car's rear door and Maundsley stepped inside.

"Get your camera out," I yelled over my shoulder at Freddie as I raced towards the Bentley.

But Blunt had shut the door on Maundsley.

As I ran up, the car's ignition fired and it shot away from the kerb.

Freddie panted after me. He lifted his camera and took a shot of the back of the Bentley as it disappeared around the corner.

Blunt was left standing in the road. He watched the retreating car, then turned towards us. His scowl moved into overdrive. He raced towards us. He looked like a charging rhinoceros. I hadn't expected such a big man to run so fast. But then even rhinos can put on a turn of speed.

I stepped forward but Blunt angled away from me towards Freddie who was busy with his camera.

Freddie looked up a second too late. Blunt cannoned into him and Freddie fell backwards. His arms went up and the camera flew into the air.

The momentum of Blunt's charge took him ten yards past Freddie. But his target was the camera. He screeched to a halt and tried to turn.

The camera was still in the air. Freddie was scrambling to his feet. But there was no way he would catch it before it smashed on the ground. And now Blunt was charging Freddie again.

I raced across the road as the camera fell. I was never going to catch it. I dived like a rugby forward heading for the touchline. I stretched out my arms and caught the camera six inches from the ground.

Now I was floundering on the road, feeling bruised. And Blunt was charging towards me. He was eight feet away. His left leg was up and he planned to treat my head like a rugby football. His shadow loomed over me. I rolled to one side. Lifted my right leg off the ground, caught my foot behind Blunt's incoming kick and twisted upwards.

Blunt toppled backwards like he was a redwood tree that had just been felled. I swear the ground shook as he hit it. Seismographs in Africa would have recorded a minor earthquake. Blunt bellowed in pain. The wind had rushed out of him. He floundered on the ground like a beached whale. He wasn't getting up any time soon.

Freddie was now on his feet. He ran towards me. I scrambled up and handed him the camera.

Freddie checked the film, adjusted the focus, and lifted the viewfinder to his eye.

He pointed the camera at Blunt.

"Smile," he said as he clicked the shutter.

Chapter 11

Freddie Barkworth said: "You'll want to see this."

It was just before nine o'clock the following morning. We were in the newsroom at the *Chronicle*. I'd finished batting out a twelve-hundred word front-page lead on the riot at the rally. I'd written a sidebar on the rumble with Captain Wellington Blunt and the camera.

Now Freddie had slapped a photo on my desk. It showed Blunt seconds after I'd tripped him up and Freddie had taken his picture. Blunt was flat out in the middle of the road. He'd lifted his head. His mouth gaped, his nose looked squashed, and his eyes were glazed with confusion.

"This is a great shot," I said.

Freddie preened himself a bit. And why not?

"Figgis plans to run it on the front page," he said.

"And to think Blunt wanted to grab your camera to stop you taking his picture," I said.

Freddie scratched his head. "I'm not so sure about that now. I think he may have wanted to stop us seeing these pictures. I've just finished printing them."

He laid three black and white eight-by-six prints on my desk. They were still damp from the fixer and rinsing solutions. The effect was a bit like looking at pictures through a shower of rain.

I leaned closer. "These are the snaps of the rear of Maundsley's Bentley disappearing around the corner," I said.

I had to admire Freddie's work. He'd had seconds to yank the camera out from under his shirt, focus it on the Bentley and snap the shutter. He'd taken three shots in quick succession. There couldn't have been a time lapse of more than five seconds between the first and the last.

The pictures reminded me of the sort of film noir images you used to get in movies like *The Third Man*. They showed a street dappled with pools of light and dark shadows. Solitary figures lingered on the edge of the shadows. Beams from a single street lamp fell on the rear of the Bentley.

I could see Maundsley in the back seat. His head was twisted round and he was glaring through the car's rear window. His upper lip was curled in a snarl. His nose cast a shadow on the left side of his face. But his right eye radiated hatred.

In the second picture, Maundsley had moved. I could see his whole face. And his eyes showed surprise, perhaps at the flashlight from Freddie's camera. He'd lifted his arms across the back shelf of the Bentley. He seemed to be lurching to his left.

The third picture showed why. Maundsley was reaching for a box perched on the shelf behind the Bentley's rear seat. He was making a grab for the box. His left hand was stretched out trying to obscure it.

I turned to Freddie. "Is there any way you can blow this picture up more so we can see what that box is?"

Freddie whipped a magnifying glass out of his pocket. "I anticipate your every need," he said.

I took the magnifying glass and focused it over the box.

"It's a hat box," I said. "A lady's hat box. And there's some writing on the side which reads..." I peered closer. "...*Pascale Dubois. Chapeaux de Dames. Faubourg Saint-Honoré.*"

"This is strange," I said. "I've seen pictures of Maundsley wearing a homburg but no way is that a *chapeau de dame*."

"Perhaps it's his wife's hat box," Freddie said.

"She divorced him. When you lose a wife, you lose her hat box and her love - and not necessarily in that order. Maundsley is not the sentimental type to hang onto mementoes. I'd guess there's a new woman in his life."

"Could be that Unity Box-Hartley," Freddie said.

"She certainly seems keen enough. But when the riot started she didn't rush to his side. That would have been the giveaway that they were having an affair."

"Interesting piece for the gossip column," Freddie said.

I leaned back in my old captain's chair. "If you're right about Blunt wanting the camera to destroy these photos there could be more to it than that."

"But what?" Freddie asked.

"I don't know," I said. "But you know what the French say when a man gets into a fight?"

Freddie shook his head.

"*Cherchez la femme.*"

"How do you manage to eat all that for lunch and still keep a model's figure?" I asked.

Shirley hoisted a forkful of shepherd's pie to her mouth and said: "I think beautiful thoughts while I'm chewing." She stuffed the pie in her mouth and munched away.

We were in the Happy Tripper restaurant, a meat-and-two veg joint on Brighton seafront where Shirley had worked as a waitress before she'd got into modelling.

She'd taken a break from her current assignment on the West Pier. A magazine fashion shoot for groovy disco wear. Shirl was wearing baggy trousers in a red and black harlequin pattern tucked into the top of snakeskin boots. She had a halter top which looked as though it had been made out of a pocket handkerchief. She'd turned a few heads when we'd walked into the restaurant.

I said: "I hope the beautiful thoughts don't include those trousers."

Shirley forked up a lorry driver's sized portion of pie and said: "These daks make some of the gear I modelled this morning look like a widow's weeds."

I ate some of my sausage and mash while Shirl chomped away.

I said: "Do you ever get to model hats?"

Shirl opened her arms in a look-at-me gesture. "Do you think a girl wearing this clobber to the disco is going to worry about head-gear?"

"It's just that I've been thinking about a hat."

"You'd look weird in a bowler or a trilby."

"I was thinking of a woman's hat."

"You'd look even more of a drongo than usual in a straw number with feathers and flowers."

I put down my knife and fork and pushed away the remains of the sausage and mash.

"I just wondered whether you'd ever heard of a Paris hat shop called *Pascale Dubois*. It's in the *Faubourg Saint-Honoré*."

"Sounds like the kind of place for snooty Sheilas who walk around like they've got a bad smell under their nose."

"That's what I thought."

"What's your interest?" Shirley asked. She scooped up the last of her shepherd's pie.

I told her about the rumpus with Blunt and how Freddie had snapped pictures of the hat box in Maundsley's car.

Shirley put down her knife and fork. "Haven't you got enough on your plate finding this Gervase Pope bludger without worrying about a hat box?"

I shrugged. "You're probably right. But I've no idea where Gervase is hiding out. And Maundsley is supposed to be his target. So I figure the more I can find out about Maundsley, the more chance I might discover a link to Gervase."

"And blagging an extra headline about Maundsley's mystery woman couldn't be further from your mind."

I grinned. "No fooling you, is there?"

"Most don't even try," Shirley said.

"So you can't help about the hat box?"

Shirley leaned across the table and kissed me lightly on the lips. "I didn't say that. As it happens there's a lighting guy in the crew for this fashion shoot. He was telling me he's done some work in Paris. I'll quiz him this afternoon and see if he's heard of it."

Shirl flicked her gaze to a tiny wristwatch. "Jeez, I'm late for the afternoon shoot. Guess I'll have to blow and leave you with the tab."

"My lot in life," I said.

But Shirl had already disappeared.

I watched as the red and black harlequin trousers hurried along the promenade towards the pier.

One thing you learn on newspapers is that there's nothing like a photograph to stir people's memories.

You can run a thousand words of perfect prose and won't have a flicker of a reaction. But print a photo, and it churns up all kinds of hidden secrets.

So I wasn't surprised to receive a call within five minutes of arriving back in the newsroom. The midday edition of the paper was on my desk. It had the picture of Blunt on the ground in New Road. It ran across six columns above the fold under the headline: DOWN AND OUT.

I was admiring the page as my phone rang.

I lifted the receiver and Sonya, the receptionist in the front office, said: "There's a man here to see you."

"Who is it?"

"He won't give a name."

"Did he say what it's about?"

"No, but he's got today's paper. He's sitting over by the potted palm, looking at the picture on the front page and laughing."

I thought about that for a moment. Quite a few newspaper informants like to play the man-of-mystery act. Especially if they're after tip-off money.

I said: "Park him in the interview room and I'll be down in a couple of minutes."

I took another look at the front page, grabbed my notebook, and headed downstairs to the interview room.

Mystery man was lounging on a chair, with his right foot up on his left knee. His gaze was locked on the front page of the *Chronicle*. He held it in both hands in front of him. The paper rustled in his grip as he chuckled at the picture.

He looked up as I stepped through the door. A weasely face was topped with a thatch of brown hair that had started to grey round the ears. There were dark smudges under his eyes and a small scar at the right side of his mouth. The lobe of his left ear was missing. He looked about fifty, but he was the kind of person who'd probably looked fifty for years.

He waved the paper at me and said: "Last time I saw old Blunty on the floor was VE night in Hamburg. He was throwing up in a latrine, the only useful thing he'd done that day. That taught him the perils of hooky vodka. He'd blagged it from a Polish infantry sergeant. The Pole had distilled it from boot polish. Blunty drank a whole bottle of the poison."

I said: "But not you?"

"Stick to stout. That's my motto. Not that you could get a decent bottle of it in Hamburg in forty-five."

I took a seat on the other side of the table.

I said: "I'm Colin Crampton."

Mystery Man put the paper down and said: "Terry Jones."

I said: "I take it you're not a fan of Captain Wellington Blunt."

"Wellington? That's a laugh, for a start. His real name is Wilberforce. He changed it when he joined the army. Reckoned the old general's moniker would give him a leg up in the promotion stakes. I guess he may have had a point. At least he ended up a captain. I never made it past corporal - and that was only for a few weeks. I got busted down to private again. By that bastard Blunt."

I flipped open my notebook. "Care to tell me about it?"

Jones narrowed his eyes. "What's in it for me?"

"A cup of tea."

"Anything else?"

"A digestive biscuit."

Jones slumped back in his chair. The corners of his mouth turned down.

"I hoped you might spring a couple of bob. Just for a bottle of stout or two."

"Tell me the tale, and we'll see."

Jones shrugged. Sat up straighter. "Hamburg in May 1945 was a bleeding mess. You ain't seen anything like it. I certainly hadn't. It was like walking through a demolition site. No electricity. No mains water in much of the city. No plumbing, half the sewers didn't work. No wonder Blunty was treated as some kind of saviour by the locals."

"How come?"

"He likes to portray himself as a bold warrior. That's a laugh. He commanded a mobile latrine unit. Bogbrush Blunt he was known as in the officers' mess. He hated the name."

"But a hero to the locals with no water and no sewers," I said.

Jones nodded. "Yeah. And didn't he just milk it. Made a small fortune on the black market."

"With a mobile latrine unit?" I said.

"You weren't there. Tell me this: what was the most marketable commodity in Hamburg's black market?"

"Bread," I said.

"No."

"Coffee."

"No."

"Soap."

"Closer but not right. It's bog paper. Toilet tissue if you want to be posh about it. Not that it was tissue in those days. After a big one, your bum felt like it had been rubbed down with sandpaper. Not that that bothered the locals. They couldn't get enough of the stuff."

"Are you saying Blunt sold army supplied toilet paper on the black market?"

"Tons of it. But too much. He could fool the brass most of the time. They had more important things to worry about than how much bog paper the mobile latrine unit was using. But Blunty didn't know when to stop. He over-reached himself."

"And was caught?"

Jones shook his head. His eyes flashed angrily. "Not Blunt. He knew how to cover his back. There were two of us who used to make the deliveries. Me and Smudger Burnley. We walked into a trap. The red-caps were waiting for us. Someone sold us out. Never found out who."

"But Blunt walked away?"

"Blunty visited Smudger and me in the glasshouse. Said he'd act as our officer advocate at the court martial. He told me that if I put my hand up and kept him out of it, he'd see me all right. I didn't see I had much choice. I was nailed whether Bogbrush was involved or not. Blunty made the same offer to Smudger. But Smudger didn't see it that way. He reckoned that if he was going down, Bogbrush would come with him. He told Blunt to his face that he'd denounce him before the court martial."

"So Blunt was cashiered, too?" I asked.

"No such luck. The night before the hearing Smudger was found dead in his cell."

I leaned forward. "Not from natural causes?"

"No. His throat had been slashed with a knife."

I rocked back on my chair so hard I nearly fell off.

I wobbled back to the upright. Straightened my tie. Tried to look as though I was taking it all in my stride.

With a mouth as dry as a sack of cement, I asked: "And you believe that Smudger was killed by Blunt?"

Jones smirked: "Who else? But it was never proved."

"Why not?"

"The turnkey - a redcap - guarding the cells that night went AWOL."

"He disappeared?"

"Never seen again. It was happening a lot after the war finished. Blokes who'd stepped up to the plate when the fighting was on, didn't see why they couldn't slope off now it had finished. Besides, in forty-five those German *fräuleins* would put it out for a box of matches, let alone a packet of fags."

I made a note in shaky Pitman's. "You're saying the redcap ran off with a German girl?"

"Helped on his way with a generous donation from Blunt's bog roll slush fund," Jones said.

"So there was no record of who visited the cell during the night," I said.

"And naturally Blunt had arranged for alibis to say he'd not been near the place."

"But you believe he'd killed Smudger?"

"Who else could have done it? Blunt was more than a ducker and diver. He had a nasty streak as wide as the North Sea - and just as murky. He killed Smudger, all right."

And, I thought, could have killed Derek Clapham in the same way. Except there was no motive for the killing. In theory, Blunt and Clapham were fascist comrades in arms.

I looked at Jones. He had the satisfied air of a man who's said his piece after a long time waiting.

"Why contact the *Chronicle* years after all this happened?" I asked.

"I served my time in the glasshouse, then came out into civvy street hoping I'd make a go of my life. But that time in the can has followed me everywhere. I've had jobs, but it's been tough to find them and keep them. Meanwhile, Blunty used his ill-gotten to start up a security business. Security - with Blunt that's a sick joke. When I saw him on the ground in that picture it gave me a real lift."

Jones stood up. Stepped towards the door.

I said: "You haven't had your tea and biscuit. Or a couple of bob for a bottle of stout."

He grinned: "Not what I really wanted, after all," he said. "I've left you with what I came for. It's made me feel good. Think I'll treat myself to a fish tea."

I hadn't expected one shock about Blunt - let alone two.

The second came after I arrived back at my lodgings that evening.

I crept silently into the hall. I hoped to sneak upstairs and avoid the Widow.

But she had ears like Jodrell Bank antennae. She shot out of her parlour waving the Night Final edition of the *Chronicle*. The Blunt picture was still on the front page.

She said: "I didn't expect to see this man on his back."

"Is that because you normally see him on his front, Mrs Gribble?"

The Widow frowned. "Don't be disgusting. It so happens I've seen him three times at my tango class in the past couple of weeks. I thought he was the kind of gentleman I wouldn't mind trying a backward *ocho* with."

I didn't ask.

But I did wonder what Blunt was doing at the Dolores Esteban Tango Academy. He didn't strike me as a man who'd be a natural at tripping the light fantastic.

So I did ask: "Was the fat old basket pictured lying in the road a dance pupil?"

The Widow sniffed. "I'll ignore the offensiveness in your question. But, no, he wasn't taking lessons. On each of his visits, he had private business with Conrad Montez, my occasional dance partner. When he called, Conrad had to leave me to speak to this gentleman in the green room. On the third occasion I was annoyed because I missed doing the Kiss of Fire with Conrad."

"It would probably have gone out," I said.

The Widow stamped her foot, stormed back into her parlour,

and slammed the door.

It left me standing on the bottom stair wondering what the hell Captain Wellington Blunt from the bog brush battalion was doing at a tango class.

Chapter 12

I was still wondering about it when I arrived at my desk the following morning.

There were certainly plenty of questions about Blunt. And I didn't have an answer to any of them.

Had Blunt murdered Smudger to protect himself, as Terry Jones had said? Blunt certainly had a motive to kill Smudger. But, then, Jones had a motive to discredit Blunt. Whose tale should I believe? As a reporter, I was used to sneaky types that tried to use newspapers to settle old scores.

But if Blunt did murder Smudger, could he have also killed Derek Clapham? The night I'd entered Clapham's flat I was certain I'd seen his killer from the kitchen window. He'd fled down the darkened alley at the back of the flat. I conjured up the image in my mind. The sturdy figure had moved at a steady pace. Yes, it could have been Blunt. But, equally, it could have been a thousand other heavy-set men in Brighton.

And, anyway, what reason would Blunt have for killing Clapham? On the face of it, Gervase Pope had a stronger motive than Blunt. After all, Clapham had been the instrument that had resulted in Gervase being interned.

Finally, the Widow's news that Blunt met Conrad Montez at the Dolores Esteban Tango Academy added an exotic touch to the mystery. Blunt's visit could have been a social call. But, from the Widow's account, it didn't sound like it. And Blunt, as I'd discovered in New Road, was an old bruiser and not light on his feet.

I was mulling all this over when my telephone rang.

I hoisted the receiver and Ted Wilson said: "You'll be a dummy if you don't land this story."

I said: "I'll be a dummy if I try. I've already got more stories than I can shake a printer's rule at."

"I'd better call Jim Houghton at the *Evening Argus* then."

"Now that's below the belt," I told Ted. Houghton was my rival on the other paper in town. "So what's the big news?"

"There's been a robbery at Louis Tussaud's."

"You mean the waxwork museum on the seafront?"

"The very same. I'm calling you from the manager's office."

"Don't tell me - somebody's nicked yesterday's takings from the ticket booth. That wouldn't make more than a paragraph on an inside page."

"It's a little more than that. Whoever gained entry made off with some of the wax models."

"Not that Ali Baba and the Forty Thieves set-up they've had in the window since I was a lad? It's about time that was changed."

Ted chuckled. "Last night's thieves were a bit more discriminating than that."

"How discriminating?"

"For starters, they've taken Marilyn Monroe."

"Not the one with Marilyn in the white dress she wore in *The Seven Year Itch*."

"Yeah, the one blowing up with air from the subway vent."

"Bad business, but good choice," I said.

"And not their only one. The thieves have also had it on their toes with Yuri Gagarin."

"The first man in space? Reach for the stars and all that."

"Yeah. But that's not all. They made a final selection. Winston Churchill."

"He's vanished? Even his cigar?"

"Gone. All of them. As though they'd walked out of the place themselves. And there's more."

"Go on."

"You'll never guess whose company once had a hand in the security for the place. Here's a clue. Look at the picture on the front page of yesterday's paper."

The paper with the photo of Blunt spread-eagled on the road was propped up against my overflowing in-tray.

"Now that gives the story a new dimension," I said. "I'll be there in ten minutes."

"I thought you might be," Ted said. He cut the connection.

I grabbed my notebook and headed for the door.

By the time I reached Louis Tussaud's, the cops had rigged up a crime scene tape across the front of the building.

A few curious rubberneckers had gathered outside the tape. They gossiped among themselves. Pointed fingers at police cars. Craned necks as cops entered or left. Swapped theories with their neighbours.

Crime as entertainment.

One of the watchers collared me as I strode up. He thumbed towards the entrance. "Any idea what's going on in there, mate?"

I said: "I believe the wax model of the Queen Mother came alive in the night and eloped with Joseph Stalin."

The bloke's eyes goggled. The cogs in his brain turned slowly. It was incredible. It couldn't be true. But it would be better if it were. He'd have something to pass on to the others. Something they didn't know. That would make him special. The man in the know. He grinned. He turned and whispered in his neighbour's ear.

The cop behind the tape was staring at the exhibit in the window. A gruesome montage based on Edgar Allan Poe's story of *The Pit and the Pendulum*. It showed some poor sap in mediaeval get-up strapped to a table while a pendulum with a razor-sharp axe descended slowly towards him.

I pulled out my press card and called to the cop.

I said: "I'm here to see Inspector Wilson about the robbery."

The cop thumbed at the pendulum. "Bad business."

"I guess Louis Tussaud must be as cut up as that bloke would be if the pendulum slipped lower."

The cop shrugged.

I dodged under the tape and went through the door.

Ted Wilson was just inside leaning on the Sleeping Beauty exhibit. ("Watch her breathe.") He wasn't. He was casting a tired eye over a couple of young detective constables dusting the place for fingerprints.

I strolled up to him and said: "I reckon Quasimodo from the Chamber of Horrors did it."

Ted looked at me like I'd just asked him to take a class-load of kindergarten kids on a summer outing.

"He's still down in the Chamber of Horrors ringing his bells," he said.

As if to confirm the information a deep "bong, bong" sounded somewhere below ground.

"Any idea what's behind this?" I asked.

"Your guess is as good as mine. But I expect when you write it, you'll make it sound that your guess is better than mine."

"Could be some weird kind of collector," I said. "I've heard of paintings being stolen to order. Perhaps this is a similar case."

"I don't buy that. The things aren't worth that much. Besides how would you hide them? Remember they're life-sized."

"That's the attraction," I said. "Picture a sad old bloke with no friends. Suddenly, he's got Winston Churchill sat at his dinner table for some brilliant conversation and Marilyn waiting for him in the bedroom with her dress already half way up her thighs."

"What about Gagarin?" Ted asked.

"Up on the roof, keeping look-out," I said. "Where were the waxworks usually kept?"

"In the main exhibition hall," Ted said. "This way."

We entered a long chamber with a tiled floor and white ceiling. It was lit with spotlights that picked out the individual waxworks. They were arranged around the walls, behind a red rope slung between metal posts. The figures had shiny hair and staring eyes. It was like walking into a party where no-one was enjoying themselves. I expected a wax museum to smell like old candles. But it didn't. There was a heavy odour of disinfectant in the air. Probably Harpic.

Ted slouched by the door, while I walked round the room. I stood in front of the empty space where Marilyn had tried to keep her skirt from blowing up. A card on a small stand read: "Marilyn Monroe 1926-1962, film star." The red rope in front of the little podium she'd stood on was still in place. I could see the outline in the dust of where her shoes would have been.

I glanced to her left. John Wayne wore a Stetson and carried a six-shooter like he did in *The Man Who Shot Liberty Valance*. Except there was no-one to shoot here. And Wayne looked a bit sheepish to me. Well, you would if you had a constant stream of gawpers sniggering because they'd just discovered your real name was Marion, not John.

On the other side of Marilyn Monroe, Elizabeth Taylor held her head high. Her hard eyes seemed to scan the room. As though she were searching for her sixth husband.

I moved on in case she spotted me.

Yuri Gagarin - born 1934, the exhibit card told me - was also absent without leave. Not circling the earth in outer space this time. Where was he, I wondered? I'd read somewhere that Gagarin dolls - fully togged out in space suit - were on sale in Gamley's. Could it be that a generous parent had decided to go one better? If so, they'd have to make sure their kids played with wax Yuri well away from the fireplace.

I turned and looked back down the hall. Winston Churchill's place had been set aside from the others. He'd occupied a tableau tricked out like his office in 10 Downing Street. There was a desk and a bookshelf holding volumes of his history of the Second World War. But the old boy was missing. I sniffed deeply as I approached the tableau. Not even the whiff of a cigar.

I wondered whether the real Winston had been told that he'd

The Tango School Mystery

been stolen from a wax museum in Brighton. In the company of Marilyn Monroe and Yuri Gagarin. I could imagine him, chewing his cigar, an impish grin on his face. "It is a riddle, wrapped in a mystery inside an enigma," he would growl.

It was certainly that.

I strolled over to Ted.

I said: "There seems nothing to connect the three waxworks that were nicked."

"I've been thinking about that."

"Come up with any conclusion?"

"Could be a country thing. One Yank, one Russkie, one true born Englishman."

"Churchill was half American," I said. "His mother came from New York."

Ted shrugged. "Bang goes my theory then."

I said: "How did the thieves get in?"

"Round the back. Door secured by an ancient Chubb lock. They brought a screw-driver and simply took the whole unit out."

"So they must have planned it."

"Sure. I guess if you're planning a date with Marilyn Monroe you look ahead."

A distant "bong bong" sounded from the Chamber of Horrors. Quasimodo was still ringing his bell.

I'd played it cool with Ted. I'd learnt from experience it was the best way to get information out of him. But it was time to bring up the matter which had made me rocket round here like a guided missile.

"You mentioned on the phone that Captain Blunt had been involved with the security."

"Yeah, thought that might get your motor turning over - especially after I'd seen that front-page picture in the paper."

"How recently has he been involved?"

"Not for a couple of years now. It seems his company was

asked to conduct a security review of the place. But apparently he gave it a clean bill of health. Said nobody was likely to scarper with a full-sized waxwork of Haile Selassie under his arm."

In that, at least, Blunt had a point. But it raised another question.

"Any leads on how the thieves made off with their haul?" I asked.

"Not yet."

"They must have had a vehicle of some sort. Probably a van."

"That's what we thought. But as the break-in occurred in the small hours, there weren't many witnesses about. Besides, a parked van wouldn't be suspicious."

"It would be if someone spotted Marilyn Monroe in the back," I said.

"Yeah, I wouldn't mind being in the back of a van with Marilyn myself. Before she killed herself, of course," Ted added, unnecessarily, I thought.

"What about the beat constables? Or were they round at the all-night café in the market stuffing their faces with bacon sandwiches?"

Ted sniffed. "One lad saw a van parked in Pool Valley."

"By the bus terminus?"

"Yes. That would have been around three in the morning. He didn't pay much attention because he thought it might belong to a night worker doing late maintenance on the buses."

"Didn't get a number plate, then."

"No. He could only see the van sideways on - so nothing on the back or front. But he's sure from the shape it was a Bedford. And it looked recently painted."

"Colour?"

"White."

"Why did he think it had been recently painted?"

"There was a splash of paint on one of the tyres."

It didn't sound like much of a lead. I changed tack.

"But does two-year old security work put Blunt in the frame for this job?" I asked.

"Can't see how it does," Ted said. "According to our information, since his love affair with the tarmac in New Road the other night, he's taken refuge at Sir Oscar Maundsley's country place."

"And he has an alibi for last night?"

"I'll have an officer checking that out. Discreetly."

"But Blunt would've known about the weakness in the place's security?"

"I suspect he knows as much about security as my Aunt Fanny. Besides, what motive would he have for a crazy heist like this?"

I shook my head. "I don't know. But it seems to me that Captain Blunt is no stranger to turning up in the wrong places."

I kept schtum about the interview I'd had with Terry Jones. It wouldn't help Ted's investigation to throw up untested allegations of murder. I couldn't substantiate them. And, besides, when I'm investigating the same case as the police, I like to keep an edge. It's only human.

I asked: "What's your next move here?"

"We'll do all the usual forensic stuff. Take fingerprints, but in a place like this, that'll be about as much use as sweeping up dead leaves."

"You'll check antique dealers?" I asked.

"I'll have someone go round the usual suspects. But I can't see even the dodgiest fence handling any of these. Too damn recognisable. If the waxworks are being sold on, it'll be a very private operation."

I nodded. There were too many private operations going on. Like the mystery caller on Derek Clapham who'd killed him. And the private rally which had ended in a riot. The clandestine theft of waxworks. Not to mention the discreet search for the whereabouts of His Holiness's brother.

Blunt's name cropped up time and again. And Blunt was close to Maundsley.

It was about time the old fascist answered a few direct questions.

Chapter 13

The butler was togged out in a black morning coat with matching waistcoat hung with a gold watch chain.

He wore a white shirt with starched collar and black tie. He sported grey pinstripe trousers.

And jackboots.

The trousers were tucked into the top of the boots so they bagged out above the knee. Like plus-fours.

He looked like a truculent bank manager on his way to give an errant client a good kicking for exceeding his overdraft limit.

I looked down, straightened my tie in the reflection from the spit-and-polished jackboots and said: "Good morning, Jeeves."

His mouth curled into a lop-sided sneer and he said: "The name is Collington, sir." His voice had the oily darkness of black treacle and the sincerity of a conman's promise.

His upper lip curled with contempt as he added: "And I'm guessing that you are not Mr Bertram Wooster."

"Colin Crampton, Brighton *Evening Chronicle*," I said a little sharply. Clearly, I needed to watch my step here.

I was standing outside Maidover Bottom, the house Sir Oscar Maundsley had rented when he'd returned to Britain earlier in the year. It was an old Jacobean place with mullioned windows and crooked red-brick chimneys. It lay in a hollow in the Downs, a few miles north of Brighton. The wooded hills formed a kind of semi-circle around the house increasing its sense of isolation. The Downs seemed to wrap the house into its place in the countryside. The trees showed the yellows and reds of their early autumn colours. The first leaves had fallen and begun to carpet the ground.

I'd left my MGB parked on a patch of bare earth next to a cart track which led up into the woods. I'd walked a couple of hundred yards to the house and then hoofed it up the gravelled carriage drive. I didn't want Maundsley or any of his Grey Shirts seeing my car just yet. There could come a time when I'd be using it to follow them and that would be more difficult if I'd stupidly blown my own cover.

Sneaky? Perhaps. But I reckoned when it came to Maundsley, I was dealing with the man who wrote the sneaky rule-book.

Collington looked down his nose and said: "Would you care to state your business?"

I said: "Kindly be good enough to tell Sir Oscar Maundsley that a member of the Fourth Estate is here to speak to him."

Collington said: "Sir Oscar is out hunting."

"Anyone in particular?"

"Sir Oscar is hunting with the Dicker and Fulking, sir."

"And not necessarily in that order, I'll bet."

"The Dicker and Fulking is the most respected hunt in the county, sir."

"Not by the foxes, I hear. But no matter. I was actually hoping to speak to Captain Wellington Blunt."

"Who did you say, sir?"

"Captain Wellington Blunt. I believe he's been staying here."

"I regret to inform you, sir, that you have been misinformed."

"Really? I thought he might be just the man to Dicker with the Fulking."

Collington managed a kind of reedy dismissive cough. It sounded like he was strangling a sparrow. "Now if you will excuse me, sir. Perhaps you will kindly remove yourself from the premises."

"Before I do, one last question. Are jackboots regulation butler wear these days?"

"They are necessary when I feed the pigs, sir."

"To make sure they give you the respect you think you deserve when you're pouring their swill?"

Collington's lop-sided sneer turned to a snarl. "Good day to you, sir."

He reached for the door handle - a polished brass number - and the old oak door creaked closed in front of me.

I trudged back down the carriage drive wondering whether I'd played it too hard with the butler.

He'd got right up my nose the moment he'd hauled that heavy old door open and sneered down at me. And when I spotted the jackboots, that set me off. Perhaps I should have played him a little more smoothly. Like a Celtic harpist plucking a watery melody from the strings. In any event, it didn't look as though I would have wangled an interview with Maundsley. He was charging across the countryside on horseback. "The unspeakable in pursuit of the uneatable," as old Oscar Wilde put it. Collington was probably telling the truth about that. Fox hunting was just the kind of pointless vandalism those upper-class types indulged in. It gave them a break from looking down on the lower orders.

But I wasn't convinced Collington had told me the truth when he said Blunt wasn't in the house. The old street brawler had to be holed up somewhere. And I was willing to bet that after the fiasco outside the rally, it was somewhere Maundsley could keep a close watch on his inept head of security. But eventually Blunt would have to show his face outside. I decided to spend a little time watching the house.

I arrived back at the car, opened the boot, and took out a pair of binoculars I kept in my emergency kit. (Don't under-estimate bins as a vital tool for the ever-ready journalist. I've known journos read letters left on a dining room table from outside the window with a pair. Not that I'm recommending that approach to scanning your own morning mail.) Then I headed up the cart track on to the Downs.

The track led up through a wood with oak, beech and horse chestnut trees. Leaves drifted down. Birds twittered in the branches. Squirrels foraged among the leaf litter. I could've made a few notes and contributed a piece to the paper's country life column. I huffed my way up the hill and scrambled round to a vantage point where I could look over the house. I was on a track which ran parallel with the contours of the land a hundred feet or so above the level of Maundsley's estate.

It was like looking down on a toy-town village. The house stood at the centre of a group of buildings. To the left of the house, there was a stable yard, ringed with horse boxes. Beyond it was a walled-garden with a couple of small flint-built huts. I guessed they were used by the gardeners to store their hoes and rakes and dibbles.

To the right of the house, the carriage drive continued into a cobbled yard in front of a large timber-framed barn. It had huge doors in the centre, which rolled back on small wheels, and a thatched roof. As I watched, one of the doors was pushed open a little and an agricultural yokel, wearing a frayed sweater and dark green corduroy trousers tied at the knee with string, stepped out. He hurried towards the house.

I looked back down the hill in the direction I'd come. I could just see my MGB on the cart track. Beyond the track a country lane wound its way around the foot of the Downs. The entrance to Maundsley's estate was further along the lane, hidden by a clump of beech trees. As I watched, two vehicles appeared in the lane. The first was a Wolseley, a fine old model with swept back wings and stand-up engine grille, bold as a castle's portcullis. It was taking the twisty roads at a stately pace. Behind it, a white van tailgated the Wolseley. It wanted to overtake, but there wasn't room in the narrow lane.

The two vehicles disappeared behind the trees and I switched my attention back to the house. The yokel reappeared and hurried over to the barn. And he had someone with him.

Captain Wellington Blunt.

So I was right. Blunt had been hiding out in the house.

Blunt waved his arms at the yokel. I heard the distant rumble of his voice as he shouted his order. The peasant got to work and pushed the barn doors wide open. I raised the bins and took a closer look. The place seemed to have a hard clay floor. But it was dark inside the barn and I couldn't see more than a few yards beyond the doors.

I swivelled the bins to look at the approach to the house. The white van I'd seen in the lane appeared on the carriage drive and headed towards the barn. Blunt started waving his arms again. He pointed at the van driver and then at the barn. I turned the bins on the van and tightened the focus. Inside the van, I could see the driver. He was a thin bloke with long sideburns and brown hair thinning at the back into a bald patch. His hands were heaving the steering wheel as the van reached the yard in front of the barn. It bounced over the cobbles.

I ran the bins over the van. It was like a thousand other white vans I'd seen.

But not quite.

I swung the bins down to focus on the rear wheel. One of the tyres had a white patch on it. The patch was smooth on one side but had smeared on the other. As though paint had dripped and run. The van slowed as it approached the barn. For a moment the wheel was stationary. Yes, it was definitely a patch of paint.

Ted Wilson had told me that a beat constable had spotted a white van with a white patch on the wheel in Pool Valley the previous night. A few steps from Louis Tussaud's. Where Marilyn Monroe, Yuri Gagarin and Winston Churchill were being moved from the comfort of their own podiums.

Could there be more than one white van with a patch of paint on the tyre? Of course, there could. It was probably a coincidence. One of those strange conjunctions of random and unrelated events that surprise us from time to time.

The van turned to line itself up with the barn's open doors. And for the first time I saw the van's rear. There were words sign-written on the back. I lifted the bins and read: "Potter & Son. Builder and Decorator." Underneath, a Brighton telephone number.

The van stopped and the driver climbed out. Blunt headed over to greet him. But not with a warm handshake. The pair stood to attention and their arms snapped up in a Nazi salute.

So if Potter was the van driver, it looked as though he was also a member of Maundsley's private army.

Potter climbed back in the van and started the engine. I watched as the van drove inside the barn and the yokel leant into the massive doors and pushed them closed.

I lowered the bins, fished out my notebook, and wrote down the name and the phone number from the van.

Of course, the fact the van had been parked in Pool Valley, didn't mean it was involved in the robbery. Potter could've been making a business call. But at three in the morning? Maybe he was in a late-night bar. Or cavorting with a woman in a nearby hotel. Or maybe he'd just left his van in Pool Valley overnight. Free parking.

Or maybe he was inside Louis Tussaud's. And, if he was, why was he now here? Was this call legitimate business and nothing to do with Tussaud's? Or was Sir Oscar Maundsley connected to the robbery? But what use would Maundsley have with a job lot of life-sized wax statues? He already had enough dummies among his party's members.

Well, coincidence happens.

No, I didn't believe that. Not this time.

The problem was I didn't know what I was going to do about it.

I heard a faint "clump" as the barn doors finally closed. The yokel shuffled off out of sight.

A deep silence settled over the countryside.

Apart from a murder of crows squabbling in a copse behind me.

The distant lowing of cattle.

The bark of a dog behind the house.

The rough growl of a tractor in the lane.

And the "view halloa" of a hunting horn.

I swivelled to my left. The sound came from beyond the cart track where I'd parked the MGB.

And there it was again.

View halloa.

This time a little closer. And this time accompanied by the high-pitched yapping of excited foxhounds.

And the rhythmic beat from the hooves of a dozen galloping horses.

View halloa.

I lifted the bins to my eyes and scanned the country beyond the cart track. Couldn't see much beyond the trees.

And then a fox dashed from the undergrowth.

It paused for a moment by my car. Looked back.

The yelps of the hounds were closer.

The fox took off again. Up the hill along the track I'd taken. Towards me.

His sides pulsed like a furnace's bellows as he gasped for breath.

He was running for his life. But he was bringing trouble my way.

The last thing I needed right now was to be caught snooping on Maundsley's estate by a bunch of toffs in hunting pink. By gad, the blighters might horsewhip me.

Just let the blood-thirsty tykes try!

Foxy was a hundred yards from me now and tiring.

He was following the track of a scent I would've laid down as I climbed the hill. Would hounds follow my scent as well as the fox's?

This wasn't a good moment to test the theory.

Down on the cart track, yelps filled the air as the hounds burst from the undergrowth.

In the lane, the rhythmic clop, clop of horses galloping came closer.

I needed a way to throw the hounds off the fox's scent - and mine. How did those hunt saboteurs fix it? I recalled Sally Martin running an interview with one of them a few months ago. What was it they said? I wished I'd paid more attention to the piece.

Aniseed! That was it. They sprayed aniseed on the ground. All I needed was a few gallons of aniseed solution and an industrial spray gun. Drat!

And then I remembered.

I didn't have aniseed, but I did have the next best thing.

I rummaged in my jacket pocket. The tube of extra strong peppermints Figgis had given me a couple of days ago was still there.

I grabbed them and pulled out my handkerchief. I fiddled with the wrapper on the tube, ripped it off, and emptied the mints into my handkerchief. I wrapped the hankie around the mints. Then I hunted on the ground for a couple of rocks. Found a flattish one and a roundish one. I put the handkerchief-wrapped peppermints on the flatish one and pounded it with the roundish one.

Crunch!

The peppermints splintered and I caught a flash of the sharp aroma they released.

This could work!

I looked up. The fox was five yards away on the track. It was looking at me with a wary eye. Or perhaps a mystified eye.

Then a horn sounded, from closer than before. The hounds' yelps were more frenzied. A horse whinnied.

At the foot of the hill I could see red-coated huntsman readying their horses for the climb. The whipper-in had the hounds gathered together.

A voice gruff with a lifetime's brandy and cigars yelled: "Tally-ho!"

With a flash of his whip, the whipper-in released the hounds and they scrabbled up the hill.

Foxy looked round - and took off.

Followed by me.

I sprinkled a little of the peppermint powder on the track behind me.

I reached a fork in the track. Foxy had taken the right branch leading further uphill. Not a wise choice, but perhaps he knew something I didn't. I could see him streaking into the woods.

I dumped the rest of the peppermint powder on the track, spread it around a bit, then headed along the left fork.

It was downhill all the way.

Story of my life.

The downhill path brought me out close by a copse of trees to the north of the main house.

As I'd descended the yelps of the hounds and the pounding of the horses' hooves had receded. I pictured the hounds foraging around the ground confused by the peppermint.

Tough, doggies. Next time I'll make it sherbet lemons.

I imagined the master of the hunt turning puce in the face as he realised his hunt had been ruined by a sixpenny packet of Trebor's.

I entertained a brief hope that foxy had made it to safety. But I had problems of my own to resolve.

From my position at the base of the hill, I could see the crazy chimneys of Maidover Bottom about a quarter of a mile away above the tree tops.

I wondered how to get back to my car, which was parked on the cart track. I guessed I'd have to make a wide circuit of the house. I wanted to avoid the grounds. There were going to be a lot of frustrated huntsmen about.

I cast about for a way around the copse and found it in a narrow path - no more than a track trodden down through the meadow.

I trudged off.

A hundred yards on the other side of the copse I came across an old Nissen hut. It would have been left over from the war. Perhaps some troops were stationed here. Maybe the house had been requisitioned for training. Perhaps the hut was now used for storage.

The thing was made from large sheets of corrugated steel which had been bent into a semi-circle and fixed into the ground to make a kind of tunnel. Then each end of the tunnel had been filled with breeze blocks roughly cemented into walls. The whole structure was about thirty feet long and twelve feet high at the apex of the roof.

There was a stout metal door on the front of the hut.

I stepped up to the door. A notice said: "Danger: Keep Out."

There was a serious padlock on the door. A heavy-duty job that mocked at intruders.

I crouched down and put my ear to the door. There were animals inside.

I heard some grunts. And some oinks. And some squeals. And what sounded like flatulence magnified through a megaphone.

Pigs.

And, if I believed the "keep out" sign, dangerous pigs.

These must be the pigs Collington spoke about feeding. Perhaps he was on his way with a bucket of swill. Perhaps he needed jackboots to keep the dangerous pigs in check.

I decided to make myself scarce. I headed into the copse and took a path that led back to the car.

I'd had enough excitement for one day.

Chapter 14

It took me almost an hour to walk back to my car.

I kept to a route well away from Maundsley's house. I tramped along muddy footpaths. Clambered over stiles. Splashed through puddles. Snagged myself on brambles. Tripped over tree roots. A walk in the country. Apparently, people actually did this for fun.

By the time I reached the car I felt like a scarecrow having an off-day.

But I'd done some serious thinking on my walk. The problem with finding Gervase Pope, I decided, was that there were no hard leads, but too many vague possibilities. His Holiness was convinced Gervase was out to kill Maundsley. But, so far, there was only one dead body - Derek Clapham. The backstory - about Clapham providing Maundsley with the letters that got Gervase interned - certainly provided a motive. But Gervase had had nineteen years since the end of the war to croak Clapham - and hadn't done so.

Yet the fact there was a link between Clapham and Gervase - and that Clapham had died - was compelling. It suggested His Holiness's fear that Gervase would pot Maundsley wasn't entirely fanciful. And the fact Maundsley had chosen to flaunt himself around Brighton as an election candidate could well be enough to awaken old hatreds. If Maundsley knew of the threats, he didn't seem concerned about them. He'd been prepared to face hostile crowds outside the Dome two nights ago to address his rally. And, this morning, he'd ridden out on the hunting field - where any enemy could be lurking behind a tree with a shotgun.

Perhaps Maundsley was better briefed on the threats he faced than I reckoned. Perhaps he knew about Gervase's plan but didn't take it seriously. If so, I wondered what part Captain Wellington

Blunt played in keeping Maundsley safe. Blunt evidently had a talent for turning up unexpectedly. He'd surprised Freddie and me when we'd popped out of the underground tunnel at Maundsley's rally. And the fact the Widow had spotted him at her tango class added a bizarre touch. I didn't see Blunt as the type to cavort to music with a dark-haired beauty's leg wrapped around him.

At least, not on the dance floor.

But, then, there was the strange case of the robbery at Louis Tussaud's and the mystery van - seen outside at the time of the robbery, and by me arriving at Maundsley's house this morning. Perhaps the van had nothing to do with the robbery. And even if it did, perhaps the fact it had turned up at Maundsley's place the morning after was pure coincidence. But I didn't think so. Blunt had opened up the barn for the van and formed the welcome committee when it turned up. So, was Blunt behind the robbery? And, if so, why? I simply couldn't construct any credible narrative that pulled together an editor's missing brother, a dead fascist above a restaurant, a hard man at a dance class, and the heist of three wax models.

I'd hoped to keep watch to see what happened after the van had driven into the barn. I wanted to see what Blunt and the van driver did next. But the arrival of my foxy friend closely followed by the horse and hound brigade had put paid to that. But I now knew the van belonged to Potter & Son, builder and decorator. It wouldn't be difficult to trace him.

By the time I'd arrived back at the car, I'd decided what my next step would be.

When you needed to break into a car in Brighton, your first choice was always Click-Click.

His real-name was Denzil Simkins. But at his first appearance in the magistrates' court he'd been asked how he managed to open the driver's door of a Jaguar XK150 Roadster with a piece of bent fencing wire.

He'd replied: "It's simple, Your Worthiness, I inserts the wire in the lock, I gives it a twiddle and a twist, and - click, click - the door opens."

Since then, Click-Click had been before the beak three more times, but had managed to avoid jail. On the first occasion, he claimed he was opening the car to save a trapped dog from heatstroke on a hot day. On the second, that he'd thought the lady owner had left her Park Drive filter-tip smouldering next to a shopping bag. And on the third, that he'd mistaken the car for one owned by a close friend on whom he planned to play a practical joke. (It was the first of April.)

Click-Click was sitting opposite me in the kitchen of his flat in Whitehawk. He was a short-house of a lad who didn't seem to have grown much since he was a teenager. If it weren't for his wispy moustache, he'd have been able to get into the cinema on a kid's ticket. He probably wangled it anyway. He was wearing a grubby sweater with a hole in the sleeve and a pair of blue denims.

We were sitting at a table laid with the remnants of Click-Click's lunch. The crust of a stale loaf. A pat of butter that had turned green. The rind of a piece of cheddar. Click-Click was no gourmet.

He said: "I'd offer you a cup of tea, Mr Crampton, but it's the butler's afternoon off."

I took a glance at the pile of unwashed crocks in the kitchen sink. A frying pan thick with congealed lard festered on the hob. Drips of fat ran down the outside. The place smelt like Click-Click had just fried a dead badger.

I said: "You can't get the help these days."

Click-Click grinned. "Ain't that just the case."

I said: "As it happens I could use some help myself."

"Wondered why you'd called."

"I want you to teach me how to open a car with a piece of

wire."

"Lost your car keys?"

"Let's just say I've developed a thirst for new knowledge."

"Unusual know-how for a reporter."

"Never know when arcane information will come in useful."

Click-Click smoothed his moustache with his fingers. "Not sure I can help after that last thing you wrote about me in your paper."

"What thing?"

"You called me an 'uncommon car thief'."

"That wasn't me. I was quoting the magistrate in your last case. Besides, you could take it as a compliment. If he'd called you 'common' it would have meant there were loads of you around. And there's just the one and only Click-Click."

Click-Click preened himself a bit. Sat up straighter. Studied his fingernails. They had grease under them. Decided there could be better ways to stroke his self-esteem.

I said: "I'm a quick learner."

He said: "Trouble is, I don't give lessons."

"Why not? You could become a professor in this stuff."

"When you're good at something, you don't encourage the competition. I mean look at that bloke who plays the violin."

"Yehudi Menuhin?"

"No, Max Jaffa. I bet he don't give lessons on playing the fiddle."

"I won't be a competitor. I only want to open one car. Van, actually."

Click-Click leant forward. Looked interested. "What van?"

"Belongs to a painter and decorator."

"Wasting your time. My experience, there'll be a few old brushes gone stiff with dried paint. And you'll end up ponging of turpentine. Dead give-away if the fuzz nab you."

"I think this one might be more interesting."

"Why?"

"It's too long a story to tell now. But if you won't teach me how to open it with wire, there's no point anyway."

I stood up. Click-Click jumped up. Put a restraining hand on my arm.

"Now, wait. Didn't say I couldn't help in any way. How about that cup of tea, after all?"

I glanced at the sink. "I'll pass, thank you."

"Suppose I open the van. You get first dibs on anything you need and I take the vehicle."

"How about you open the van, we take a look inside, and then lock it again without taking anything?"

"What's the point in that?"

"Information."

"Information don't pay my rent."

I reached inside my pocket and took out a pound note. Handed it to Click-Click. "Another one when the job's done," I said. "I'll contact you later about the time and the place."

The edges of Click-Click's mouth turned down in a moue of disappointment. "First time I've ever taken a fee. Next thing I know I'll be on wages and stamping my card every week."

Shirley was in a bubbly mood when I met her after work.

She looked great in red Capri pants and black tee-shirt with the slogan "On paper, you're my type…" printed on the front. On the back, it added: "…Pity you come in flesh and blood."

Her photoshoot on the pier had ended well and she'd been told she could expect more work from the magazine in the future.

That pleased me. I love seeing Shirl happy. Especially when I've got a big favour to ask. But I needed to pick my moment carefully.

We went for an early supper at the China Garden in Preston Street. I had sweet and sour pork with special fried rice. Shirley had chicken chow mein and some bean sprouts. We sipped jasmine tea from delicate willow pattern cups without handles.

Shirl scooped up some chow mein and said: "I've had a great day, reporter boy. How about you?"

"Interesting," I said. "Even lively." I told Shirley about my experience with the hunt.

"Jeez! All those hounds. They could have done some serious damage."

"Thanks for your concern."

"I was thinking about the fox."

"I'll pass on your best wishes next time I see him."

Shirl dug into the bean sprouts. "After the day you've had, we ought to have a night out."

"That's just what I was thinking. Why don't we go dancing?"

Shirley gave me a sly grin. "I know your dancing. Last time you suggested it, we ended up doing the horizontal hokey-pokey back at my flat."

"I believe we call it hokey-cokey in England."

"Only when you're doing it standing up," Shirl said. "Anyway, what's with this sudden urge to cut a rug? I don't mind if we can bop at Sherry's to that new Supremes' number, *Where Did Our Love Go?* It's great."

"Sure. But I was thinking something a bit more ballroom."

Shirley put down her fork and looked at me like I'd just suggested we don space suits and swim the English Channel.

I took another mouthful of sweet and sour pork and chomped at it while I thought about what to tell Shirley.

"It's all to do with this mission I've been given by His Holiness. Find Gervase. There's a dance school in Kemp Town called the Dolores Esteban Tango Academy and I think there's more to it than 'take your partners, please'."

I described how the Widow had enrolled herself at the school to find a new husband. I told how she'd started to imagine the new man in her life was Conrad Montez, the dance instructor. I explained how she'd seen Blunt at the school three times, each time meeting with Montez. I mentioned how the Widow had recognised Blunt from his picture on the front of the *Chronicle*. And I added that Blunt's presence made me suspicious that the Academy was a front for other activity - perhaps political, perhaps criminal, perhaps both.

Shirl grazed at her bean sprouts while I spoke. She had that tiny wrinkle in her forehead which meant she was frowning. You wouldn't have known otherwise.

She said: "If we go there, looks like we could tango into trouble." She grinned. "I'm up for it. But we'll need a good story."

I said: "We'll just say we've always been crazy about the tango and we want to learn how to do it properly. Perhaps we could say we're hoping to win a dance competition."

"Think they'll buy that?"

"Why not? I guess it's why most of their other pupils are there. The difficult bit is finding a way to snoop around while we're in the Academy. We won't be able to work that one out until we've had time to see what the place is like."

"Haven't you forgotten something, mastermind?"

"What's that?"

"Blunt is a regular. After last night, there's no way he won't recognise your ugly fizzog. What's the big plan if he blows in?"

I took a final mouthful of the sweet and sour pork and chewed.

"I don't think he will. For starters, he'll still be nursing a few painful bruises after I tripped him up in New Road. I guess he won't fancy dancing. But, most important, I think after the rally fiasco, Maundsley will be riding him hard. He won't like a security chief who fouled up so spectacularly. And, besides, he'll want to keep Blunt away from the press. Especially yours truly. The last thing Maundsley wants is more bad publicity. I don't think Maundsley will let Blunt stray far from his mansion."

Shirley leaned back on her chair. She had a sly smile.

"And how will you explain it away to your landlady if she

turns up. I thought you said she had the hots for the dance instructor."

"She had, but it cooled after he stood her up during the Kiss of Fire. Besides, tonight's the night when her friend Mrs Blagg from the Beauregard Hotel comes round. They share a bottle of cream sherry and talk about how to bilk their tenants."

"So, I guess there's nothing to stop us," Shirley said. "Except one thing."

"What's that?" I asked.

"Neither of us knows anything about the tango."

"It's a dance," I said. "All you need is two feet and a floor. How hard can it be?"

Chapter 15

It was half past seven when I pulled the MGB into a parking space a few steps from the Dolores Esteban Tango Academy.

The place occupied a converted church hall in a street just off the seafront at Kemp Town. It was a single-storey building at the end of a terrace of neat houses with white stucco frontages. The Academy had been painted a shade of grey which made it stand out from the terrace like a rotten tooth.

The old church hall would have been the kind of place where pensioners gathered for a game of bingo. Or wolf cubs mustered for lessons in tying knots. Or the mother's union swapped recipes for Victoria sponge cake.

I wondered what we'd find inside now.

I turned to Shirley. "Are you ready for this, Twinkletoes?"

She grinned. "And I suppose you're the original cobber with the dancing feet."

"That's the word down at the Palais."

Shirley rolled her eyes.

We climbed out of the car.

The front of the Academy had a pair of double doors. There was a small window to the right of the doors.

I stepped up and peered through it.

I turned to Shirley. "Look at this. There are bars behind this window. Impressive security. Surely they're not worried about Burglar Bill breaking in and pinching their dancing pumps."

"The bars could have been installed when the place was a church hall," Shirley said. "Perhaps they stored valuable church stuff here."

"Perhaps," I said. "But in my experience the most valuable thing you'd find in a church hall is an old tea urn." I shrugged. "Anyway, let's get into the dancing mood."

We pushed the doors open and stepped into a small foyer lit

by a couple of low-wattage lamps. There was a rush mat on the floor and a couple of upright chairs pushed up against the wall. There was a noticeboard with information about forthcoming classes, dancing competitions and second-hand records of tango music ("in good condition") for sale. Beside the noticeboard was a large print of Eva Peron. Her blonde hair was tied back in a bun. She wore a large pink flower like a gardenia on her black dress. She had a woman-of-the-people smile on her lips which faded when you looked at her eyes.

I said: "I guess they're trying to summon up the Argentinian atmosphere as soon as you step through the doors."

"Yeah, like a night on the Pampas with only your horse for company," Shirley said.

I pointed to a door off the other side of the foyer. "That must lead into the room with the barred windows," I said.

I tried the door. Locked. "There's something in there they don't want anyone to know about," I said.

"Probably just their personal bits and pieces. A girl's got to have somewhere to park her handbag while she bops," Shirley said. "Trouble with you is that you've got a suspicious mind."

"The best kind for a reporter. It's what helps me get front-page stories."

Shirley was about to say something. But before she could get any words out, music started up from further inside the building. A couple of violins began a mournful tune. Like a woman wailing over something sad. Perhaps the loss of a lover. Perhaps a ladder in her stockings. And then a man began to sing in Spanish. He had a soft tenor voice, loaded with sorrow. The kind of voice you'd hear at a nightclub. In the early hours, when the air is fogged with cigarette smoke and the punters are drowsy with drink.

The music came from behind a door at the far end of the foyer. I looked at Shirley and nodded. We walked towards the door and opened it.

We stepped into a Buenos Aires nightclub. The kind of club where there's a spyhole in the door and the drink comes served in bottles with no labels. The kind of club where the barmen look like bouncers and the bouncers look like gorillas.

At least that's what the room felt like.

The place had black walls and no windows. It was bigger than the *Chronicle's* newsroom, smaller than Woolworth's in Western Road. It smelt like the perfume counter in Woolworth's on Christmas Eve, when the last-minute rush is on. The room was lit by two droopy chandeliers. A glitter ball hung from the centre of the ceiling. It reflected shards of light that circled the room, like a drunk flashing an Aldis lamp. There were small round tables, each set with two cane-backed chairs, spaced around a polished dance floor.

The music came from an old wind-up gramophone with a huge horn. It sat on a table at the far end of the room. Three couples were dancing anti-clockwise around the floor. A woman with dark hair piled in a beehive, tied at the base with a red ribbon, stood in the centre of the room.

She tapped a foot to the beat of the music.

She had to be Dolores Esteban.

In appearance, she lived up to her exotic name. She wore a red dress which Shirley later told me had a scalloped neckline and puff sleeves. The dress hugged her hips like a second skin. It was slit to the thigh and revealed a leg in a fishnet stocking. She wore a pair of stilettoes you could have used to punch holes in steel plate. She had a clutch of chunky rings on her fingers and a pair of dangling hoop earrings (thanks again, Shirley) that looked big enough to pick up the Home Service.

She was waving her arms and shouting at the dancing couples as they glided by.

"Ralph, no. *Está incorrecto*. Shift your weight to the left foot. And Maudie, *abrazarlo*. Keep in hold." This to an old bloke with white hair and a military moustache and a thin woman with worried eyes and twitchy lips.

"Humphrey, *darse tono*! Keep that spine straight." A tall man pushed back his hunched shoulders. "And Lavinia, look at your partner. *Lo deseas*. You desire him." The lady in question twizzled her head and gave Dolores a look that could have dropped a carthorse in its tracks.

A young couple swept into Dolores' view. He wore glasses with thick black frames. She had her long blonde hair held back from her face by a pink Alice band.

"*Muy bien*, Tom and Val. But don't play safe. *Ser peligroso* - try a *salida*." They turned together and moved forward in time to the beat. They giggled at one another, which rather spoilt the effect.

Dolores frowned.

The violins reached a crescendo and the music ended with a few soulful chords. The couples released one another from their holds and politely applauded. They moved off to the tables and sat down.

Dolores turned and saw Shirley and me standing by the door. She had an oval face with dark watchful eyes that were too close together.

She crossed the room towards us like a panther stalking its prey.

"*Buenas tardes, senor. Buenas tardes, senorita,*" she said. "*Bienvenido a la Academia de Tango Dolores Esteban. Has venido a bailar?*"

She walked up to us with her arms spread as though expecting an embrace.

"Remember our backstory," I whispered to Shirley. We'd worked out what we were going to say earlier at the China Garden.

Dolores extended an elegant hand with scarlet painted nails. I took the hand and shook it. It was smooth to touch and strangely cool.

"I am sorry," she said. "When I see new people and *gente tan hermosa* - such beautiful people - I am so excited, I speak in my native language."

"Don't worry about it," I said. "I have the same problem every time I walk into the office."

"You and your beautiful lady are here to learn the tango?" Dolores asked.

"That's right," I said.

"Sure, we'll give it a go," Shirley added.

"But why the tango?"

"Well, it's like this," Shirley said. "My boyfriend and me go for our holidays to Butlin's every year. They have this dancing competition and if you get through your heat, you get to go to the finals and you pick up a free holiday. Well, we think we can get into the finals with the tango."

Dolores clapped her hands. "A competition! I, too, am winning competitions for tango. In Buenos Aires, you understand. Not Brighton. The judges, they say I am unbelievable. You think I am unbelievable? You better believe it."

I said: "As soon as I stepped through the door I said to Shirley, 'That woman is unbelievable'."

Shirley nodded. "'Totally unbelievable,' I said to Colin."

"But we must dance. Your first lesson will be free. *Gratis*. You like, then you pay for the lessons. No?"

"Yes," I said.

"For the first lesson, I dance with the man," Dolores said. "It is good, no? My partner, Conrad Montez, dance with the lady. Also good. But not good because Conrad he is not here. So you dance together. You share the passion? No?"

"As long as there's enough to go round," I said.

"Always with the tango, there is much *pasión*," Dolores said.

"Same with the hokey-pokey, when Colin's around," Shirley said.

The other dancers had been chatting at the tables around the room. Dolores clapped her hands. They turned towards her.

"*Atención, por favor*. We have two new pupils. We are going to teach them the tango's basic eight-step move."

The other couples shuffled to their feet. Dolores hurried to the far end of the room and wound up the gramophone. Selected another record. Lowered the arm and more scratchy violin music started to play.

The other couples took one another in their holds.

Dolores swept into the middle of the room. "And so first, gentlemen, make a small back step. Ladies, right leg forward. Wait for the first beat of the bar."

We tried the move. I slipped. Shirley giggled.

Dolores shouted above the music: "Gentlemen, make a side step. Ladies, follow. Gentlemen, third step forward, fourth step forward. Ladies, third step back, fourth step cross left over right foot. Gentlemen…"

But we never found out what the gentlemen had to do next.

Because the door to the room opened and a man hurried in. He was tall and had a slim wiry body. I put him at about fifty. He had a thin face with an aquiline nose and compressed lips. His left eyelid drooped a little. When I looked closer I saw that was because he had a small scar between his eye and his ear. He wore wire-framed glasses. He had thinning brown hair combed back from his forehead. He carried a black bag which sagged heavily from his hands.

He stood in the doorway and looked around the room. He seemed flustered. Angry. He saw Dolores. He dumped his bag on one of the tables and hurried across the room towards her.

Dancing stopped. Eyes focused on him.

Ralph called out: "Evening, Conrad. Everything all right?"

So this was the missing Conrad Montez. The Widow's new heart-throb.

Conrad closed on Dolores.

I whispered to Shirley: "I don't think he's going to ask her to dance."

Montez grabbed Dolores's elbow and whispered something in her ear.

She shrugged. He let go of her elbow and said something sharply.

She walked towards the far end of the room. The end where the gramophone was grinding out the tango tune. The violins were giving it everything they'd got and a contralto had joined in.

Humphrey and Lavinia tangoed by as though nothing had happened. Tom and Val swayed to the music. They couldn't decide what to do. Ralph and Maudie broke from their hold and watched Dolores and Montez cross the room.

I whispered to Shirley: "Keep dancing."

"How? We don't know the steps."

"Let's do anything. Just dance towards the table where Montez has left that bag."

We shuffled across the floor trying to look like a couple of old pros.

Dolores and Montez were at the far end of the room, close to the gramophone. They were whispering to each other intensely. Not yet an argument, but it had the potential to be a big one.

Shirley and I slid alongside the table. I took a good look at the bag. It was a black holdall arrangement made from real leather. An expensive item. I wondered what it held. I ran my hand lightly over the outside. The leather was smooth. But I couldn't feel what was inside.

But wait.

At one end there was a warm patch on the leather.

Shirley and I danced a few steps on the spot while I felt the patch a little more. Yes, definitely warm. I wondered what had made that part of the leather warmer than the rest. Had it been resting against a radiator? Perhaps on a hot part of his car? Or had there been something hot inside the bag? But who would put something hot in an expensive leather bag? Unless they had no choice.

The music rose in a crescendo. A duet of a man and a woman belted out a song of passionate love. Perhaps for one another. Perhaps for their dog. I couldn't tell. They were singing in Spanish.

Shirley and I danced a few steps away from the table and the bag. We ignored that move where you snap your head back and forward like you're doing a double take. We kept our gaze on Montez and Dolores.

At the far end of the room, the pair now squared up to one another. Pointing fingers. Shaking heads. Rolling eyes. The argument had begun. They didn't want the rest of us to know. But they couldn't help themselves.

Montez wagged his finger at Dolores and spat out a few words. She shook her head angrily and stamped her foot. Turned her back on him. He grabbed her shoulder and forced her to face him. She slapped his face. He raised his fist. Thought better of it. Stomped back through the room. Grabbed his bag from the table and went out.

The door behind him slammed as the music ended.

Dolores moved away from the gramophone. There were pink spots on her cheeks. Her eyes flashed but she was trying to hide her fury. She stood in the room and motioned for everyone to gather around her.

Dolores held up her hands. "*Lo siento.* I'm sorry. Tonight, we must end the lesson early. We have more dancing next time. I see you all next week. *Buenas noches.*"

She turned and marched swiftly out of the room.

We all stood around and gawped at one another.

"Well, it was only a matter of time," Ralph said.

"What did you mean, 'it was only a matter of time'?" I asked.

Shirley and I were sitting opposite Ralph and Maudie in The

Jolly Boatman, a pub round the corner from the Tango Academy. The dance class had broken up in confusion after Montez and Dolores had left. We'd looked at each other in an embarrassed kind of way. As we'd filed out through the hall, we could hear Montez and Dolores arguing in the office. In the room with the barred windows.

I'd invited Ralph and Maudie to join us for a drink. They'd accepted with the enthusiasm of a couple who have a thirst which needs urgent refreshment.

Ralph raised his pint of Harvey's best bitter and said: "That pair have had their knives out for each other since the day Conrad Montez turned up. I don't understand it. Dolores told us he'd been her tango partner in Buenos Aires."

"But we don't think they'd ever danced together until he came to the Academy," said Maudie. She raised her glass and took a refined sip of Advocaat. It left a pencil moustache of yellow along her upper lip. "When we first saw him, he stumbled over the eight-step basic, let alone any of the more exotic moves."

"When did he turn up?" I asked.

Ralph took a good pull at his beer and sighed. "It was a couple of months ago. But if he was Dolores's dancing partner in Argentina, I'm the Queen of Sheba."

Maudie giggled and had another dainty sip of her drink.

"What does the guy do there?" Shirley asked.

"He dances with some of the older women who come, one in particular," Ralph said.

I nodded. That would be the Widow. She wouldn't care whether Montez could tango or not. She was after a husband, not a dancing partner.

"So why do you think he's there?" I asked.

Ralph shook his head. "No idea. But I do know the pair can't stand one another. It's as though Dolores has Montez there against her will."

"Could he have some hold over her?" I said.

"It's possible," Ralph said. "I haven't considered that. But I suppose he must have something that prevents her throwing him out."

Maudie drained the last of her Advocaat. "Don't forget to mention that other man who's turned up a few times, Hunky Boots," she said.

Ralph patted Maudie's arm. "Thanks for reminding me, Pinky Petals. Large geezer. Fancied himself. Ex-army, I think. Maudie heard Dolores call him Captain Blunt. But what a Captain wants at a tango school, I can't imagine. He didn't join in any of the lessons."

"Just used to disappear into the office and gossip with Conrad Montez," Maudie said.

"That's another thing," Ralph said. "That office is always locked now. It never was before Montez turned up."

"And you never saw Blunt at the school until Montez arrived?" I asked.

"No," Ralph said.

"And you don't know what they talked about?"

Ralph shook his head. "No. But there is something. Last week, I happened to step into the foyer just as Blunt and Montez were coming out of the office. They had their backs to me. I heard Montez say, 'I'm ready'. And then he shook Blunt's hand and said *'Auf Wiedersehen, mein Freund'*."

"What did you make of that?" I asked.

Ralph raised his glass and drank the last of his beer. "I don't think Conrad Montez is Argentinian at all. I think he's German."

"What do you make of that?" Shirley asked after Hunky Boots and Pinky Petals had left.

"I'm not sure," I said. "It certainly looks as though Montez has some kind of hold over Dolores. Plainly, she doesn't want him there - but she's got no choice. Perhaps it's something to do with Dolores's life in Argentina."

"Yeah," Shirley said. "I've known whackers like that back in Oz. They're slime-balls."

"I think Montez may be more dangerous than a slime-ball."

"You do?"

"If Ralph is right and Montez is German, I think he could be a fugitive."

"From what?"

"From justice. After the Second World War, some Germans who'd committed war crimes escaped to South America. Remember Adolf Eichmann who was captured in Buenos Aires in 1960?"

"Sure, the guy was one of the worst Nazis. You think this Montez could be one also?"

"Perhaps. But if he is, why has he come to Britain? He'd be more likely to be exposed and captured than in South America."

Shirley shrugged. "Beats me."

"It must be because he has some job to carry out here."

"Not dancing the tango, that's for sure."

"No," I said. "And whatever it is, the fact Montez meets with Blunt must mean that Sir Oscar Maundsley is behind it."

Chapter 16

"I'd have hated to be a locksmith," Click-Click said.

"Why's that?" I asked.

We were in my MGB driving up the Ditchling Road in Brighton. Half an hour earlier I'd dropped Shirley at her flat in Clarence Square after our drink with Ralph and Maudie. I'd then picked up Click-Click from outside a breaker's yard in Portslade. He was sitting in the passenger seat nursing a large canvas pouch in his lap. He smelt of brown ale.

He said: "Why'd I hate being a locksmith? It's because if you're a locksmith, you know you're going to be a failure."

"Not if you were Jeremiah Chubb. He patented the detector lock and made a fortune."

"Money made on a false promise. He claimed the lock couldn't be picked. He challenged people to do so - and someone did. A few years later. It was a geezer called Alfred Hobbs. So, you see, Chubb failed. He hadn't built an unpickable lock."

"What's all this got to do with opening a rusty old van, Click-Click?"

"It's like a philosophical puzzle. You see what locksmiths don't get is that the real winners in life are not the ones who set the puzzles. It's the geezers like me who solve them."

I turned off the Ditchling Road and drove towards Hollingdean. We were heading for Potter's house. I'd looked up the address in the telephone book.

Crampton, the master researcher.

I reckoned Potter would keep his van close to his house. Not exactly a brilliant deduction, but probably a reliable one. Not too close to the house, I hoped. We would need a bit of cover while Click-Click exercised his talents. In lock-picking rather than philosophy.

I said: "Why were you hanging around that breaker's yard

when I picked you up?"

Click-Click rubbed his chin. "Just keeping an eye out for anything that might be useful."

"Such as?"

"Odd bits of wire. You see, some of your lock-picks buy their kit ready-made or, even worse, second hand. But when you buy, you don't learn. That's why I've made all my own picks from selected bits of wire. I've learnt what kind of wire works when you're opening a car, what kind cracks a safe or just trips the lock on one of them fancy bureaux you see in posh houses. You understand how the wire works and you're way ahead of the others."

"Let's hope you've got the right wire for this van."

Click-Click patted the pouch on his lap. "It'll be in here," he said.

I turned off the main drag leading through Hollingdean into a side street of well-tended council houses.

"Potter lives near here. We'll drive by a couple of times to see if we can spot the van," I said.

Potter's house was a semi-detached place with a small front garden. He'd fixed a notice to his garden gate which read "Potter & Son, Builder & Decorator. Enquire Within."

The power of advertising.

We didn't notice the van when we drove by and I wondered whether my deduction had been wrong. But we spotted it on the way back. It was on a piece of rough ground at the side of the house. And, most importantly, in the shadows.

"Even better," Click-Click said. "I hate it when there are bright lights everywhere. Makes me feel like I'm doing a turn at the Brighton Hippodrome."

I drove the MGB a hundred yards down the street and parked. I looked at Click-Click. "Are you ready for this?" I said.

"Ready and willing."

"Let's hope you're also able."

"Never failed yet."

"Before we start, if we're spotted, you leg it and leave me to talk my way out of trouble."

"Now that sounds like worth hanging around to hear. But, I'll accept your offer. It's not long since I was last up before the beak and I want to give him time to forget my face before I put in another appearance."

"Come on," I said.

We climbed out of the car and headed down the street. It was deserted. There were lights on in a few houses, but most residents had already gone to bed. Somewhere a dog barked. An angry voice shouted and the barking stopped.

As we approached Potter's house, I looked up and down the street. Decided nobody was watching us. Stepped smartly onto the rough ground beside Potter's house. We crept round to the back of the van.

Click-Click whispered: "I'm going to try the back doors rather than the driver's or passenger's."

"What for?"

"Curious, aren't you?"

"It's my inquisitive nature."

"Reason is that where you've got two doors coming together like this, parts of the lock are on each door. Over time, the hinges of the door sag a little and this creates more give in the latch part of the lock which holds the doors together. Sometimes, I don't even need one of my wires - by shifting each door more tightly onto its hinges I can get the catch to release."

"Will you be able to do that this time?"

"I'm going to try something else first."

Click-Click reached for the handle on the left-hand door. He turned it. Something clicked softly. And the door opened.

"How did you do that?" I asked.

"Door wasn't even locked. About one time in five it isn't. Makes it easy for me. But less fun."

"I could've opened that myself."

Click-Click looked worried. "I still want my fee."

"And you'll get it." I took out my wallet and handed Click-Click a pound note. "Now you'd better beat it," I said. "This next bit's down to me."

"You not giving me a lift back into town?"

"The exercise will do you good. If you walk down to the Ditchling Road, you should catch a late bus."

Click-Click shrugged. "Glad to be of assistance."

He turned and I watched his jaunty swagger as he headed down the road.

I turned back to the van. Took a small torch from my jacket pocket. Switched it on and looked inside. The van contained a couple of ladders, three buckets, half a dozen pots of paint (two green and four crimson), a couple of bottles of turpentine and a box of brushes. There were also two rolls of wallpaper (one sprigs of climbing roses, one regency stripes), a paint roller and tray, and a stack of dust sheets.

I climbed into the van and pulled the door behind me, but made sure it didn't shut. If Potter found me trapped in his van in the morning, it would test even my ability to talk myself out of trouble. "Er, well Mr Potter, I thought I heard the plaintive meow of a trapped moggy and climbed in to rescue him." No, I didn't think that would work. The best way to avoid being caught was to search fast and get out.

So I crouched down and shuffled to the front so that I could have a look around the driver's and passenger's seats.

The first thing I found resting on the dashboard was a thick notebook. Its cover was stained with paint blotches. I rested against the back of the driver's seat, opened the book and shone my torch on the pages. The book seemed to be a record of Potter's jobs. He'd recorded the name of the client, a brief note on the work they wanted, and the date he planned to do it. When he'd completed the work, he wrote "DONE" in capitals against the job and entered the price he'd charged.

I flicked back over his last couple of weeks' work. Not surprisingly, there was no reference to stealing three wax models from Louis Tussaud's.

But Potter had painted the front door at a house in Tivoli Crescent. "Awkward customer," he'd noted.

He'd wallpapered the front bedroom in an unoccupied top-floor flat in Brunswick Road, Hove. "Passed on duplicate key," he'd written.

He'd mended a gutter and downpipe at a fish and chip shop in Moulsecoomb. "Free chips!" he'd added.

He'd repainted the front of a house (but not the sides or back), the hallway and one other room in a house at 29 to 30 Brunswick Road. He'd marked the job "Urgent. Complete by Friday 25th September." He'd added a note: "Booked after they saw board outside Brunswick Road flat."

I noted down the addresses where Potter had worked just in case I needed them. But it was small pickings for the risk I'd taken in searching the van.

I'd hoped to find hard evidence I could use in print to link Potter to Blunt. Even better, direct to Sir Oscar Maundsley. But there was no mention of Blunt or Maundsley in Potter's job book. No incriminating note from either of them in the van. Not even a business card. And nothing which suggested Potter had taken part in the Tussaud's heist.

I scrabbled back through the van. I'd knocked the pile of dust sheets over as I'd climbed through to the front. I had to pick them up and repack them in the pile I'd found them. I shoved them up against the ladders and went to move forward. The torch light glinted off something on the floor.

I leant forward and picked it up. It was an earring. A white earring. And not any old white earring, either. It was the same kind that Marilyn Monroe wore in *The Seven Year Itch*. The same kind Marilyn's waxwork had worn at Louis Tussaud's.

It was proof that Potter had had the waxworks in his van.

Mr Potter had some questions to answer. And I didn't plan to waste any time asking them.

I climbed out of the van and closed the rear doors.

I didn't bother to check that everything in the van was just as I'd found it because I would have to admit having had a shufti inside. Potter would no doubt start hurling accusations of illegal searches at me. But I wasn't the police. And, besides, he had more pressing questions to answer.

The front of Potter's house was dark. At this time of night, a man who spent a good part of his life climbing ladders would be in bed. Perhaps he was having a pleasant dream. Maybe it involved Marilyn Monroe. Perhaps it included her earrings.

If so, a nightmare was about to arrive on his doorstep. Me.

A short path led up to Potter's front door. I rapped on it loudly. Like I was a bailiff come to collect a debt.

No answer.

I knocked again. This time with the ball of my fist so that the door shuddered in its frame. It was a knock that would have raised Rip Van Winkle. But not Potter.

I leant down, pushed open the letter box and peered through. The hallway provided a narrow passage to the rooms at the back of the house. To the right was a staircase. A finger of light from an upstairs room filtered down the stairs. Presumably from a bedroom.

The fact there was a light on meant Potter was still up. Unless he left it on for security. But that didn't make any sense, because you couldn't see it from outside the front of the house.

Perhaps Potter was cowering in his bedroom. Perhaps he had good reason not to open the door. Especially when the knocking was so urgent. Which made me wonder whether Potter had good reason to be scared of person or persons unknown. Perhaps persons connected with the Tussaud's robbers. Perhaps persons who were part of Maundsley's stage army of Grey Shirt thugs.

I walked away from the front door and back to the rough ground at the side of the house. Potter's back garden was behind a high wooden fence. I walked along outside the fence and looked at the back of the house.

The rooms on the ground floor were dark. But in one of the rooms upstairs a light was on. The curtains were open. And something was wrong.

There was a hole in the glass.

I went back to Potter's van, opened the back doors, and took out the extendable ladder. I pushed open the gate leading into the back garden and carried the ladder through. I set it down and pushed up the extension so it leant on the wall just below the lighted window.

Then I climbed up feeling a bit like a sweaty voyeur looking for a cheap thrill.

As I neared the top of the ladder I could see the window had been broken in one place. A jagged hole about six inches across had been punched in the centre of the glass.

I climbed the final three steps of the ladder and looked into the room.

It was a sparse room with an ugly lump of a wardrobe, a small chest of drawers and a bed.

Potter lay spread-eagled on the bed.

He had a hole in the middle of his forehead.

He'd been shot as precisely as if he'd had a bullseye tattooed between his eyes. There was a smear of blood on the bed's headboard, but none of the usual carnage of violent death. No brains splattered on the wall. No pool of blood on the carpet. No face contorted in a final agony. Potter's eyes were open and his lips were parted as if he'd just been promised a nice surprise. If death can ever be tidy, this was as neat a slaying as anyone was ever likely to see.

And there was a witness.

Marilyn Monroe was propped on the side of the bed. She was missing the earring, but otherwise dressed as she'd been in Louis Tussaud's. As she'd been in *The Seven Year Itch*, when she'd stepped out of a cinema after watching *The Creature from the Black Lagoon* and stood over a subway vent to cool her ankles.

I gripped the top of the ladder like it was my final handhold in an ascent of Everest. It felt like my heart was doing the eight-step tango basic. In double time. For a moment, I wondered whether my legs would have the strength to climb down. I took a couple of deep breaths to steady myself.

Then I had a thought.

The broken window meant Potter must have been shot by a sniper operating at a distance. Suppose he was still there. And I was lined up in his cross-hairs.

I found some strength in my legs and scurried down the ladder. But by the time, I'd reached the ground, I'd thought again. No sniper hangs around after delivering his *coup de main*. He'd be long gone.

But he must have fired from somewhere. Beyond the fence at the end of Potter's garden I could see the flat roofs of some single-storey buildings. I made my way through the undergrowth and looked over the fence. The roofs belonged to a compound of garages, deserted at this time of night and unlit. The garages had been built on ground that rose away from Potter's house. I estimated the roofs would have been at the same level as the window of Potter's bedroom. An ideal vantage point to line up a shot. Perhaps the sniper had left some trace. But I didn't think so. A marksman with enough skill to fell Potter with one shot didn't leave a mess behind him when he quit the scene of the crime.

I made my way back to the front of the house. I knew I had to call the police. But I also wanted to alert the paper so that we could get a photographer on the scene.

When Click-Click and I had been reconnoitering the area I'd

noticed a telephone box two hundred yards down the street. I'd make a call from there, but first I had a job to do.

Chapter 17

The fact Potter was dead could make my breaking into his van look a bit suspicious.

So I had to cover my tracks.

There was no reason the cops should even suspect I knew Potter if I played my cards right. Chances were Brighton's finest wouldn't consider the van part of the crime scene. That meant no hunt for fingerprints. But, anyway, I'm a blameless citizen. My prints weren't on file.

Even so, when there's a dead body around, it pays to be cautious.

So I took down the ladder and shoved it back in the van. I took Marilyn's earring out of my pocket and left it on the floor of the van. Somewhere even the dimmest cop with pebble glasses would find it. Ever helpful, that's me.

Then I scooted down the road to the phone box. I called the office and got through to Jake Harrison, the duty reporter. Jake was a night owl. He claimed he liked working through the wee small hours because he suffered from insomnia. I had something that would definitely keep him awake.

I said: "Jake, I've got a favour to ask, but it's not something you'll have picked up on your National Council for the Training of Journalists course."

Jake gave a throaty chuckle. "I thought it mightn't be."

"I need you to find a public phone box at least a quarter of a mile from the office and make an anonymous call to the cops. Tell them you've heard what sounded like breaking glass coming from a house earlier this evening."

"Which house?"

I gave Potter's address.

"What do I say if the cops ask why I didn't report it earlier?" Jake asked.

"You could say you were on your way to do your cleaning shift at the bus depot and couldn't find a phone. That should also throw the cops off your scent."

Jake chuckled again. "Consider it done."

"One other favour, Jake. Contact one of the photographers and get him up to the street in about an hour's time. By then, the cops should be on the scene in force."

"What are you going to do?"

"I'm planning to call on the neighbours," I said. "I need to pick up some background about the dead man."

"Would you like a ginger nut with your cocoa, Mr Crampton?"

Betsy Threadgold offered me biscuits on a willow pattern plate.

Her husband Wilf sidled up to me with a bottle of whisky and added a good slug to the cocoa.

"The lad needs a strengthener at this time of night, dearest one," he said to Betsy.

I was sitting in their best parlour. A set of chintzy armchairs had lacy antimacassars and arm covers. There was a fireplace with a set of brass fire irons. There was an Ekco television set with a nineteen inch screen in the corner. There was a coffee table in the centre of the room. It held copies of the *Radio Times*, *Woman's Weekly* and couple of Alistair Maclean paperbacks.

Betsy and Wilf reminded me of that old rhyme about Jack Spratt who could eat no fat, his wife could eat no lean. Betsy was a plump motherly type with smiling eyes, pouched cheeks like a hamster's and a pair of double chins. Wilf had a body that was lean and whippy. He had a face that seemed set in a permanent smile. He had white hair with a bald patch at the back of his head..

I'd waited at the end of the road until the cops had arrived before knocking on their door. Sooner or later, one of the brighter coppers would ask how I came upon the scene so soon after the alert was sounded. I'd say I just happened to be in the area and decided to see whether anything was doing. They wouldn't believe me. But, then, they rarely did.

I said: "Good of you to see me so late."

Betsy grinned. "Not often we have a bit of excitement in this street, is it Wilf?"

Wilf paused from pouring a knockout slug of scotch into his own cocoa. "No, dearest one."

I said: "From what I've heard, your near neighbour Mr Potter has been shot."

"Is he dead?" Wilf asked.

"Yes. I believe being shot between the eyes can do that to you."

Wilf nodded. "Saw enough killing in the war. Hoped never to see any more."

"And this used to be such a nice neighbourhood," Betsy said. "Now I suppose we'll all be in the newspapers."

"Not all of you. Only Mr Potter. And he's in no position to complain about it. I'll keep your names out of the *Chronicle*. That's a promise."

Betsy's chins wobbled with pleasure. "I told you he was a nice young man, didn't I Wilf?"

"Yes, dearest one."

I said: "What I'd like to do is get some background information about Mr Potter. Have you lived near him for long?"

"About four years, since Wilf retired. He was on the railways, you know."

"And Mr Potter was a decorator," I said. "And his son was in the business with him."

Betsy leaned closer, the way people do when they're planning to tell you something they think is confidential. "That's what it said on the back of the van," she said. "Potter & Son. But he had no son. Never even had a wife."

"Why did he call his business Potter & Son?" I asked.

"Asked him about that once," Wilf said. "He told me it was because it made his firm sound more reliable. Like it weren't just him and a paint brush."

"But I think there was more to it than that," Betsy said. "I think he was living a - what do you call it? - a fancy."

"A fantasy," I said.

"Yes, a fantasy. I think the truth is he wanted a son but never had the chance to have one. He just didn't have a way with women. Not like my Wilf. He'd have his way with them all if I let him."

Wilf blushed. "You know you're the only girl for me, dearest one." He took a slurp of his cocoa.

I said: "Was Potter's decorating business successful, even without the fantasy son?"

Wilf said: "I think it was up and down, the way these self-employed decorators are. I remember about a year ago - it was a Sunday morning and I was out front washing the car - he came up the road with a pint of milk and his *Sunday Express*. We got talking and he seemed quite chipper. He'd just picked up a job to redecorate the flat of some toff who lived in a posh penthouse flat on the seafront at Kemp Town. I remember I said to him, 'That's a step up in the world for you. Quite a few steps if it's a penthouse.' And he said, 'No steps at all, Wilf. The place has got its own private elevator.' It was the only time I ever saw him grin."

"He didn't tell you who the client was, by any chance?" I asked.

"He did but I can't remember the name. I think it was something to do with the church. Priest, possibly? Or Parsons?"

"Could it have been Pope?" I asked.

Wilf clapped his hands. "Yes, that's it - Pope."

"Did he know this Pope well?" I asked.

"Couldn't say," Wilf said. "Potter just seemed pleased he had a job that would pay well and give him the chance to know more clients in a higher income bracket."

I guess I should have been surprised that Potter had known Gervase Pope. Perhaps I should have gasped. Slopped my cocoa over myself. Held my hands up and yelled: "I don't believe it." But I did believe it. After all, I'd already seen Potter at Maundsley's place snapping into a Nazi salute with Blunt. But the news that Potter had worked for Gervase added a new strand to the cat's cradle of connections I was trying to untangle. After all, Pope and Maundsley were hated enemies. So if Potter was helping them both out - Gervase with decorating, Maundsley with nicking waxworks - whose side was he on?

I asked: "When did you last see Potter?"

"Haven't set eyes on him for at least a couple of weeks," Wilf said.

Betsy put down her cocoa. "I saw him a couple of days ago. I was just heading off to the shops when he came out of his house and got into his van. I called out 'good morning' to him, but he virtually ignored me."

"Perhaps he was feeling under pressure," I said.

"Perhaps. But common civility costs nothing," Betsy said.

"Did Potter have any enemies that you knew of?" I asked.

"We never knew him that well, did we, dearest one?" Wilf said.

Betsy shook her head. "Glad we didn't now."

I drained the last of my cocoa and put the mug on the coffee table.

I said: "You've been a great help. Thanks for your time."

"Don't mention it, dear," Betsy said. "I suppose at the end of the day Mr Potter was just an unlucky man who didn't have much success with the ladies."

Wilf flashed Betsy a beaming smile. "We chaps can't all attract such a precious one as you," he said.

This wasn't the moment to tell them about Marilyn Monroe.

*

I arrived in the newsroom at the *Chronicle* before seven the following morning after barely five hours sleep.

I was feeling about as fresh as a week-old halibut. I'd spent the previous night playing hide-and-seek with the cops. I was anxious not to get pulled in as a witness in Potter's murder. I'd be tied up at the cop shop for hours answering their damn fool questions. That would mean I couldn't turn out the front-page exclusive I was about to write.

But that posed another problem. I couldn't use much of the information I'd garnered while up the ladder peering into Potter's bedroom without revealing what I'd done. So I had to find a way of persuading the cops to tell me what I already knew.

I lifted the phone and dialled a number at Brighton police station.

Ted Wilson answered with a yawn.

I said: "Wakey, wakey. Anyone would think you'd been up all night."

Ted said: "I have. The Hollingdean shooting."

"You're heading the case?"

"If only. Your favourite detective has decided he's going to crack this one."

"Detective Superintendent Alec Tomkins."

"I don't know how a man with an empty mind can be so full of himself."

"Can I quote you on that?"

"You dare and I'll arrange for something nasty to happen to you on a dark night."

"Ooooh! I'm scared. But, seriously, I'd like some information."

"You know the score. Turn up at the press conference this morning."

"Haven't got time, Ted. Help me out. Perhaps we can help each other."

"Why? What do you know that I don't."

The Tango School Mystery

I grinned. "That list would take all day to read. But let me ask you one question. I gather someone was shot at a house in Garland Street, Hollingdean. What was the name of the victim?"

"Can't tell you that until next of kin have been informed."

"Was it Stanley Potter?"

"How did you know that?"

"By noting the house the cops had cordoned off and looking up the name in the electoral register. Besides, the neighbours also knew him."

"And he was the same Potter whose van was seen in Pool Valley the night Louis Tussaud's was robbed?"

"Where did you get that from?"

"The van is parked at the side of his house. Anyone can see it - and the identifying paint splash on the tyre you told me about."

"Yes, it looks like the same van," Ted conceded.

"I believe Potter was killed in his bedroom?"

"Who told you?" Ted said.

"No-one but you can see the hole in the bedroom window from houses in the next street. Not hard to work it out. Any unusual features to the killing?"

Ted put on his official voice. "Too early to reveal what we've found at the scene of the crime."

"Was the shooting connected to any other crime?" I asked.

"We're keeping an open mind on that."

"As Potter's van was in Pool Valley, he could be connected to the waxworks heist. I wondered whether any of the stolen waxworks were in his house."

"I can't comment on that."

"If I were to speculate in my piece that Potter had at least one of the waxworks would you deny it?"

"Er, not exactly deny..."

"So which waxwork?"

"Tomkins will have my lights for a clothesline if I revealed that."

"A bloke of Potter's age is unlikely to have much interest in Yuri Gagarin or Winston Churchill. That just leaves Marilyn Monroe."

I heard Ted sigh. I could imagine his shoulders sagging and his frown becoming deeper. He'd be stroking his beard for comfort. He'd have to explain all this to Tomkins.

I said: "Don't worry, Ted. There'll be enough hints in my piece to suggest the information came from another source."

"Which source?" he asked hopefully.

"Detective Superintendent Tomkins," I said.

I put the phone down before Ted could ask any more questions.

And then I pulled my old Remington towards me and hammered out a story that would lead the front page.

Twenty minutes later Frank Figgis bustled into the newsroom.

He spotted me and hurried over to my desk.

"Where is he?" he asked.

I gave him my wide-eyed look and said: "Where's who?"

"The man you're supposed to be tracing."

I made a show of looking all around the newsroom and then stooped down and peered under my desk.

"He's not there," I said.

"This isn't a joke."

"Too right," I said. "Two men have died so far and, if His Holiness is right, a third is in line for a trip to the Pearly Gates."

Typewriters at nearby desks fell silent as fellow journos suddenly realised they needed to consult their notes. All the better to earwig the argument Figgis and I were having.

Figgis picked it up immediately. "Come to my office," he said.

He marched off across the newsroom. I followed with stooped shoulders like a slave being led into captivity. I could hear suppressed sniggers behind me.

In his office, Figgis reached for his peppermints, ripped off the paper, and shoved three of the things into his mouth. His teeth crunched viciously on them.

I slumped in the guest chair and said: "I've landed us an exclusive on the Potter murder. I've linked the killing to the Tussaud's robbery."

Figgis asked me how and I told him how Potter had made Marilyn Monroe his bedroom playmate.

Figgis's eyebrows arched in disbelief. "Good heavens. I can just imagine what Mrs Figgis would say if I tried that."

"Would she notice?" I asked.

"As long as I kept Marilyn properly dusted, probably not." Figgis said. "But don't think you can change the subject. I want to know what progress you've made in tracing Gervase Pope. I've been ordered to report back to His Holiness this morning."

I leaned back in my chair.

"You can tell His Holiness, I've no evidence that Gervase has killed anyone - yet. But I've also got no lead on where he's hiding. If Gervase were plotting to kill Maundsley, it's possible the Clapham murder may have spooked him. Even the cops will discover that Clapham was linked to Maundsley. That means there will be an increased police presence around the old fascist."

"A ring of steel?" Figgis asked.

"Knowing the Brighton cops, it'll be more like a ring of rusty old tin. But it may persuade Gervase to back off - if he were planning an assassination attempt in the first place."

"His Holiness can't think of any other reason for his disappearance."

"Pope may not know as much about his brother as he'd like to think. When I visited his flat, it was clear he's still deeply involved in extreme right-wing politics."

"But he hates Maundsley."

"That makes no difference to fanatics like Gervase. They remain faithful to the cause and regard those who let them down as traitors."

"So you're saying that Gervase looks on Maundsley as a traitor?"

"Could be. But there's a broader picture here. The Clapham and Potter killings suggest to me that there's something big about to happen in Maundsley's organisation. I don't know what it is, but I'm beginning to wonder whether Gervase could be involved. Perhaps he knows what's going to happen and wants to be part of it. Perhaps he wants to stop it. Perhaps he just wants to find out more. If we could get to the bottom of that, I think we'd have a clue where we can find Gervase."

Figgis swallowed his peppermints and reached for another.

Before he could do so, there was a rap on his door. The door opened and Cedric's face appeared.

"Urgent call for Mr Crampton at his desk," Cedric said.

"Get the switchboard to put it through in here," Figgis said.

Cedric disappeared and thirty seconds later Figgis's phone rang.

I lifted the receiver and a voice taut with tension said: "This is Estelle Daventry. Something terrible has happened. It concerns Gervase Pope. I need to see you immediately."

"I'll be with you in ten minutes," I said and replaced the receiver.

Figgis's eyes asked the question.

"Gervase's housekeeper," I said. "It sounds like bad news. I'll call you when I've seen her."

I jumped up and hurried from the room.

Chapter 18

The doors of Gervase Pope's private lift opened and I stepped into his apartment.

Estelle Daventry was over by the window looking out to sea. She turned as I walked into the room. She was holding an envelope like it was a live hand grenade.

Her eyes were moist and her nose was pink. She'd been crying. She hurried across the room to me holding out the envelope. She said: "I'm beside myself with worry."

I took the envelope. Whoever had sent it chose quality stationery. It had been made from thick bond paper. With an envelope like this, you'd be impressed even before you discovered what was inside. This was the kind of envelope you'd get if you were being invited to take tea with a duke. Or you were being offered a knighthood by the Queen. Or, perhaps, you were getting one of those chance-of-a-lifetime investment opportunities from a scam artist in Bermuda.

I looked closely at the envelope. Just eleven words had been typed on the front: Private and Confidential: For the attention of Mr Gervase Pope only. The counter - the area enclosed by a letter's form - of the "e" was smudged. The e key on the typewriter had probably filled with paper dust and not been cleaned.

I said: "Do you know when this letter came?"

Estelle sniffed. "I couldn't say. It must've been during the night. I noticed it in our post box in the lobby when I went to collect the milk about half an hour ago."

"Why does it worry you?"

"Because the envelope is the same as the one Mr Pope received before he left."

"The letter you told me about last time - the one he locked in his desk drawer?"

"Yes."

"And the one he replied to and posted himself?"

"Yes."

I held the envelope up to the light. Couldn't see anything inside. I squeezed the envelope. Its texture compressed pleasingly between my thumb and forefinger. But it didn't feel as though there was much in the envelope.

I said: "I'm going to open this."

"No, you can't." Estelle said. "It's private."

"And confidential," I added. "But Gervase Pope has too many secrets and it's about time some of them were made to blink in the light of day."

I inserted a fingernail under the envelope flap and flipped it up.

I took out a single sheet of paper and a photograph.

The photograph showed the stretch of a river as it passed through a sweeping curve. From the white caps on the water, the river was flowing fast. Perhaps because at that point the river passed through rapids. Or perhaps because there'd been heavy rain before the photo had been taken. To the right side of the photo a rough track passed close to the riverbank. Reeds had grown to obscure part of the track. It looked like the kind of place that rarely saw even a horse and cart.

I unfolded the sheet of paper. My eyes widened in surprise. The paper held a poem - typed using the same typewriter as the envelope. The poem read:

Once was a beauty, loved as a sister,
Then came a man who loved her as well,
Won over her heart 'cos he couldn't resist her,
Asked her to marry him and with him dwell.
Took her one night for a drive by the river,
But the car plunged in and then she was gone.
Failed to rescue her, failed to deliver
Her. Now he must pay the price, forty years on.

I handed the paper to Estelle. She read it and looked at me. Her eyes were misty.

"What does it mean?" she asked.

I frowned. "It means someone is planning to kill Gervase."

My brain had just stepped up a gear. I could almost feel the neurons tingling.

So this was why Gervase had disappeared. He wasn't planning to kill Oscar Maundsley. An assassin was planning to murder him.

I said: "The poem suggests Gervase had a love affair with a girl forty years ago - that would be in 1924. But the girl died when a car Gervase was driving went into a river. I imagine this photo shows the spot where it happened. This poem has obviously been written by the girl's brother. He's Gervase's potential killer. Has Gervase ever talked about any of this?"

Estelle slumped on a chair. "No."

She leant back and looked out of the window. I waited while she gathered her thoughts.

She turned back to me. "Mr Pope has never mentioned anything like this directly. But I remember a few years ago, he'd had a little too much brandy after his dinner one night. He was looking at old photographs from his album and became quite maudlin. I recall he rambled on about a girl. Something about having loved and lost being better than never having loved at all."

"Did he say who this girl was?"

"No."

"Had he been looking at her picture in the album?"

"No. I remember he'd had so much to drink I had to help him to his room. When I came back into the sitting room, I noticed he'd left the album open at the page he'd been looking at. It showed a group of young men in a formal kind of pose. I think it was a photo from his university days."

"Does Gervase still have the picture?"

"I don't know. He still has the album because he keeps it in his study. But whether the picture is still in the album…"

Estelle voiced the thought running through my mind. If Gervase had taken the first envelope from his mystery correspondent when he disappeared, perhaps he'd taken the photo as well.

"Could I see the album?"

"I'll fetch it." Estelle hurried from the room. She was back in less than a minute, carrying the album. It was one of those old-fashioned jobs, bound in brown cloth with stiff card and pages separated by tissue paper.

Estelle put the album on a table by the window and flipped the pages.

"The photo's not here. No, wait…"

I hurried to her side. Estelle had opened the album at a page near the back. There was a single photo held on the page with little stick-on corner pieces. The photo showed two rows of young men dressed in white tie and tails. In the front row six men were sitting on chairs. In the back row seven were standing behind the chairs. Thirteen men. Unlucky for some. Certainly, it seemed, for Gervase.

Five of the men had moustaches. Two wore glasses. Seven had folded handkerchiefs in their breast pockets. All had the glassy eyes and slouched postures of men who've dined well but not wisely. Three held brandy snifters. Two were smoking cigars. One was laughing. Four looked bored.

The photo had been taken indoors in a room with oak panelling and hung with fancy chandeliers. One of the chandeliers appeared on the right of the picture. The floor was made of dark flagstones. There was no carpet. No pictures on the wall behind the men. The men were sitting on upright wooden chairs. The kind not made for comfort. The kind you find in British Rail waiting rooms.

I gently pulled the photo out of its corner-piece fixings and turned it over. In neat script, someone - presumably Gervase - had written on the back of it: Cambridge University Blunderbuss Club dinner, Lent Term, 1923. Then followed a list of the names of the six men in the front row: Toby Herrington, Jarvis Plunkett-Winterbourne, the Honourable Richard Gascoyne, Lord Timothy Bridlington, Harry Williamson, J G McMasters.

Then came the names of the seven in the back row: Glyn Olwen-Thomas, Freddie Harbottle-Smythe, self - as Gervase had identified himself - Felix Delaunay, the Honourable Charles Stuart, Archibald ffoulkes, Tarquin Tirconnel O'Henry.

I showed the back of the photo to Estelle.

I said: "Have you ever seen any of these names before?"

Estelle said: "I didn't know the gentlemen in the photo were identified on the back. But, no, none of the names are familiar."

"You don't remember Gervase mentioning any of them?"

"No."

"Did he ever speak about the Blunderbuss Club?"

"No."

"But presumably you knew he'd been at Cambridge University?"

"I did know that. I remember once the subject of universities came up in conversation and I asked him whether his days at Cambridge were the happiest in his life. He muttered something I didn't hear and walked out of the room. I never raised the subject of his time there again."

I said: "I need to keep the envelope with the paper and this photo for the time being. Thank you for your help."

I moved towards the door.

Estelle hurried after me.

She said: "Do you think Mr Pope is safe?"

"I don't know," I said. "Perhaps for the moment, but it's clear from this paper that someone intends to kill him."

Estelle slumped down on a sofa. Her mouth had dropped open in a silent scream. Her hands trembled.

"Who would want to kill him?" she asked.

"I don't know, but I think we'll be able to find out. I need to use your phone."

Estelle's arm quivered as she pointed at it.

I strode across the room, lifted the receiver and called Figgis. He was silent while I explained what I'd discovered.

I said: "If Gervase was in love with a girl who died in a motor accident, His Holiness must know who she was. If he can give me the girl's name, we can track her brother down."

"Leave it to me," Figgis said. "I'll speak to Pope immediately. Come straight back to the office. I'll have the name by the time you get here."

"What do you mean you don't know where His Holiness is?"

I was in Figgis's office. It was less than twenty minutes since I'd left Estelle at Gervase's apartment.

Figgis had slumped in his chair. He looked smaller than usual, as though he'd been dipped in a bath and shrunk. He seemed distracted. He picked up a tube of peppermints and put the end in his mouth, as though it were a cigar. Realised what he'd done and tossed the mints back on his desk.

"What do I mean? Just what I've told you," he said. "Our editor has left the building and I don't know where he is. And it's at times like this that I miss my Woodbines."

"But you told His Holiness about the girl, about the accident, about the death threat in the poem?"

"Yes."

"What did he say?"

"He sat there looking as though the gates of Hell had just opened in front of him. His face couldn't have looked paler if you'd slapped on a coat of whitewash. Then he stood up and left the room. I assumed he was making for the lavvy. He looked as though he wanted to throw up. The next thing I know Joan Fotheringay, his secretary, is in the room telling me Pope has left and she doesn't know when he'll be back."

"So you didn't get to ask him the name of the girl?"

"No."

"From which we could have discovered who the brother was. The brother that wants to croak Gervase."

"No."

Figgis's shoulders sagged. The lines on his forehead looked deeper than ever. There were black smudges under his eyes. His right hand worried away at a stray paperclip on his desk.

I said: "I think we may be able to work out who Gervase's stalker is."

Figgis looked at me with a flash of hope in his eyes. "How?"

I showed him the photograph of the Blunderbuss Club members.

I said: "Estelle told me she once caught Gervase looking at it and he seemed moved. At least his eyes were moist, which may not be the same thing. But I think we can conclude the photo meant something to him. This photo is dated to 1923, so it was taken a year before the motor accident mentioned in the poem."

"So how does that help us?" Figgis asked.

"I think the girl who died was the sister of one of the men in the picture. That's why Gervase was getting sentimental about it."

"But we have no idea which one - there are twelve of them, apart from Gervase."

"We can narrow the field. I think the brother we're looking for attended Harrow, the public school."

"How can you know that?"

"The poem reads like a verse from Harrow's school song. It even ends with the song's title - *Forty Years On*. The first time I visited Gervase's flat, I saw a picture of him at Harrow. The man we're looking for knows that Gervase would recognise the poem and take it as a serious threat."

"So get on the dog and bone to Harrow and ask for a list of

old boys who were at Cambridge in 1923."

"I don't think so. For a start, the school would ask why I wanted the information. I could probably come up with a false answer but when they discovered the real reason they'd be off to the Press Council with a complaint. We'd both be in the firing line."

"So what?"

"We know the Popes have been a Sussex family for generations. Wherever this accident happened, there would have been an inquest on the girl's death which would have involved Gervase and possibly other members of the family. There's a strong chance we'd have carried a report of the inquest. The answer could lie in the morgue."

Now there was a bit of hope, Figgis had regained his customary vigour. He reached for the peppermints and fiddled with the wrapping. Looked up and saw me watching him.

"So why are you still sitting there?" he said.

Henrietta Houndstooth crossed her arms and gave me her stern-eyed schoolmarm look.

"We can't possibly do that today," she said. "Do you know how much extra work a general election creates for us in the morgue?"

She was sitting at her desk. Two tall heaps of files threatened to topple onto the floor. Across the room, the Clipping Cousins - Mabel, Elsie and Freda - looked up from the files they were leafing through.

"We have to check the file on every candidate," Mabel said.

"Of every party," Elsie said.

"In every parliamentary seat in Sussex," Freda added.

"They're for the profiles the political reporters have to write," Henrietta explained. "So we simply don't have time to do what you want."

Because the clippings files went back just twenty-five years, they wouldn't contain any information from 1924. So I'd need to look in the bound copies of the newspaper held on shelves at the back of the morgue. A much bigger job than pulling a clippings file.

I'd asked Henrietta and the Cousins to help. If there was a report on the inquest it would carry the name of the dead woman. Depending on whether the reporter had stayed awake during the proceedings, it might also include more detail about what had happened when the car plunged into the river. And, if I was really lucky, it might even tell me which reach of which river.

But it looked as though I'd have to do the job myself.

I'd hefted one of the volumes of the 1924 copies off the shelf. It was bound in heavy cloth-covered board and smothered in a thin film of dust. It smelt like I'd just opened an old sock drawer. I leafed over a few pages to see what the job would involve. The paper ran to an average of twenty pages a day back then. So with six papers a week, there'd be 120 pages to scan each week, 6,240 pages during the whole of 1924. Double that if I had to look at 1925 - because inquests don't always happen soon after a death, especially if the circumstances are complex. Especially if lawyers get briefed. And as this involved the Pope family, I was certain m'learned friends would have been crawling all over the case.

It would take me days to search through all the papers. I could never do it. Especially as Figgis would be pressing me for copy on the Clapham murder investigation and the Tussaud's robbery.

But wait a minute... Would I need to search all the papers? Was there any way I could narrow down the hunt? The poem sent to Gervase had said that it was "forty years on" from the date when the events it described happened. It was now 1964 - so when I'd read the poem I'd taken it to mean what happened had taken place any time in 1924. But suppose the meaning was more precise than that. It was curious the writer had taken the trouble to deliver the poem in the early hours of the morning. Could that mean the forty year reference was more precise? Could today's date, in fact, be an anniversary?

Today was Friday 25th September, 1964. Could the tragic event have taken place on the 25th September 1924?

I marched over to the shelf holding the bound back issues of the paper. Took down the volume for September. Turned to the paper for the 26th September, which would report events that took place the day before. The pages of the paper had become stiff and fragile over the years, but I turned them as quickly as I could.

And there it was on page four.

I felt my heart do a tango that Dolores Esteban would be proud of. It beat to a faster rhythm and I felt the flush that always appeared around my neck when I was excited.

The story was a down-page piece because there were few facts. But there were enough. A Sunbeam 14/40 two-seat tourer had plunged into a stretch of the river Ouse at Barcombe Reach. The driver was a Mr Gervase Pope, an undergraduate at Cambridge University. He'd had a passenger, Miss Harriet Delaunay, believed to be from a well-to-do family living in the West Country. Miss Delaunay had drowned in the incident but Mr Pope had managed to scramble to safety.

I followed the running story in subsequent issues of the paper. The pay dirt came in the report of the inquest. I used the report and the earlier cuttings to construct a narrative of the events that night.

Gervase and Harriet had been on their way to a fancy-dress party at the country house of some friends. Gervase was dressed as a wizard in a long cloak covered with stars. Harriet was dressed as a witch, complete with conical black hat and a besom broomstick. On a lonely stretch of road by the river, the car slipped sideways. It hung suspended from the river bank with the two passenger-side wheels in the water, the two driver's side wheels clinging perilously to the land.

In evidence, Gervase claimed he tried to pull Harriet to his side of the car. But the car slipped further. He climbed out hoping that he could gain a foothold on the bank and hold the car steady. But the loss of his weight from the land side of the car made the whole vehicle topple over into the water. Harriet slipped from the passenger seat and was trapped under the car. Gervase claimed he'd plunged into the water to pull Harriet to safety, but that she'd drowned before he could do so.

Gervase didn't strike me as the hero type. After all, he was now running for cover.

Gervase was asked by the coroner, Dr Timothy Pocklington, how, if he had been submersed in the water, his magician's cloak was largely dry when help arrived. According to the *Chronicle's* reporter, Gervase looked shamefaced and was unable to reply.

I was right! So the weasel had stood on the riverbank and watched the poor girl drown. Or he'd panicked and fled the scene.

Mr Josh Gorringe, a motor mechanic, said he had examined the Sunbeam after it had been pulled from the river. He found that the steering mechanism was incorrectly adjusted so that the car had a tendency to over-steer. With the car in this potentially dangerous condition, Gorringe was surprised it was being driven by someone who was not its owner. There was a gasp from the public seats when Gorringe named the owner of the car. Gerald Pope. Gervase's brother.

So could this explain why His Holiness had now scarpered? As Pope owned the car in which Harriet died, was Pope also in the assassin's cross-hairs?

Mr Gerald Pope was called to the witness box. He admitted that the car's steering was faulty. He claimed the vehicle was still safe to drive if the driver took care. He said he'd warned his brother about the problem when he handed over the Sunbeam's key. He admitted to the coroner he should never have allowed the car to be driven.

No wonder His Holiness now wanted Gervase's problems tidied away with no official involvement.

There was an outburst on the public benches when the jury delivered a verdict of accidental death. Harriet's brother, Felix Delaunay, leapt to his feet and shouted abuse. Before he could be dragged from the court he'd screamed: "Gervase Pope, I'll kill you. No matter how long it takes - even if it's forty years on. You're dead, Pope. Dead!"

I looked again at the date of the accident: 25th September 1924.

I looked again at today's date on the Clipping Cousin's wall calendar: 25th September 1964.

Today was the last date of the promised execution.

Forty years on.

Chapter 19

I closed the heavy board cover of the bound newspapers and sat back in my chair.

If Felix Delaunay was true to his threat, he would kill Gervase Pope today.

But was it sensible to take seriously a threat uttered in anger forty years ago? I could just imagine what Detective Superintendent Alec Tomkins would say if I called him with the news. Scorn wouldn't even begin to describe his reaction. I couldn't even get my old mate Ted Wilson to abandon his lunchtime pint and pork pie to follow up the lead on the strength of the evidence I had.

But not everyone knew that Gervase had disappeared. Or that he'd received an old Harrovian poem threatening retribution. In fact, it was a song rather than a poem. If Delaunay really did plan to top Gervase, was he going to set it to music?

Tra-la-la-la-li, you're dead.

But I was allowing my mind to wander into flights of fancy.

There was a simple way to discover whether Felix was serious about his threat to kill Gervase. I could ask him. He wouldn't admit it. But I'd know from his reaction what he planned to do. Besides, just asking the question would prove a deterrent. He'd know his name would be in the frame if any mishap befell Gervase.

There was only one problem with that plan. I had no idea where Felix lived. He could be anywhere. The inquest report said the Delaunays lived in the West Country. That was a start, but the West Country covered a huge tract of territory from Gloucestershire to Cornwall. I considered working my way through telephone directories covering the area. But that would take hours. There'd be at least fifteen directories. There could easily be several Delaunays in each. Calling each one in turn would take more time I didn't have.

And, anyway, I couldn't be sure Delaunay still lived in the West Country. Those old families put down roots for centuries but they have to move some time. Generally when the death watch beetle moves in.

Besides, what would I say? "Excuse me. Are you the Felix Delaunay who plans to murder Gervase Pope?"

There had to be another way to discover Delaunay's whereabouts. And, I realised with the customary flash of genius about which I'm normally so modest, there was. I didn't know Delaunay's address, but Gervase must do. After all, if the first letter Gervase received - the one he'd hidden from Estelle - had come from Delaunay, he'd replied to it. Estelle had spotted him sneaking off with the envelope.

I was betting that an organised old gent like Gervase would have Felix Delaunay's whereabouts neatly written out in an address book.

I could look it up. But only if Gervase hadn't taken the book with him.

There was only one way to find out.

To say that Estelle Daventry was pleased to see me would be pushing it a bit.

She stood in the middle of the sitting room at Gervase's apartment with her arms crossed. She had a scowl on her face that could have curdled milk.

She said: "You march in here and expect me to hand over Mr Pope's address book, one of his most private possessions. I won't do it."

I said: "First, I didn't march in here. I came up in the lift. And, second, if you don't hand it over, I shall have to search the flat and take it anyway."

Estelle advanced towards me. She was shaking with fury. "You'll do no such thing. I shall call the police."

I held up my hand in what I hoped looked like a calming gesture but probably made it look as though I was waving goodbye to someone I didn't like.

I said: "I wouldn't do that, if I were you. I'm sure Gervase wouldn't want the cops crawling all over his flat. Especially when they came to the display cabinet in his office."

"There's nothing illegal about Mr Pope's collection of memorabilia."

"Perhaps not. But what remains of Gervase's reputation would be shredded if it was generally known he had a soft spot for old Nazis. That's one reason why his brother wants all this investigated discreetly."

Estelle sat down heavily. Her eyes were watery. She sniffled. She pulled a lacy handkerchief out of the arm of her cardigan and blew her nose.

I sat down beside her. Rested my hand gently on her shoulder.

"I know this isn't easy for you. But you need to think of yourself. If Gervase becomes an object of scorn - even hatred - as a result of his, er, unusual hobby, your life would also be more difficult."

Estelle nodded reluctantly. "I suppose so," she whispered.

I said: "Where does Gervase keep his address book?"

"In his study. In the top right-hand drawer of his desk."

I stood up and headed for the study.

The billboard-sized photo of Mussolini still presided over the place.

I stuck out my tongue at him and plonked myself down in the chair behind Gervase's desk.

The desk drawer was still locked. But armed with the brief tutorial Click-Click had provided when he'd opened Potter's van, I went to work.

The desk was old and the wood had warped a little so the drawer sat a little loose on its runners. Gervase had a whippy little paper knife on his desk. I inserted the knife through a gap between the drawer and the desk frame. I pushed down on the lock.

I didn't think it would give. So I pushed down on the drawer handle at the same time as I pressed on the lock. I used force. My fingers holding the paper knife turned white. The drawer wasn't going to open.

Click.

Just one. Not two. Like Click-Click's. But it was enough.

The catch came free and I yanked open the drawer.

I uttered a simple prayer to Tyche, the Greek goddess of good luck, that Gervase had left his address book behind.

And there it was, nestling in the corner of the drawer. I reached in, took it out and put it on the desk. It would have been a handsome item in its day. It was covered in tooled brown leather. The words "Address Book" had been picked out on the front cover in gold leaf. But the book was old. The leather had faded in parts. The spine was cracked. The gold had faded.

But hopefully the information inside was still intact.

I opened the cover. The book had been bound with marbled endpapers which looked like a psychedelic dream. An old-fashioned bookplate was headed *Ex libris Pope*. The bookplate had some fancy heraldic stuff I've never been able to follow and a motto: *Ducit amor patriae*. I applied my schoolboy Latin to the translation: love of country guides me. I wondered how far that applied to Gervase with his cabinet of Nazi junk.

The bookplate had been inscribed in now faded ink: "To Gervase, on your 21st birthday - from Mater and Pater. 4th April 1923."

So it looked as though Gervase's address book might have become over the years something of an heirloom. The book had an alphabetic thumb index cut into the side of the pages. Ever hopeful, I flipped straight to the Ds.

There was a jumble of names, addresses and phone numbers. Here was a forty-one year slice of Gervase's life profiled in the contact details of people he'd known. At least, the people he'd known well enough to record in his book.

But Gervase would have been no great shakes as a filing clerk. Or a librarian. Or a Ministry of Bumf bureaucrat. Anyone, in fact, who had to keep information in alphabetical order.

He'd jotted down entries at random. Sometimes he'd used the person's real name. Sometimes a nickname. Sometimes he'd written the full address. Sometimes just a telephone number.

I ran my finger down the D pages. I guessed the earliest names were at the top of the page, the later further down. Gervase had started by writing them clearly in blue ink using a pen with a thick nib. Later he'd changed to a black pen. Later still to a red Biro. One or two of the entries had been added in pencil. I started at the top and moved through the entries. It was like passing through the geological layers of Gervase's life.

There was a Dickie De Lisle, a Hector Doddington, a Sheldon Doubleday and others with names that spoke of comfort and prestige.

Then there were the women, usually just a given name. There was a Doreen, a Dulcie, a Daphne (with two exclamation marks in brackets after her entry) and a Deborah (not Thursdays, Gervase had noted gnomically).

And then there were the nicknames for people Gervase obviously knew - or had known - well. There was a Dog Biscuit, a Doughnut Face, a Drab Derek, and a Doubting Thomas.

But I didn't find an entry for Felix Delaunay.

Which left three possibilities.

One, Gervase could have entered the name under the Fs - for Felix.

Two, he could have entered it as a nickname anywhere in the book.

Three, he may not have included it at all.

If it was the third possibility I was as sunk as a shipwreck. But if it were possibilities one or two, I might have a chance.

I flicked to the Fs and hunted for Felixes. No dice.

So that left the nickname option. I sat back in Gervase's chair and thought about that for a moment. On the face of it, the idea of guessing the nickname that someone I'd never met had given to someone I didn't know seemed impossible.

But perhaps there was a way to do it. For starters, the nickname would have to be one of those written in the address book. That limited the selection from the millions of pet names people give their friends - and occasionally their enemies. I could go through the book, study each nickname, and decide whether it might be the one.

I flipped back to the As and then had a quick look at the Bs. There were about a dozen nicknames across the two letters. If that average applied through the rest of the alphabet, I'd be looking at more than one hundred and fifty - although I could probably reduce that by twenty or thirty as there'd be fewer for uncommon letters such as K, Q or X. Even so, I didn't fancy my chances of cracking the puzzle that way.

But there might be a way of narrowing the choice even further. For a nickname often relates either to some physical characteristic (Fatface Fred) or a personality feature (Dithering Delia). But as I had no idea what Felix Delaunay looked like that wouldn't be much help.

Sometimes a nickname becomes a variation of a real name. Like when White becomes Chalky White. I didn't think that would apply in Delaunay's case. Unless his name had some posh connotation I'd never heard of. So how the hell was I going to work out whether any of the nicknames belonged to Delaunay?

I sat back in the chair, frowned at Musso, and gave the matter some more thought.

Gervase had known Delaunay since their days at Harrow. Then they'd both been members of the Blunderbuss Club at Cambridge - in the days when they were friends. Gervase had received his address book when he was twenty-one - and still at university. So if Delaunay was in it, he'd be one of the early entries under whichever letter his nickname began with. That could still leave three or four dozen nicknames to check out - and I didn't have time for that.

But, I realised, I also knew something else which could help me reduce the number. Gervase had recently been in touch with Delaunay. He'd written at least one letter to him - the one Estelle saw him sneaking to the post. So the original forty-year-old entry could have been updated recently. I could be looking for an entry originally written with the thick nib in blue ink and then updated with the red Biro. I'd seen several of these through the book, but there weren't more than a handful of them.

The first one was under the As - Apple Chappie. There was an address in Norfolk which had been changed to one in Nottingham. No phone number. I made a note of the name on a pad lying on the desk.

There was no altered name under the Bs, but there were two under the Cs. The first was a cove called Christian Larry. The original address had been a vicarage in Shropshire. It had recently been updated to the Deanery in a northern England cathedral city. I didn't think Larry would be my mark but I made a note anyway.

The second name was Catnap. No address this time but the original phone number - Shepton Beauchamp 27 - had been updated to a Bristol number I didn't recognise. I wrote Catnap on my pad. I sat and stared at it.

It was one of those moments when you think you know something important, but don't know what it is. But, wait a minute. I did know what it was.

I flipped back to the bookplate at the front of the address book. Read the motto again: *Ducit amor patriae*. Not English, but Latin. I put myself in Gervase's shoes. He came from a family with Latin bookplates. Attended a school where a boy offering round his toffees would shout out "Quis?" (who wants one?) and expect the reply "Ego" (me). Went on to a university which had a public orator who'd spout a mouthful of the dead language before handing over your degree.

For Gervase, Latin would be as familiar and insistent as a ruck in his socks.

And Delaunay had a name - Felix - which in the Latin *felis* meant cat. True, not the ancient Latin which old Caesar would have spouted round the Forum - *Et tu Brute,* and all that. This was mediaeval Latin which scientists took over so they could give those long Latin names to animals and plants.

Felis catus - a domestic cat.

Felix Delaunay - Catnap.

And a would-be killer.

I picked up the telephone and dialled the Bristol telephone number, not knowing who would answer.

At the other end of the line a woman's prim and proper voice said: "University of Bristol. Carol Dawlish speaking. How may I help you?"

I said: "I'm sorry to trouble you, but I'm trying to get in touch with Felix Delaunay."

"Hold the line, caller," Carol said primly.

There was a silence, then paper rustled, like a file had been opened.

"I'm afraid Professor Delaunay is currently on leave for two weeks," Carol said.

"I'm sorry to have missed him. Could you tell me which department Professor Delaunay works in?"

"The professor is one of our leading lights in the history department."

"Ten sixty-six and all that."

"There is no 'all that', as you put it." Carol put me in my place. "Professor Delaunay is one of our country's leading experts on the history of witchcraft."

The line went dead.

I sat for a minute in Gervase's chair. I felt cold and goose bumps had risen on my arms and back.

Gervase and Harriet had been dressed as a wizard and a witch when they'd been on their way to the fancy dress party. The party Harriet never reached because she died.

And now the professor of witchcraft wanted to kill the wizard who had let her drown.

Chapter 20

I left Gervase's apartment with the distinct feeling that time wasn't on my side.

I'll admit I couldn't figure out why Felix had waited forty years to kill Gervase. I could understand Felix being devastated by Harriet's death. I could understand why he blamed Gervase. But I would've expected Felix's fury to cool as the years passed. Had there been some kind of trigger which had reignited his passion for revenge? I couldn't think of one.

But perhaps it was the symbolism of the forty years on. That would have deep meaning for both Felix and Gervase. They'd both been schoolboys at Harrow. It was as though Felix had set a date for Gervase's execution. The poem I'd seen and the letter which Gervase had received earlier would have been Felix's way of taunting him. A way to make Gervase fearful. To create true terror in his heart. No wonder Gervase had fled.

On the way down in the lift, I glanced at my watch. Four-thirty. If Felix was planning to use the fortieth anniversary of his sister's death to kill Gervase, he had just seven and a half hours to do it.

Unless, of course, Gervase was already dead.

Which raised another question in my mind. Had Felix found Gervase? I'd tried and failed. If Felix had been similarly unsuccessful, Gervase's date with death would be off. At least for today.

The lift doors opened. I stepped into the lobby, and made my way out into the street while I thought about the implications of that. The Forty Years On poem had been delivered to Gervase's apartment in the early hours of the morning. That implied Felix thought Gervase was still holed up in his flat. Or perhaps he didn't know where Gervase was. Perhaps he sent the poem to the flat in the hope it would reach him. Either way, he hadn't been able to kill him yet.

But events were moving fast. Could Felix have found and captured Gervase since he'd sent the poem? If so, Gervase might already be dead. It seemed the forty years stuff was important to Felix. Maybe he planned to kill Gervase to the exact hour when Harriet died. If so, that would be in the evening, because the pair had been on their way to a party.

And there was something else about Felix's approach. The date was important - but so was the location. Why include a photograph of the exact spot where the poor girl drowned? This whole thing was taking on the gruesome features of a ritual killing. And Felix was an historian with an expert knowledge of mediaeval witchcraft. How did they kill witches? I'd read enough books, seen enough Hammer horror films to know the answer to that. They burnt them to death at the stake.

I reached my car, took out the key, and unlocked the door. I climbed inside and sat staring out of the windscreen.

I wasn't sure what I should do next. I could go to the cop shop and tell them what I knew - a local fascist was about to be burnt at the stake by a witch fancier. They'd laugh so much the place would sound like the Palace of Varieties.

I could return to the office and pursue my day job - reporting crime stories rather than chasing my editor's brother. But that would place me in line for months of revenge from His Holiness. It would make my life a misery.

Or I could drive to the supposed location where, if my deductions were correct, the denouement to this whole grisly business would take place. I didn't expect to find anything. There'd be no sign of Gervase. But at least I could report back to Figgis that I'd tried.

I rummaged in the back of my car for the Ordnance Survey map of East Sussex. The exact spot - Barcombe Reach on the river Ouse - had been mentioned in the coroner's report of Harriet's inquest. From the map, it looked like a lonely spot, far from the nearest village. I folded the map so I could see it on the passenger seat beside me.

Then I pressed the starter button, revved the engine a couple of times, and pulled out into the traffic.

The sun was low in the west by the time I pulled the MGB into a passing place on a narrow country track.

There were thick woods on either side of the track - tall trees like larch and birch, with an undergrowth of holly and brambles. The trees grew so thickly I couldn't see more than ten yards into the wood.

I picked up the Ordnance Survey and applied my map-reading skills to the problem. (Thank you, Brian Alner, geography teacher.) If Mr Alner had taught me correctly, the river Ouse lay about five hundred yards to the east, through the woods. The map showed another small stream coming down from the higher ground. The stream seemed to flow into a pool which then connected to the main river through a thin tributary. The map indicated that the stream and pool lay in the thickly-wooded country.

The track on which I'd parked the car forked about three hundred yards ahead, round a bend. The right fork continued to re-join the main Lewes to Uckfield road. The left fork ran past the stream-fed pool and then continued on to the village of Chailey. When Gervase and Harriet set off to their fancy-dress party forty years ago, this would have been the route they'd taken. But since then a new road had been built to the west, so these tracks were now little used. They'd become overgrown, like an untended garden.

I debated driving down the left-hand fork, but dismissed the idea. If Felix were lurking by the pool - with or without Gervase - the sound of the car would alert him. Better, I decided, to risk snagging my trousers on the brambles and sneak through the woods. If my trousers were ruined, I'd claim for a new pair on expenses. And if Figgis jibbed at that, I'd go to His Holiness's tailors and order a pair on his account. And maybe a pair of spats to go with them.

Fifty yards into the wood, I decided I would need a new pair of shoes and a jacket as well. The ground was covered with thick leaf mould. The leaves disguised marshy hollows filled with brackish water. The first one I stepped into filled my right shoe so I squelched as I walked. Every time I put my right foot to the ground it sounded like a plunger unblocking a drain.

It was difficult to keep a sense of direction among the trees. I must have drifted off to the left because when I came into a small clearing I could see the pool through the trees about seventy yards to my right.

I couldn't see anyone - and I strained my ear to hear voices. But all I heard were the squawks of squabbling pigeons in the tree canopy above me. I crept forward as quietly as my squelching shoe would allow. I positioned myself behind the thick trunk of a sycamore about five yards from the edge of the pool.

Trees surrounded the pool except for a grassed area where the route of the track had created a small clearing. I peered around the edge of the tree and almost let out an involuntary gasp. I pulled back out of sight and put my back to the tree for support. I was breathing like a fell runner. My heart was pounding like a steam-hammer. And my legs wobbled like the raspberry blancmange my Aunt Tilda used to serve on birthdays.

I took a couple of deep breaths to steady myself. Balled my fists and flexed my shoulders. Felt a bit calmer. Took another peep around the tree.

On the far side, one of the trees on the bank of the pool had been cut down. A stump of trunk about three feet high had been left in the ground. Across the stump a thick crossbeam of some rough wood had been balanced, like a see-saw. One end of the beam was lashed to the ground with a rope. The other end of the beam hung over the pool. The seat and back of a wooden chair had been lashed to the beam at the pool end.

And I should have known.

I cursed myself for being so slow. I should have made the connection as soon as I discovered Felix was an expert in witchcraft.

And now I knew where Felix had obtained this contraption. From Unity Box-Hartley, the queen of reproduction antiques. The clue had been staring me in the face ever since I'd visited her shop. I'd taken a peek in her day's to-do list and seen a reference to "Delivery. Cucking St." I'd taken that to mean she had something to deliver in Cucking Street. That the St abbreviation was short for Street.

But St wasn't short for Street at all.

It was short for "stool".

Unity Box-Hartley was delivering a cucking stool.

And there it was on the far side of the pool balanced across the tree stump. It was a nasty implement, used in the Middle Ages to punish - and often drown - witches. What was I thinking? There were no witches - never had been - just unfortunate women who for one reason or another didn't fit in and so were picked on by bullies. And as for cucking stools - better call them ducking stools, because that's how they worked.

The poor girl who'd been fingered as a witch was sat on the chair end and plunged into water. If she floated she must be a witch - because she was in league with the Devil. She'd rejected the water that baptises a true believer in God. If she sank, she'd embraced the baptism and must be innocent.

But usually she drowned.

So this was how Felix planned to kill Gervase.

His sister had died dressed as a witch. And now Gervase would die as one.

As if to confirm it, Gervase appeared from among the trees on the far side of the clearing. I recognised him from photos I'd seen at his apartment. There was the shock of wild hair, brown in the photos but now traced with grey. There were the haughty arched eyebrows, the beaky nose, the thin lips permanently compressed into a sneer. Gervase was wearing a brown seersucker suit and a light blue shirt, open at the collar. The suit was the kind of gear I imagined he'd turn up in at Henley or Goodwood or one of those posh summer events. Except that today he was turning up to his death.

That was clear because his hands were bound behind his back. Gervase turned away from me to follow the path and I saw they'd been fastened with a neck tie. The tie was a dark blue number with a double stripe pattern. I'd bet his old school tie.

Gervase was stumbling along with hunched shoulders. He glanced behind him with the look of a man who knows there's nothing good there. And within a couple of seconds I saw what it was.

Or rather who it was. A tall man with a rangy figure carried a shotgun. The breech was closed. I was willing to bet the thing was loaded with two cartridges. And it was pointing at Gervase's back. The man had to be Felix Delaunay. He had the weathered complexion of a man who spends much of his time outdoors. He was wearing a checked jacket and brown corduroy trousers. He had a moleskin flat cap on his head. He wasn't dressed like your typical executioner. But, then, he wasn't your typical executioner. He was a man with a grudge he'd nurtured for a lifetime.

Which, in this situation, made him more dangerous than your average executioner - who's under orders to top his victim swiftly and pick up his fee. Felix was out for revenge. He'd be deaf to orders - or reason.

Gervase said over his shoulder: "I understand your pain, Felix." His voice quavered like his voice box was wobbling.

Felix raised the shotgun so that it pointed at the base of Gervase's neck. "You understand nothing about how I feel," he said. "You never have."

"Can't we talk about this?"

"We've done all the talking that's needed."

Gervase stopped. Turned round and faced Felix. Took a step closer, but Felix raised the gun and Gervase stepped back.

"I tried to save Harriet that night," Gervase pleaded. "I really did."

"How could you? Your clothes were dry."

"I tried to keep the car from falling into the water. But I wasn't strong enough. It kept dipping in. I managed to pull it back twice, but on the third time it just fell."

"And Harriet with it. Why didn't you pull her out of the car? You got yourself out."

"I was on the landward side, Harriet was closest to the river."

"You should have jumped into the river and pulled Harriet out after the car fell in."

"But Harriet was under the car. I knew I couldn't move it without help."

"You should have tried."

Gervase fell to his knees. "Please, Felix. It doesn't have to be like this. I can't bring Harriet back and I regret that every day. Genuinely, I do. But I can make amends. I'll pay you anything you ask."

Felix threw back his head in a scornful laugh. "There's no amount of money can compensate the loss of a sister like Harriet. What is it the Good Book says? 'An eye for an eye.'"

"You don't have to shoot me."

"I'm not going to shoot you." Felix pointed at the ducking stool.

Gervase swivelled on his knees. I saw his mouth drop open. He scrambled to his feet. He turned back to Felix, like he was about to beg for mercy.

Felix gave a dry little laugh. "Harriet lost her life dressed as a witch. Now you'll die as one. Climb on the seat, Gervase."

"No," Gervase screamed.

"Climb on the seat or I shall shoot you in the legs and load you onto it."

Events were getting out of hand.

It was time someone tried to lower the temperature.

I looked around. There wasn't anyone.

So, as usual, it was going to be me.

I stepped out from behind the tree and walked into the clearing. I sauntered along like a country type out for an evening stroll.

"Good evening, gents, lovely evening," I said. As though coming across a mad gunman and his tied-up victim was part of the simple country life.

The pair of them looked at me like a caveman from the stone-age had just appeared on the scene. Gervase's eyes lit with hope. Felix turned the shotgun on me.

"Is this some ancient country custom or are you making a film?" I said.

I twizzled my head about a bit as though looking for a film crew. "I don't see any cameras."

Felix's eyebrows beetled together. "We're not making a film. And you're on private land. You should leave immediately. That is unless you want to feel the prickle of lead shot in your backside."

"I know it's the open season for grouse and pheasant, but I didn't know journalists were also fair game."

"You're a journalist?" Gervase blurted.

"Colin Crampton, *Evening Chronicle*. And I have a feeling this is a David Livingstone moment."

"What do you mean?" Felix said.

"I can just imagine the scene somewhere in Africa when Henry Stanley - he was a journalist too, you know, working for the *New York Herald* - stumbles into a clearing, sees the man he's been searching for, and utters those immortal words."

"What immortal words?" Felix asked testily.

"'Dr Livingstone, I presume?' Except in my case, I have to say, 'Gervase Pope, I presume?'" I turned to Gervase as I said it.

He stepped towards me, but Felix raised his gun, twitched it towards Gervase as a signal he should move back.

I said: "This has gone too far. You're behaving like a mad man."

"No, like a brother who loved his sister dearly," Felix said. "You know nothing about me."

"I know enough to realise that what you're planning is crazy."

I tried sweet reason. "I can understand you want revenge on the man you blame for Harriet's death. I can understand the weird logic that makes you want to extract that revenge on the anniversary of the tragedy. I can even understand the desire to kill Gervase the same way Harriet died. But do you really have to make a freak show out of it? I mean, what's with the cucking stool? If you use the damn contraption the way you intend, you'll end up in Broadmoor, the high security psychiatric hospital. You'll spend the rest of your life bouncing off the walls of your padded cell and swapping gothic fantasies with the craziest goons in England."

Felix said: "I've had enough of your interference. You have unfortunately arrived on a scene that does not concern you. I had hoped to send you on your way none the wiser, but it's clear that you know this man." He twitched a thumb at Gervase. "I can't discount that you know about my purpose. As you're a journalist, I can't have you writing about it for your rag, so I must kill you as well."

In one swift movement, he swung the gun back towards me and fired.

Chapter 21

At first, I thought the bells ringing meant I was dead.

Perhaps they were the church bells pealing for my funeral. Or perhaps they were celestial bells welcoming me through the Pearly Gates. Or maybe it was the bell you ring to summon the boatman who ferries you across the river Styx, when you turn up at the entrance to the Underworld.

No.

It was none of them.

It was a ringing in my ears. It sounded like my brain had become a set of cymbals pounded by a demented drummer.

I clapped my hand hard against the side of my head and the bells toned down a few decibels.

And then I realised what had just happened. Felix had tried to shoot me. He had a shotgun with two barrels. He'd missed first time but he'd make sure it was second time lucky.

I looked around confused. I couldn't see him.

Gervase stumbled towards me, his hands still tied behind his back.

He nodded his head towards the ground. I followed his gaze. Felix was lying on the grass looking dazed.

Gervase said: "I shoulder-charged him as he fired. Just like I used to do playing rugby at Harrow. The shot went loose in the trees. I saved your life."

The arrogance of the man!

I squared up to him. Let him see there wouldn't be any gratitude from me.

"I didn't come here to pick flowers," I said. "Where do you suppose you'd be now if I hadn't pitched up? I'll tell you: doing an impression of Lloyd Bridges but without the snorkel."

Gervase shrugged. Not easy with hands tied behind his back. It made him look like a duck about to lay a difficult egg.

I stepped over and undid the tie binding his wrists. He rubbed them to get the blood circulating again. Stuffed the tie in his pocket. Didn't bother to thank me.

I said: "Besides, we're not out of trouble." I pointed at Felix. "He's still got the shotgun."

Felix was lying on the ground with the shotgun tightly gripped in one hand. He scrambled up on one knee and pointed the gun at us. It wavered between Gervase and me as though he couldn't decide who to shoot first. But he'd only pot one of us because he hadn't reloaded the empty barrel.

He said: "I gired the fun."

I said: "What?"

He said: "I mean, I fired the gun."

"I had noticed. It's not something I recommend."

Felix stood up unsteadily. He crouched in front of us with knees half bent. He waddled towards Gervase. Kept the shotgun pointed at his chest.

He came right up to Gervase and swayed a bit. He looked straight into Gervase's eyes and said: "I'm going to kill your friend first."

Gervase said: "He's not my friend."

"Then that will make it easier for you."

"But not for me," I said. "Don't I get a say in this?"

Felix turned to me. His head drooped and his eyelids looked heavy.

He said: "Only got one…"

"One thought," I said. "To end this madness."

"No. One cart."

"You mean cartridge."

"So I've got to use my stool." He gestured with the gun towards the contraption. "Go over there or I'll shoot you in the bells."

"Bells?"

"I mean balls."

The Tango School Mystery

Felix briefly pointed the gun at Gervase. "You'll tie him in the chair," he said. "Follow him."

"Or he'll shoot the clappers out of your bells, too," I said.

We trooped across to the ducking stool. On the business end, the chair was suspended over the pool. The other end was fastened to a peg in the ground by a short rope. Closer up, I could see that the main crossbeam was pivoted on a peg which stuck vertically out of the tree stump.

Felix turned to Gervase "I want you to release the rope on the land end of the crossbeam but keep hold of it."

Gervase gave me a quick glance. Like he didn't really want to, but knew he had no choice.

Felix stumbled a bit and his knees wobbled. I thought he was going to fall over, but he regained his balance. But he stepped back and pointed the gun at Gervase.

"Now rotate the crossbeam so the end with chair is over the ground," Felix ordered.

Gervase moved away from me on the other side of the tree stump as the chair moved towards me.

"Now let out the rope so that the chair is lowered to the ground," Felix said.

Gervase shrugged, like he couldn't be bothered not to, and the chair came down in front of me.

"Get in the chair," Felix said.

"Make me," I said.

Felix gestured at Gervase. "Come here," he said.

Gervase stepped reluctantly around the tree stump.

Felix pointed the gun at Gervase's head and said: "I am going to shit."

I said: "What?"

"I mean shoot."

Felix's head drooped but he made an effort and pulled it up to look at me. His eyelids sagged like they were weighed down.

"He means it," Gervase said. "Shoot not shit, that is," he

added unnecessarily.

I climbed into the chair. I didn't like the look of it one bit. There was a waist strap to hold the victim in and arm straps so that he couldn't get out.

"Tie the strips," Felix said to Gervase.

"He means straps," I said.

Gervase stepped forward. The straps had buckles, just like a belt.

"I'm sorry about this," he whispered as he fastened the buckles. "I've got no choice."

"Me, too," I said.

With me safely tied in, Felix ordered Gervase back to the control end of the crossbeam.

"Lift the boom…"

"Beam," I shouted.

"And rotate it over the pill."

"Pool."

Gervase looked like he'd been invited to join a lunatic asylum. I felt I was already in one.

But he did what he was told. Like a good Nazi. Just obeying orders, they'd explained at Nuremberg. But there wasn't going to be any Nuremberg for Gervase or Felix. Because I wasn't going to be around to point my finger at the guilty.

Gervase had the damned ducking stool rotated just as Felix liked it. I looked down. I was about three feet above the water.

"Let go," Felix shouted.

And down I went. I was still sucking in the air I knew would be my last breath when I hit the water.

Splosh!

I sank with all the grace of a dead body dumped from a bridge. Every muscle in my body tensed as the freezing water engulfed me. It was ten times worse than being in the cold showers after PE at school.

The coldness dulled my senses and for a moment I couldn't

figure out what had happened to me. Then I realised I was submerged in water and that my eyes were cold. I opened my eyes, blinked as the water stung. Then looked around. It was quiet and still. So this is what it was like to be a salmon. Or an eel. Or perhaps a jellyfish.

But then I realised it wasn't like that at all. Because they didn't have to breathe oxygen from the air. And I began to panic. I had air in my lungs and was holding my breath. I was good at it. I'd won competitions among school friends doing it, only cheating a bit. But there'd be no cheating down here. I'd managed to hold my breath for two minutes. Two and a half with a bit of cheating. But how long did I need to hold it?

I struggled with the straps on my arms, but I couldn't move them. And as bubbles floated past my eyes I realised I'd wasted some of the air with my effort. I dribbled the air out as slowly as I could. But I was running out. I wondered what would happen when it did. How long would it take me to drown? It could be a lengthy business.

It was going to start any moment. The last bubbles passed before my eyes. My head felt light. I knew I would faint soon.

And then the chair began to move. But I was still under water. Perhaps the chair was just being moved sideways by the current. Yes, that was it.

No, it wasn't. The chair was moving upwards.

My head emerged from water and I sucked in a huge gulp of air.

And then the chair began to rotate towards the land.

I glanced around. My vision was blurred. But I could make out Gervase on the control end of the crossbeam. He manoeuvred the chair onto the land and let it down on the ground. He hurried round and unbuckled the straps.

I climbed down from the chair with my mind still dazed.

I said: "What happened to Felix?"

Gervase said: "He fell asleep."

He pointed to the ground. Felix was lying on the grass, under the crossbeam, close to the tree stump. His snores sounded like a chainsaw.

"Narcolepsy," Gervase said.

I should have worked it out for myself. Felix's nickname was Catnap. I'd figured out the cat part of it, but never asked myself why the nap bit had been tagged on. Felix could have been slipping into uncontrolled short sleeps for years. No wonder his school chums had given him the nickname.

Gervase said: "I remembered about the narcolepsy just after I'd lowered you into the water. Felix developed it at school. It lasts a lifetime, you know. Confused speech is one of the sure signs that an attack is coming on."

I said: "He's cradling that shotgun like a teddy. I'm taking charge of it."

I crawled under the beam and pulled the gun from his arms.

For the first time since I'd stepped off the chair, I realised I was standing in dripping clothes. I shivered in the cool evening air.

"I need some clothes and Felix needs the police," I said. "I'm going for help, but keeping the gun. While I'm gone, you can tie up the Sleeping Beauty with your Old Harrovian tie. No need to worry. He was at the school, too."

I trudged off feeling like I'd just walked out of the Niagara Falls. About fifty yards across the clearing, I heard a shout.

I turned around. Felix had woken up and was scrambling to his feet under the crossbeam.

But Gervase was on the move, too. He was holding the control end of the beam.

Felix's eyes widened with fear. He reached for his gun. Realised he no longer had it.

He moved away from Gervase. And as he did so Gervase swung the beam. I heard a crack like a coconut breaking as the heavy end of the beam - the end with the chair - crashed into the side of Felix's head.

His head flopped unnaturally to one side and he stumbled. Then he fell backwards. For a moment, it was as though he was suspended in air by gossamer-thin wires. His arms flailed. His legs pounded like pistons. His mouth dropped open and he uttered a long ululating wail. Like a cry from his heart that vented all the emotions he'd ever felt.

And then he splashed into the water.

I raced across the clearing, but Felix had floated ten feet into the pool before I'd reached the bank.

His lifeless eyes were open and I fancied there was a smile on his lips.

"You murdered Felix," I said.

"It was self-defence," Gervase whined.

"How could it be? I'd disarmed him of the shotgun. Or, rather, he'd disarmed himself by falling asleep."

"He planned to kill both of us."

I nodded. There was truth in that.

We were sitting in the back of a hired van parked on the track fifty yards from the clearing. It was the van Felix had used to bring his ducking stool and Gervase to the spot.

I'd had to strip off and swim into the pool to drag Felix's body to the side. I hauled him up onto the bank and left him there. I'd have to call the police soon. But not yet. I had unfinished business with Gervase.

I'd found some sheeting in the back of the van which Felix had used to cover up the ducking stool. I'd used it to dry myself off. I'd run the engine and was drying my clothes as best I could on the van's heater while I sat swaddled like a baby in the sheets.

Gervase gave me a cunning look out of the corner of his eyes. "I shall tell the police that I saved you from drowning. I'll be feted as a hero."

"That depends on what I tell them." I said.

"You'll corroborate my story."

"As far as it goes. But there's also the little matter of a dead body. The cops will want to know how it came to be dead. That's the bit where you'll find you have some questions to answer. You swung that crossbeam deliberately to kill Felix."

"I just thought he might go to sleep again."

"The cops might buy that. But it only reduces the charge from murder to manslaughter. You're still looking at a long spell inside. Not an attractive prospect for an old fascist like you. You won't be popular with the old lags and hard cases in jail. They may be crooks, but they're patriotic crooks."

"Keep my politics out of it."

"I don't see how I can. It seems to permeate this whole business."

Gervase fell silent. He was thinking.

He said: "Is there any way out of this?"

I pulled the sheet more tightly around me. Felt my trousers that were hanging over the steering wheel. They seemed a bit drier.

I said: "There might be. If you tell me everything you know, I can put that into context. It might help me understand how you came to swing that beam."

Gervase shrugged. "I suppose being a journalist you've already poked your nose into the root of all this."

"If you mean have I diligently researched the background, yes. I know about the motor accident when Harriet died. What I don't know is how you came to be marched into a remote forest clearing with your hands tied behind your back."

"About two years ago, I heard through some friends that a woman in Brighton was dealing in memorabilia from the Third Reich."

"That would be Unity Box-Hartley," I said.

Gervase nodded. "The Third Reich has always been a consuming interest for me and I contacted her. Over the weeks,

I bought a few small items for my collection. I discovered that we held similar political views."

"You were both fascists."

Gervase stiffened. "I'm not ashamed of the fact. But I'll admit it pays to be discreet. As I got to know her better, I found that Unity was less cautious in broadcasting her views. She had embraced the cause with more passion than me. She had a close attachment to Sir Oscar Maundsley."

"The leader of the British Patriot Party and the man who had you interned during the war?"

Gervase nodded. "When I discovered this, our relationship cooled. But I kept in touch with her because I thought she might be a source of information about what Maundsley planned to do. I regard the man as a traitor to our cause and I would do anything to destroy him."

"You used Box-Hartley as a way to spy on Maundsley?"

"In a manner of speaking."

"But that can work both ways," I said.

Gervase's shoulders sagged. "Yes. Unity discovered about my wartime internment and how it happened. Perhaps Maundsley told her. On the surface, she seemed as friendly as ever. But I had the distinct impression that she'd adopted a different attitude towards me. But she tried not to let it show and she still shared titbits of gossip about Maundsley with me. Looking back, I think the aim was to keep me involved. I think they knew I could make trouble if Maundsley ever decided to return to Britain."

"And six months ago, he did." I said. "Do you know why?"

"I asked Unity about it. She told me he missed England and wanted to see it again before he died."

"Missed England. Not Germany?"

Gervase ignored that. "I didn't believe her. When I knew Maundsley well in the nineteen-thirties he never did anything without a reason. He was up to something."

"Standing as a candidate in the general election," I said.

Gervase shook his head. "He knew he'd never be elected in Britain. Besides, he only announced his candidature a few days ago. Maundsley only pays lip service to democracy. He believes in direct action."

"What kind of direct action?"

"The violent kind. You should have seen him back in the old days - those marches through the east end of London. He'd be in the thick of the fight with the commies. Loved it when stewards beat up a heckler at one his rallies. I discovered he'd recruited an army officer and a gentleman to run his security."

"One Captain Wellington Blunt," I said. "He may have been an officer, but he's no gentleman."

"I thought I'd be able to find out by subtly pumping Unity for information. But I got a bit careless. Asked too many pointed questions. Unity backed off. And the next thing I knew, Felix was sending me weird poems and threatening to kill me."

"I don't get it," I said. "What's the connection between Felix and Maundsley?"

"I knew Felix well before the tragedy with Harriet. Even after, I hoped we could rebuild our friendship. We were so alike. Been to the same school, same university. Shared the same political views."

I jolted in shock at that news - and almost split the sheeting.

"Felix was a fascist?" I asked.

"An enthusiastic one, ever since Mussolini's march on Rome in 1922. Of course, he kept the information to a close circle of friends. They included Maundsley. Because of that Maundsley knew of my part in Harriet's death."

Another surprise.

"Are you saying Maundsley put up Felix to kill you?"

"I've no proof, but it's the way Maundsley works. He keeps at arm's length from the criminal stuff."

"But why should Felix want to do it?"

"Felix has never forgiven me. He's always wanted to kill me. If he thought he could, and get away with it, he would. Besides, Maundsley helped him a lot in his career. The narcolepsy made it hard for Felix to find university jobs. Maundsley helped him with money over the years - thousands and thousands, I suspect."

"The elaborate ducking stool charade seems a mad way to kill someone."

"Maundsley knew it would make the idea attractive to Felix. He told him that Unity Box-Hartley would use her contacts in the reproduction furniture trade to get one made. And, besides when the killing was complete, the ducking stool could be removed and my body left floating in the pool. When I was discovered, it would look like an ordinary drowning - an accident. No evidence to connect anyone to the killing."

"Certainly not if Detective Superintendent Alec Tomkins was on the case. But you've killed Felix, so we've got no chance of linking the plot to Maundsley."

"There's still the big thing Maundsley is planning."

I arched my eyebrows to show scepticism.

"The big thing that's still baffling me is how Felix found you," I said. "I couldn't trace you anywhere."

"It was a letter," Gervase said. "He wrote to me saying he wanted to discuss the past. He said he thought it was time for both of us to put Harriet's death behind us. He said we couldn't let an old friendship die over the issue."

"This would be the letter you hid from Estelle," I said.

"I answered it and posted the reply myself. I told Felix I wasn't sure he was sincere, but I would have to think over what he'd said. The following evening, he telephoned me. I was having dinner at the time. Felix was friendly. He said it was time to let bygones be bygones. He wanted to meet me immediately to show how sincere he was. I knew it was a trap and that I wasn't safe in my apartment. So I left immediately, taking only some bare necessities with me - and the SS dagger from my display cabinet for protection."

"Where did you go?" I asked.

"I hid out in a small bed and breakfast place in Rottingdean. But yesterday I needed more money to pay the landlady and came into Brighton to go to my bank. Two thugs grabbed me before I had a chance to get inside the bank. They disarmed me of the dagger and bundled me into a car. They delivered me to Felix. Felix gloated when he saw me. He told me that before he'd sent the letter, he'd hired a private detective to follow me and find the places I regularly frequented. No doubt the detective was financed by Maundsley. After I'd disappeared, the detective staked out the bank with the thugs knowing I'd eventually need money."

Gervase was alive but he looked like a beaten man. I decided I couldn't bring myself to feel sorry for him.

I felt across to my clothes. They were still wet but not sopping.

"I'm getting dressed," I said. "Then we're transferring to my MGB and driving to Brighton police station."

Gervase smiled, the first time I'd seen him do so. He reached inside his pocket and pulled out his Old Harrovian tie.

"I better put this on, then," he said. "I don't want to face the full majesty of the law under-dressed."

He knotted the tie and examined his effort in the van's rear-view mirror.

"I think that looks good," he said.

"I preferred it when it was binding your wrists," I said.

Chapter 22

Three hours later I was sitting in a cubicle in the men's lavatory at Brighton Police Station.

I'd delivered Gervase to the cops. I'd phoned Figgis to say I'd found Gervase alive and well (just). I'd dictated a piece about the death of Felix to a copytaker.

I'd had a busy day which had ended with me giving Detective Superintendent Alec Tomkins a long statement about everything I knew. Or, to be strictly accurate, about everything I thought Tomkins needed to know.

There was one point which I hadn't resolved in my own mind. I wanted to check it out before I told the cops. I knew the ducking stool, which had almost killed me, and which did for Felix, had come from Unity Box-Hartley. No doubt she'd had one of her reproduction antique craftsmen knock up the thing. Goodness knows, what he'd thought about it. No doubt she'd spun him a convincing cover story. Trouble was, I had no evidence that Box-Hartley had provided the stool. And I doubted there'd be any incriminating evidence at her shop. Besides, I wanted to find out whether Maundsley really was behind Gervase's attempted murder - and Box-Hartley could hold the key to that information. So, for the time being, I was keeping that to myself.

I was waiting for my witness statement to be typed up so I could sign it. All the interview rooms were busy and I didn't fancy hanging around in reception. There'd be other reporters on the prowl now they knew there was a big story brewing. If they cornered me they'd start pumping for information.

The cubicle was the one place I could sit in peace and quiet while I waited for the typist to do her work.

The door to the loo opened and a pair of feet shod in heavy boots clumped in. I leant down and peered silently under the gap at the bottom of the cubicle door.

The feet belonged to Tomkins. They moved swiftly to the urinals.

The door opened again and two more feet entered.

A voice said: "Didn't know you were in here, guv." Ted Wilson.

"You'll always find me where the big knobs hang out," Tomkins said.

Ted dutifully chuckled at a joke he'd probably heard ten thousand times.

Tomkins said: "Talking of big nobs, is your team all lined up for the visit tomorrow morning?"

"I briefed them this afternoon," Ted said. "Told them we had a big name visiting, but didn't say who."

"Good man. Keep the location secret as well."

"They'll be told forty-five minutes before the arrival at eleven o'clock, guv."

All four feet moved and running water suggested they were washing their hands.

"Remember, secrecy is everything," Tomkins said.

"With all the preparation, I'm amazed we've kept it under wraps," Ted said.

"Keep it that way," Tomkins said.

The feet moved towards the door. It opened and they went out.

I left it a couple of minutes before standing up, pulling the chain, leaving the cubicle, and washing my hands.

I'd cracked cop secrets before and I was determined I'd discover this one.

But an hour later it looked like this was the one secret I wouldn't crack.

I was sitting at a table in Prompt Corner opposite Shirley. I'd zipped back to my apartment and changed into fresh clothes before meeting her at the restaurant.

The Tango School Mystery

I was busy getting myself on the outside of my second large gin and tonic while Shirley sipped at a Campari and soda. I'd told Shirley what had happened. I'd tried to make light of my brush with death. Shirl's hand had reached across the table to stroke mine when I told her about the ducking stool and my trip in it.

"Jeez, that's barbaric," she said.

"Sure, but only if the witch floated. Then she was taken out, dried down, and burnt at the stake. I sunk without trace."

"But you came back up again."

"You can't keep a good man down," I said. "Let's order. Being nearly drowned gives you an appetite."

Shirley grabbed my wrist to stop me opening the menu.

"Just a minute, whacker," she said. "You haven't heard my news yet."

She grinned the way she did when she had a secret. She reached under the table for her bag and rummaged inside it.

"You remember you asked me to find out about that hat box," she said.

"The one Freddie Barkworth photographed in the back of Maundsley's Bentley?"

"Sure. It came from that posh milliner in Paris. I asked Tom Arkwright who's been the lighting guy on that West Pier photoshoot I've been in. He'd just been in Paris working on a fashion shoot, and had brought back a couple issues of *Paris Match*."

"Great magazine," I said.

"Tom hadn't heard of *Pascale Dubois* but he said he'd have a quick look through them for me. He came up with this."

Shirley opened her bag, reached in, and pulled out a press cutting. She unfolded it and passed it across the table.

It was a cutting from the magazine dated two weeks earlier. A colour picture showed a tall woman with blonde hair stepping into a first-class railway carriage. I'm no fashion expert but I'd be willing to bet the canary yellow twin-set she was wearing hadn't come from Woolworth's. If I'd seen this picture in any magazine I'd have dismissed it as a filler. Woman climbs into train. Big deal.

But not this time. Because the woman was carrying a hat box from *Pascale Dubois.*

The caption below the picture read: "*Françoise Dior a l'air d'avoir fait ses courses avant de prendre la Flèche d'Or à destination de l'Angleterre.*"

Shirley leaned over and translated: "Françoise Dior seems to have done her shopping before taking the Golden Arrow to England."

I said: "This could be important. Do you know who Françoise Dior is?"

Shirley shrugged. "Something to do with the famous fashion house, I suppose. The one started by Christian Dior."

"Françoise is Christian's niece. Her own father Raymond was the heir to a fortune from a family fertiliser business. But wealth didn't stop him being an ardent communist."

"So Françoise is a red?"

"Not at all. She swung the other way. She's a fanatical Nazi sympathiser. Was during the war and still carries the swastika with pride. If she was coming to England, there's one man she'd want to see."

"Sir Oscar Maundsley."

"You've got it."

"And I think I know why," Shirley said.

"You do?"

"It's obvious. Look at the photo again, bozo. Dior is carrying two boxes. And the other one's not her hat."

I picked up the cutting again and studied the picture.

I said: "I can just about read the name on the other box. *Couture Mon...* something."

"That's *Couture Monique,*" Shirley said. "It's the best bridal shop in Paris. World famous. And if that box doesn't hold Dior's trousseau, I'll eat Ned Kelly's daks."

I leant across the table and kissed Shirley. A real loving plonker on the lips.

"You're brilliant," I said. "If Maundsley and Dior really are planning to get married, it changes everything we know."

"It doesn't change the fact I'm starving," Shirl said.

This time Shirley didn't stop me passing her the menu.

"Let's eat first and talk later," I said.

I pushed away my plate, lifted my glass, and took a last sip of my wine.

I put down the glass and said: "It's strange how childhood memories stick in the mind. I remember a day one summer when I was sitting in the garden wondering whether to go to the park or read a book. I was watching an ant scurry along the edge of the path. I noticed a second ant run down the trunk of the apple tree. Then I noticed a third ant crawling over the watering can outside the greenhouse.

"I sat there for a few minutes watching them. Just thinking there are three random ants, each unaware of the other two. But eventually they all headed for the same destination - a large stone slab at the foot of the rockery. They all scurried under the stone. I went over and lifted it up. There was a whole colony of ants under it. There was a tracery of passageways and tunnels and a queen ant at the centre of it all."

Shirley finished her chicken and put down her knife and fork.

"Except in this case the queen ant is a king ant - Maundsley," she said.

I grinned. "You're ahead of me."

"So what's new?" she said.

"I started off looking for an ant who'd gone missing."

"Gervase Pope."

I nodded. "I discovered three more ants - Wellington Blunt,

Unity Box-Hartley and Conrad Montez. At first I thought they weren't connected. Now I'm not so sure. Besides, apart from these three, there are other ants in the nest. Some are also players and some are victims."

"Like Derek Clapham, the poor sap who was killed above Antoine's Sussex Grill."

"Yes. I'm sure Clapham was killed by Blunt and now I think I know why. There was a pile of old newspapers and magazines in Clapham's apartment with a couple of *Paris Match* among them. If Clapham had seen the photo you've discovered, he'd immediately understand the significance of it. Maundsley has always tried to give his brand of fascism a patriotic British slant. But if it became known he was having an affair with an unapologetic Nazi, and a French one at that - even planning to marry her - it would wreck any last vestiges of credibility he had."

"But if Maundsley married a bad girl like that everyone would know about it," Shirley said.

"Not if the wedding was in secret. In the 'thirties there were all kinds of weird Nazi wedding ceremonies between fanatics. Swearing life-long devotion over *Mein Kampf*. Mingling of their blood and stuff like that. If I'm right, Maundsley wouldn't be walking his bride down the aisle of some ancient country church. This would be a secret ceremony in a back room somewhere."

"So anyone who knew about it - or who'd worked it out for themselves, like Derek Clapham - would be a big threat to the old fascist," Shirley said.

I nodded. "I saw letters in Clapham's flat which showed he was strapped for cash. I think he was blackmailing Maundsley over his connection with Dior. Maundsley had to silence him - and Blunt was the faithful follower who completed the job."

"So you think Blunt is Maundsley's hired killer?" Shirley said.

"One of them."

Her eyes widened in surprise. "You think there's more than

one."

"Remember that Potter was murdered."

"By Blunt?"

"I'm not sure, but not in person. I think he may have subcontracted the job."

Shirl's eyes lit up with an idea. "To Conrad Montez, the tango instructor with two left feet."

"You've got it."

"But why should a tango teacher turn to murder?"

"I don't think he is a tango teacher. Remember that Wilf and Betsy told us he turned up at the school only a month or so ago. They also said the relationship between him and Dolores was strained. We saw that ourselves when he barged in half way through the lesson and they had a row in their office. And that's another point. Wilf said the office was rarely locked before Montez appeared on the scene. Now it's always locked."

"Because he's hiding stuff in there?"

"I guess so."

"But what?" Shirley asked.

"Stuff that reveals who he really is."

"You don't think he's Conrad Montez?"

"It's not the name his mother and father knew him by. We know that Montez came from Buenos Aires, where he originally knew Dolores Esteban. After the war, a lot of Nazis fled to Argentina to escape justice for their war crimes. If I'm right, Montez is one of them."

"A real live Nazi?"

"I'd prefer a real dead one."

"So what's he doing in Britain? Surely he risks being exposed and put on trial."

"He must be here for a reason. I think he killed Potter the night we visited the tango school. That's why he arrived late with that bag - it had something warm in it. We know Potter had been shot with a rifle - I think the warm item was a silencer."

"I don't see why Potter had to die."

"He'd been mixed up in the heist of those waxworks from Louis Tussaud's. A cop spotted a van like his on the night of the theft. I saw the van the following day at Maundsley's country estate. I guess Potter was a worker ant who had to die because he knew too much."

"Too much about what?"

I shrugged. "I don't know, but it must be something big because Montez has to be a key player in it. And he wouldn't risk exposure for a minor caper. Which just leaves the third ant."

"Unity Box-Hartley. How does she fit into the picture?" Shirley asked.

"She seems to be the ant who stays in the background but knows what all the others are doing. We know she's pally with Blunt because we saw them together at Maundsley's rally. She knew Clapham because he'd asked her for a loan. I've remembered that Clapham had scribbled a note about it on the bank manager's letter he'd been using as a bookmark. And Unity must know Montez because there was a business card for the Tango Academy on her corkboard. To top it all, she also knows Gervase Pope and Felix Delaunay."

"Little Miss Popular," Shirley said.

"Perhaps. Perhaps not. Either way, I'll have a few questions for her to answer tomorrow morning."

"I'll come with you," Shirley said.

"Sorry, you can't do that. This is official *Chronicle* business. Figgis would have my press card and ritually burn it if he knew I'd taken a guest along to an interview."

"I'll take another look at the Tango Academy, then."

I reached across the table and took Shirley's hand. "Don't do that. Please. We don't know what's going to happen next, but I have a feeling it will be dangerous. I couldn't bear to lose you."

Shirley grinned. "For a minute, I thought you almost meant that."

"I do," I said. "I do."

The notice in the front window of Box-Hartley's shop read: "Closed for annual holiday."

I stamped my foot and cursed under my breath. It was nine o'clock the following morning. I'd spent a restless night turning over and over in my mind the questions I needed to ask Box-Hartley. Now I was fired up to ask them. I was determined not to leave until I had some straight answers.

But Unity Box-Hartley was not on the premises.

I discounted the blarney about a holiday. Box-Hartley was away from her business because she was up to no good. No doubt with Maundsley.

I hung around outside the shop wondering what the hell to do next. Random thoughts were racing through my brain. The vision of some terrible atrocity haunted my mind. But I had no firm evidence to support that idea. Nothing I could take to the police.

Perhaps I would've been able to prise the information from Box-Hartley. Perhaps I could have tricked her into an indiscretion which would have led me to the truth. But Box-Hartley had vanished. Made herself scarce while Maundsley and his storm-troopers - no doubt cheered on by Françoise Dior - went about their evil business.

But wait a minute. Had Box-Hartley vanished? I looked again at the small shop window and the signboard above it. "Reproduction Antique Furniture" it said. Box-Hartley had a thick catalogue of the stuff. I'd seen it on my visit. She wouldn't keep all that in the shop. There simply wasn't room. She had to have some storage space somewhere. Perhaps a warehouse. One without a sign over the door. A private place where she could keep her cabinets and commodes as well as the Nazi junk she didn't want everyone to know about. If she was mixed up in nefarious business, that's where she'd be.

It took me ten minutes to find the address of the place by asking around the nearby shops. An old boy running a second-hand book store just around the corner had once mistakenly taken delivery of an item meant for Box-Hartley. The package had the address of Box-Hartley's shop as well as a place on an industrial estate off Carden Avenue. He couldn't remember the exact address.

But I knew that there was only one industrial estate off Carden Avenue. The estate had fewer than a dozen units. It wouldn't be difficult to trace Box-Hartley's. It would be the one without any sign on the outside.

Fifteen minutes later, I pulled the MGB onto the forecourt of a small warehouse.

The place had walls which looked like they'd been built out of breeze blocks and whitewashed. There were large double doors at the front. I suppose that made it easier to deliver the big stuff. There was a wicket gate in one of the larger doors.

I climbed out of the car, walked towards the door and tried the handle.

To my surprise, the door opened. I stepped inside.

The place was arranged in aisles lined with repro furniture, much of it covered with dust sheets. There were no windows but my eyes squinted at the glare from the fluorescent lights which hung low beneath a metal vaulted ceiling. Somewhere towards the back of the warehouse, I could hear *Housewives' Choice* playing on the radio. Pete Murray was introducing the next record. Apparently, Doreen from Scunthorpe was celebrating her fortieth birthday and was desperate to hear Herman's Hermits singing I'm into Something Good.

Perhaps Doreen was. I had the distinct impression I wasn't.

I headed towards the back of the warehouse. A door off to the right led into a small office. A sign on the door read: "Private".

I ignored that, opened the door, and stepped into the office.

Box-Hartley was on the far side of the room behind a desk. She was shuffling some papers and putting them into a file.

She looked up as I entered the room. Her eyes were wide with surprise. Then she recognised me and the look changed to hate.

Did I say hate? I should have said deep visceral loathing. Her eyes flashed like they'd just loosed nuclear missiles in my direction.

But I didn't have more than a moment to take that in. Because my attention was riveted on the figure standing in the corner of the room.

I felt like my stomach had just gone into orbit and circled the earth. I forced down something warm and sticky that rose in my throat. I felt light-headed, like I'd just drunk a whole bottle of champagne at a single gulp.

And I knew that I'd just stepped into a horror beyond my darkest imaginings.

Chapter 23

The figure in the corner was Winston Churchill.

He was standing upright with a cigar between the second and third fingers of his left hand. His right hand was raised in his trademark V-sign salute. He was wearing a black jacket, striped trousers, and a blue bow-tie with white spots.

And he had a bullet hole right in the middle of his forehead.

Just like the hole Potter had had in his.

I counted seven other bullet holes in Churchill - three in the chest, one on each shoulder and two towards the back of his head.

He was the wax model stolen from Louis Tussaud's.

He'd been used for target practice.

And now I knew why.

I turned to Box-Hartley. She stood behind her desk frozen like another waxwork.

I said: "You're part of a plot to assassinate Churchill." My voice sounded thin and reedy - like it was coming over short-wave radio from the middle of Australia. I realised I was shaking. I tensed my muscles to get a grip.

Box-Hartley's eyes fired off a couple more missiles in my direction. Then she lunged for a drawer in her desk.

She yanked open the drawer and rummaged furiously in it.

I raced across the room. I thrust my left hand onto the desk and jumped.

I vaulted the thing, knocking the telephone and a glass bubble ornament of the Royal Pavilion in a snowstorm to the floor. The telephone came loose from its wire and crashed into the wall. The bubble smashed sending splinters of glass in all directions.

I slid across the desk and crashed into Box-Hartley.

She fell backwards, stumbled across a chair, and landed in an ungainly heap on the floor. Her arms waved. Her legs flailed.

She screeched like a banshee.

The dagger she'd grabbed from the drawer had a vicious six-inch blade. It flew from her hand and skittered across the floor. I picked myself up and leapt after it.

I grabbed the dagger from behind a filing cabinet and turned back towards Box-Hartley.

She was flat on the floor. She was dressed in a tight grey business skirt and a white blouse. Her skirt had ridden up her legs and she fumbled furiously to pull it back. Now she was screaming with a high-pitched shriek. It sounded like the kind of alarm that would go off to warn of a nuclear attack.

I moved towards her and brought my fist down on the desk with the force of a pile-driver.

The desk shook and a calendar and a couple of pens fell off.

I shouted: "Shut up. Listen to me and you may just avoid hanging by the neck until dead in Holloway Prison."

Box-Hartley's scream died away, like a siren had just been killed.

She tried to stand up but I gestured to her with the dagger. "Sit on the floor and don't move," I said.

Box-Hartley pushed herself upwards and rested her back against the wall.

I said: "You planned to use this knife on me so don't for one minute imagine that I won't use it on you."

"I'm saying nothing," she said.

"You don't have to," I said. "I've worked it out. I should have done earlier. But I've done it now."

"Tough. You'll be too late to stop it."

In the background, the Light Programme radio announcer was telling listeners that *Five to Ten* - "a story, a hymn and a prayer" - was about to start. I wasn't going to have time for any of them.

When I'd been in the cop shop loo the day before I'd overheard Tomkins tell Ted: "Don't forget the VIP arrives sharp at eleven o'clock. He's never late."

I had sixty-five minutes to warn the cops. I picked the telephone off the floor and listened to the handset. No dialling tone. The thing was bust.

I had to stop this happening. But I couldn't leave Box-Hartley. She'd do her best to warn her co-conspirators.

I looked desperately around the room. On the far wall there was a door. A sign on it read: "WC". I gave a grim little smile. The initials didn't stand for Winston Churchill.

I said to Box-Hartley: "On your feet."

She didn't move so I walked across to her, grabbed an arm and hauled her up. She turned and spat at my face.

"And I mistook you for a lady," I said.

I marched her across the room, opened the lavvy door, and pushed her inside. I scanned the room. No window. A loo and washbasin and nothing else. Nothing Box-Hartley could use to escape.

She turned and tried to push past me, but I shoved her backwards and she sat involuntarily on the seat.

I reached smartly for the key and took it out of the inside lock. I slammed the door and locked it from the outside.

Box-Hartley hammered on the door and screamed: "Let me out."

"At least you're being detained at your own convenience," I said.

I could hear Box-Hartley still thumping the door as I ran from the building.

Albert Einstein said: "Imagination is more important than knowledge."

This thought popped into my mind as I floored the accelerator and sped the MGB out of the industrial estate into Carden Avenue.

What the old brainbox meant was that you can stuff your

mind with facts but they won't mean much unless you can work out how they all relate to one another.

I'd been slow. I had all the facts, but I hadn't joined them together. I should have used my imagination.

I started to use it now as the speedo on the car climbed past sixty.

I saw the fact which should have triggered my imagination in Potter's job book, the night I'd searched his van. He'd had a painting job at 29 to 30 Brunswick Road in Hove. It was the building that housed the school Churchill had attended for a couple of years as a boy. I'd even told Shirley about it that night we'd had dinner at Antoine's Sussex Grill. Perhaps now he was retiring from Parliament he was making a sentimental journey back to the haunts of his youth.

I let my imagination rip. What do you do when you're having guests round? You spruce the place up a bit. It would be natural if you were about to host Churchill, to make sure the building was looking good. At least, the front he'd see when he arrived and the rooms he'd visit while he was there.

And if you had to get the job done quickly, what more natural than to call in a painter who just happened to be working in an apartment across the road?

When I'd overhead Tomkins in the cop shop loo, he'd said the visit was top secret. But the owners of the house would have to know in advance otherwise they couldn't prepare. They'd be sworn to secrecy, too, but it would be easy for something to slip out. Perhaps Potter picked up the reason for the rush job and passed it on to friends in the British Patriot Party. Perhaps Blunt. He'd have told Maundsley, who nurtured a deep hatred for everything Churchill stood for.

I jumped the lights at the bottom of Carden Avenue and powered the car towards Hove. I passed a telephone box and briefly wondered whether I should stop and call the cops. But would they take me seriously? As soon as Tomkins heard the tip-off had come from me, he'd dismiss it as a journalist's stunt. So I sped on.

I put my imagination to work some more. Potter struck me as being a lowly member of Maundsley's party. But after he'd provided the intelligence about Churchill's visit, he would have risen in the leader's opinion. Perhaps that was why he'd been given the job of picking up the waxwork figures after the theft from Louis Tussaud's.

And now I knew why Maundsley wanted the waxwork of Churchill. He had an assassin, perhaps a former Nazi with wartime experience as a sniper, to shoot Churchill. But if the sniper hadn't worked his craft for years, he'd need some target practice. What better than to try his skills on a life-sized model of his prospective victim? And of the people I'd encountered in this saga, there was only one person who fitted the bill as the assassin.

Conrad Montez.

The tango teacher with two left feet.

He would have been paid a bonus for bumping off Potter. Because Maundsley knew that Potter was a loner - and loners can be dangerous. But for Montez it would have been a useful dress rehearsal.

Maundsley had been clever. He'd distanced himself from the assassination plot by using Blunt to liaise with Montez. It was the Widow Gribble who'd first alerted me to the fact Blunt was a visitor at the Tango Academy. I imagined that if Maundsley used Blunt to liaise with Montez, he used the same ploy when dealing with Potter. Which underlined just what a ruthless bastard Maundsley was. Prepared to work with someone one day, kill them the next. For all his high-falutin' talk about a legacy for the future, the man was just a thug.

I avoided a milk-float by inches as I sped across Seven Dials. The milkman leaned out of his cab and shook a fist at me. I accelerated into Goldsmith Road wondering whether I was too late.

And whether I could do anything to stop the killing even if I wasn't.

The MGB's tyres squealed as I jammed on my foot brake and pulled the car into the kerb.

I was in York Avenue, just north of the junction with Lansdowne Road. Churchill's former school was around the corner.

I scrambled out of the car and hurried to the corner. I looked west along Lansdowne Road to the junction with Brunswick Road. An estate car, a Morris Minor, and a builder's van drove by. Nothing unusual there.

I was surprised there were few pedestrians in the street. But if the visit had been kept secret, there'd be no reason for people to congregate. A couple of uniformed coppers patrolled up and down outside the old school, about fifty yards along the street from where I was standing.

It looked as though the cops' aim was to keep the event low-key. It made sense. Keep the crowds away and the visit is simpler to manage. Besides, if this was a private visit, the low-key approach probably matched Churchill's wishes.

There was no sign of Tomkins. No doubt he'd wheedled his way into the official party. He'd be travelling in one of the back-up cars with Churchill's staff.

I'd decided what to do during my madcap race across Brighton. I'd warn the cops on duty that a sniper was planning to shoot Churchill. His car could be diverted to a safe place while cops were drafted in to search the area.

I sprinted up the street towards the two plods. I didn't recognise them. One was tall with a beaky nose. The other was fat with a double chin.

I said: "I'm Colin Crampton from the *Evening Chronicle*."

Beaky Nose said: "We know who you are. Trouble. Buzz off."

I said: "I know that Winston Churchill is due to arrive here in…" - I glanced at my watch - "…eight minutes."

Beaky Nose shot Double Chin a worried look.

Beaky Nose said: "How do you know that?"

Double Chin said: "It's secret."

I said: "Not to the people who plan to shoot Churchill when he arrives."

Beaky Nose laughed. "Yeah, and then Martians will land in a space ship and cart his body off to a distant planet."

I said: "This is no joking matter. I've uncovered a plot to assassinate Churchill. I haven't got time to explain it all now. But we must stop him arriving and then search the surrounding buildings."

I grabbed Beaky's arm to emphasise the urgency.

Beaky brushed my hand away. "Assaulting a police officer in the execution of his duty. I can arrest you for that."

"We've got handcuffs," Double Chin piped up.

"And we'll put them on you unless you bugger off," Beaky added.

I was getting nowhere with these two.

I turned my back on them and walked away. I crossed the road thinking hard. If Montez was, as I suspected, the assassin, where would he hide out?

The building that had been Churchill's old school was on the west side of Brunswick Road. It occupied a site at the junction with Lansdowne Road. Montez would have two thoughts in his mind. First, he'd want a spot where he could get a clear shot across the junction as Churchill stepped out of his car. Second, he'd want a simple exit so that he could make a getaway before the cops had worked out where the shot had come from.

I had a quick look round. The east side of Brunswick Road had a row of four-storey terraced houses. If Montez could get into one, he'd have that clear shot across the junction.

Potter, I remembered, had been painting one of the apartments in the road. According to his job book, that was why he'd landed the school job. The owners had seen his board in the street. But there was no board there now.

I looked at the fronts of the houses. They'd once been grand residences. But now they'd been converted into apartments. It was easy to tell because the curtains were different on each floor. Except for the first house on the east side of the road. The house with the best view of the junction. The top apartment had no curtains. Perhaps that had been where Potter was redecorating.

I glanced around. Beaky and Double Chin had disappeared around the corner into Lansdowne Road. Probably on a look-out for Churchill's car.

I hurried up to the front door. There was a row of four bells, one for each storey. Three had names against them. The top one was blank. The apartment must be empty. That would be why Potter had been painting it.

The front door was locked. But that wouldn't have troubled Montez. When Potter was painting the apartment, he'd have had a key. Even if he'd had to hand back the original, he could have had a copy cut for Montez.

The lack of a key was a trouble for me. I couldn't ring bells and announce there was a dangerous gunman in the top apartment. If there were, it would put the other residents in harm's way as they rushed out to see what was happening. If there weren't, I'd be in even more trouble with the cops.

I was wondering whether to ring one of the bells and blag my way in when the door opened. An old bloke with white hair and a walrus moustache stood there. He was holding two empty milk bottles in his left hand.

I glanced at the bell nameplates and said: "Thanks. Just come to visit Sarah Wainwright on the second floor."

He said: "She's at her sister's this morning."

I said: "No, her sister called to say she had a cold."

"How come I saw Sarah leave in her overcoat and that horrible brown felt hat not half an hour ago? And who are you anyway?"

Behind me a car horn blared. I glanced round. A Rolls Royce turned into the street followed by a police car.

I pointed. "Who's that in the big car?" I said.

The bloke stepped out to take a look. I nipped round him into the house and slammed the door behind me.

I could hear him hammering on the door and shouting as I powered up the stairs.

On each landing, there was a window out on to the street.

I glanced out of the window on the first floor as I raced by. The Rolls Royce had stopped.

I was panting by the second floor. The chauffeur had climbed out and opened the Rolls's rear door. A plume of cigar smoke blew into the street.

I was retching for every mouthful of air at the third. Churchill was out of the car and shaking hands with a little knot of people who'd come out of the house.

I staggered towards the door of the apartment. I was wobbly on my legs, like I'd spent a night on the tiles. My breathing was coming in gulps.

And then I heard a loud crack.

And my breathing stopped.

My first thought was: too late.

But perhaps not. The crack came from outside. I glanced out of the window. A police motorcycle had ridden into the street. It backfired again. The same crack.

My legs felt firmer. My breathing had steadied.

The door to the apartment was ajar. I charged towards it and barged through.

I was in a room filled with the acrid tang of new paint. The colour was deep red. So was the smell.

Montez was kneeling by the window. The leather bag I'd first seen at the Tango Academy was beside him. He'd raised the sash window - must only just have done it - and a rifle rested on the sill. It was like a short-barrelled hunting rifle I'd once seen as evidence in a court case about a bank robbery. Ideal for carrying discreetly in a leather bag. The rifle had a silencer fitted. Just as it must have had for Potter's slaying.

Montez looked my way as I stumbled into the room. His eyes were part surprise and part determination. I'd added the surprise. The determination was already there.

And the determination was winning over the surprise.

But for a decimal point of a second he was confused. His brain gave him two orders at the same time. But one contradicted the other.

The first said: shoot Winston Churchill.

The second said: shoot the man who's just blundered into the room.

There was a pause - barely as long as one beat of a butterfly's wings - before his brain told him which voice to obey.

He had to shoot Churchill. It was why he'd risked his liberty to travel to England. Why he'd sacrificed his dignity to masquerade as a tango dancer. How he'd regain his pride after a lifetime living as a fugitive.

He clamped his eye over the rifle's telescopic sight, adjusted the direction of the barrel, and fired.

But before he'd viewed his target, I'd spring-heeled off the floor.

Before he'd adjusted the barrel I'd taken three leaps towards him.

And before another beat of a butterfly's wings, I'd crashed into his prone body.

He cannoned sideways. The rifle barrel swung into the air as it blasted off. Somewhere in the street I heard glass breaking.

Montez retained his grip on the rifle. But he'd had to withdraw it from the window. He scrambled to his feet and stepped back. He wanted to get enough distance between us so that he could aim the rifle and shoot me.

His mouth twisted into a snarl that would have looked great in the Kiss of Fire. But his eyes burnt with a fiery rage that suggested a kiss was the last thing on his mind.

He stepped backwards and swung the rifle in an arc. I moved towards him. Tried to kick him in the balls. A sneaky trick I learnt on the rugby field rather than the dance floor.

But Montez saw my kick coming and sidestepped it.

He nearly had the rifle on me now. I rushed forward, pushed the barrel away, and tried to crush him in a bear-hug. It would have been easier to try it on a real live grizzly.

But Montez couldn't push me away easily without letting go of the rifle. Somehow I found the strength to cling on to him. We shoved back and forth around the room, like we were dancing.

Montez tried to break free but I pushed in again. Back and forth we went, watching our footwork so we didn't over-balance. We both knew the first man down would die. Would have to die.

Only one of us would walk away from this.

We moved towards the corner near the door. I shoved to push Montez against the door, but he shifted to one side. I slipped and Montez snapped free from my grip and stepped away. He moved his hands along the rifle like a man who treated it better than a woman. He had his hand on the trigger before I could rush him.

I closed and gripped him hard.

The rifle pivoted upwards between our bodies. Its barrel pointed at the ceiling. I crushed in harder and grabbed for Montez's throat. His hand let go the rifle and he shoved hard on my arm to stop me throttling him.

The rifle slipped between our bodies. I caught a flash of fear in Montez's eyes. He knew that if he lost the rifle, he'd be finished. He pivoted back from me and reached for the rifle. But it had slipped towards the floor. I could feel the stock resting on my knee.

Montez snatched at the rifle and I felt its length twist towards us. Beads of sweat glistened on his forehead as he grappled with the gun. It was pointing upwards at my head. I felt the sinews in Montez's arm stiffen as he grasped the trigger. I pushed back hard.

And then the rifle fired.

An explosion filled the room. So much for the silencer. I'd be asking for my money back. My ears popped and the rest of the world sounded a million miles away.

And then I realised the left side of my face was covered in blood.

It ran freely across my cheek and dripped off my chin. My left eye was sticky and my hair matted. And still more blood poured down my cheek.

I gripped Montez like he was a stair rail and there was a thousand feet drop below. But Montez was gripping me.

More blood flowed across my face. It seeped down my neck, inside my shirt.

And then we fell.

We lay on the floor, entwined in a death embrace, as the blood continued to flow.

Chapter 24

I was breathing like there were only two gulps of air left on earth and I had to have them.

My vision had faded. It was like a gauze blind had been drawn down over my eyes.

A heavy weight was pressing on my stomach. I realised that Montez was lying on top of me. I reached out and found the rifle had fallen to one side of us.

The blood had stopped pulsing over my cheek. But it was still sticky to touch.

I shook my head and the gauze lifted from my eyes. I glanced at Montez. His mouth gaped open.

But it wasn't his mouth. There was a hole in his cheek. When the rifle fired, he'd shot himself. I was covered in his blood.

I forced myself to look more closely. The bullet had passed through his brain. There was an ugly exit wound in his scalp.

I started to shake. Perspiration flooded my pores. My chest felt like it was tied with rubber bands. I knew that if I couldn't climb out from under Montez I would die of shock.

I shifted under him. I felt I'd used a year's worth of energy just to do it. But I had to find more. I struggled furiously. I freed my right arm. Which meant all Montez's weight was now on my left. I took a deep breath and heaved. I pushed him roughly off me. He rolled over onto his back and lay still.

It wasn't going to take a doctor to tell he was dead.

I stood up, tried to calm my breathing. Took a couple of tentative steps. Felt more confident I could cope with what I had to do next.

I hurried over to the window and looked out. Beaky Nose and Double Chin, the two cops, were blundering about. They looked confused. They pointed at the motorcycle. They exchanged baffled looks. They'd put the crack of the rifle down to the cycle backfiring.

I saw Tomkins climb out of the police car and hurry over to Churchill. The old war leader seemed unharmed. Tomkins took Churchill's arm and ushered him towards the door of the old school building.

I felt a hot anger building inside me. Maundsley's plot to kill Churchill had failed. But if the cops continued to blunder around, he would get away with it. He could be out of the country in hours.

In days he could be holed up in a hideout. In Argentina. Or Paraguay. Or wherever the *Mon Repos* Home for retired Nazis was these days.

Right now, I pictured him lurking in his mansion. He'd be tense by the telephone. He'd be waiting for word from Montez that his mission had been a success. But the word wasn't going to come.

I thought about that for a moment. Maundsley's plot had failed, but with Montez dead, there was no evidence to connect him to it. As I'd already seen, Maundsley was clever in keeping himself clear of the dirty deeds done in his name.

There would always be a faithful cut-off - Blunt in the case of Clapham's killing, Montez in the case of Potter's murder. But what evidence was there to link Maundsley to the attempted assassination of Churchill? I could explain what had happened, but with Montez dead, there was no hope of establishing the kind of hard evidence that would lead to Maundsley standing in the dock.

He was going to walk free. Worse, when the news broke of the failed assassination - I'd see to that in the *Chronicle* - Maundsley would use it to whip up support for his extremist views. He'd claim the plot was part of a breakdown in law and order. He'd demand a strong man in power to take back control.

There wouldn't be any doubt about who that strong man should be. Maundsley would be the winner from a plot he'd engineered.

I couldn't let that happen.

I glanced once more at Montez's body. I left him lying on the floor and hurried through to the back of the apartment.

In the kitchen I found an old dust sheet left behind by the decorators. I ripped pieces off it, doused them in cold water, and cleaned myself up. I couldn't do what I planned if I was still covered in blood.

There was a door in the kitchen which led onto a metal fire escape. The steps ran down the back of the building.

I unlocked the door, stepped outside, and headed down the stairs like a man fleeing the Four Horsemen of the Apocalypse.

It took twenty minutes of hard driving to reach Maundsley's mansion.

His Bentley was parked outside on the carriage drive.

I jumped out of my MGB and marched up to the front door. I was reaching for the bell pull, when I noticed the door was ajar.

I glanced behind me. Was this a trap?

I couldn't see anyone. I put my ear to the crack in the door and listened. In the hallway a grandfather clock tick-tocked. There were no voices. No stealthy footsteps snuck up the hall.

I pushed the door open some more.

The hall had a chequerboard floor in black and white tiles. There was a red Persian carpet in the middle of it. The grandfather clock tick-tocked away to the left.

I stepped into the hall and called out: "Is anyone home?" Felt a bit stupid, but even in a crisis it's hard to stop yourself behaving as though things are normal.

No-one answered.

Better still, no-one appeared and fired a gun at me.

I was beginning to feel at home. Or I would've done if I didn't have a job to do.

There was a door on the right side of the hall. I stepped

through it. It was a sitting room. Plenty of chintzy chairs. Faded Wilton carpets on the floor. Oil paintings on the walls of old buffers with scowling faces and fusty clothes.

At the far end of the room, there was a circular coffee table. It held a coffee pot, one cup and saucer, and a plate of biscuits. I walked over to the table and had a closer look.

The cup was half full. There was a custard cream with one bite taken out of it resting in the saucer. I felt the coffee pot. It was still warm.

I resisted the temptation to pour myself a cup and forced myself to think.

I'd made mistakes already chasing this story. I'd assembled facts but failed to imagine the links between them, as the old relativity man had reminded me.

I was determined not to make the same mistake again.

The facts - the unlocked front door, the half-drunk coffee, the uneaten biscuit - led to only one conclusion.

Maundsley realised his plot had failed.

But how, I wondered? Maundsley would have known that if his plot had worked, Montez or one of the conspirators would have passed the news by telephone. But if the plan failed, the conspirators would be under arrest - or dead. There'd be no message. The phone wouldn't ring. According to the wartime saying, "no news is good news". But not in this case. For Maundsley, no news would definitely be bad news. So there'd be a deadline for a message. If the deadline passed with no message, Maundsley would assume the assassination had failed.

So what would Maundsley have done then?

He'd have to get away. But that might not be easy if Montez had been captured. Maundsley would believe he could rely on Montez's silence. But killing a painter and decorator like Potter wasn't in the same league as assassinating the world's most famous statesman. Local cops wouldn't interrogate Montez. It would be the security services. And they wouldn't care what methods they used to break Montez fast.

So, I imagined, Maundsley would want to flee the country in secrecy. An old schemer like him would have had two plans. Plan A for success. Plan B for failure.

Well, he wouldn't be needing Plan A now.

Plan B would be a scheme to spirit himself out of the country. But that would take time.

So where would Maundsley hole up while he waited?

I wandered around the room deep in thought. I stood at the window and gazed out over the Sussex countryside. A manicured lawn with croquet hoops ran down to a line of trees. Beyond the trees, the land rose in thick woodland. I'd hidden in those woods, when I'd spied on the house. I knew there was a path which led down to the farm at the back of the house. The farm with the long Nissen hut which held the pigs.

The hut with the super-strong padlock that mocked intruders.

The pigs that needed a danger warning.

When I reached the hut, the door was closed but the padlock was gone.

There was no keyhole to peer through. So I put my ear to the door and listened.

Oink, oink.

Well, it wasn't Maundsley.

Grunt, grunt.

Not Blunt either. But, perhaps, a close relative.

The hut had no windows, but there was a gap under the door. Not enough to see into the hut, but sufficient to see a light was on inside. There would have to be lighting in there when the pigs were being fed, but would it be left on at other times? Someone had once told me that pigs were social creatures. Perhaps they liked some light so they could rub snouts with their fellow porkers. But perhaps the light was usually turned off.

In which case, it would be on because someone was inside.

There were too many maybes in my reasoning.

Either Maundsley was in there or he wasn't.

Either he had a gun pointed at the door or he didn't.

Either he would pot the first person who walked through it or he wouldn't.

I'd come too far to walk away without knowing the answer.

And there was only one way to find out.

I opened the door and stepped inside.

Maundsley was sitting on a bench at the far end of the hut. He was wearing a dark black coat and a homburg hat. He stood up when he saw me. All aggression with his arms akimbo. He looked like a bit-part actor in a B-movie western. Just at the point where the villain draws his six shooters.

But Maundsley, I was relieved to see, had no gun.

At least, I reminded myself, not one he'd yet produced.

I took a quick look around as I walked the length of the hut towards him. The pigs - about fifty of them - were penned off to the left-hand side by a low wall made out of breeze blocks. Half way down the hut there was a gate in the wall. It was closed.

The air was heavy with a musky stink I knew would take days to wash off. It wasn't quite like bad breath. It wasn't quite like rotting manure. It wasn't quite like over-boiled cabbage. But mix all three together and it wasn't far off.

The pigs snuffled and snorted. They seemed restless. Their sty was equipped with two long troughs - one for water, the other for food. The food trough was empty. Licked clean by the greedy porkers.

To the right of the hut, there was a row of boxes filled with sacks of feed. There were shelves and buckets and ladders. There were mops and brooms and shovels. Everything the well-equipped pig-keeper could ever want.

The place was lit by bright fluorescent lights hung from the ceiling. The lights were mounted on overhead ducts which held the power cables that came into the hut through the roof.

I stopped two feet from Maundsley. His face was set in a frown, his lips compressed in annoyance.

I said: "Conrad Montez, your hired assassin, has danced his last tango."

Maundsley's eyebrows lifted, but not more than if I'd told him it was about to rain.

"And the target?"

"If you're referring to the Right Honourable Sir Winston Leonard Spencer-Churchill, very much alive. But I see him more as a Viennese waltz type."

Maundsley's shoulders sagged. For the first time, he looked like an old man.

I said: "The police will be here shortly to quickstep you into custody."

Maundsley smirked. "If the police were coming they would be here now. Especially if the information you've just given me about Montez is correct."

That worried me. It could take the blundering Tomkins hours to discover Montez dead in the empty apartment. And when he did there would be nothing there to link Montez with Maundsley. Besides, Maundsley wasn't hanging around with the pigs because he enjoyed their company. This would be a pre-arranged place where he'd meet whoever it was operated the plan B to spring Maundsley to freedom.

Maundsley must have read the thoughts running through my mind.

"You've worked it out," he said. "Help is on the way. My transport to safety. Don't worry, we won't kill you. At least, as long as you don't make a nuisance of yourself. We'll just lock you in here. You can keep the pigs company."

"That will be an improvement on having you about the place."

"Brave words - even if insulting."

"Before you leave, tell me why you wanted Churchill dead."

Maundsley folded his arms tightly across his chest. Stuck his chin out in the aggressive pose he loved photographers to catch.

"Winston Churchill failed the country in its hour of greatest need." His voice cracked with contempt. "Great Britain could so easily have come to an agreement with Herr Hitler. We would have had our Empire and Hitler would have had Europe. Together we would have controlled the world."

"I don't think the United States would agree with you."

"Together Hitler and I would have kept America in her place. Instead the war ruined us. Look at our country now - saddled with debts and most of the Empire gone. Churchill has lived on this occasion, but the time will come when people will see the truth. They will cherish my legacy."

"The only thing people will cherish about you is that you're six feet under and can be long forgotten."

Maundsley smirked again. "Not forgotten. My book will see to that."

He gestured at the bench he'd been sitting on. For the first time, I noticed there was a thick ring binder stuffed with papers.

I looked back at Maundsley. A flash of worry clouded his eyes. He'd realised he shouldn't have mentioned the book. He moved towards it, but he was old and I was young.

I grabbed the folder. He lunged towards me but I held up my hand.

I said: "One more step and this goes as feed for the pigs."

He said: "Give that back to me. It's the only copy of the manuscript."

"Sounds like a collector's item. A rubbish collector's."

I flipped open the binder and read the title page: My Legacy. I turned the page to chapter one. It was entitled: The Morality of Strength.

I read aloud a couple of sample sentences: "When a nation possesses a supreme moral purpose, it is right that it should be the strongest of nations. It should use war and conquest to impose its moral purpose on weaker nations, whatever the cost in human life."

I looked at Maundsley: "So the strong should always beat up the weak. That's your morality, is it?"

"It's like all life - the survival of the fittest," Maundsley drawled.

"And the weak go to the wall - or, if you get your way, to an early grave. Well, I think the world can well do without this part of your legacy."

I grabbed a handful of pages and yanked them from the folder. I tossed them into the pig sty. The porkers fell on them like they hadn't eaten for a week.

"I hope that lot doesn't give them indigestion."

Maundsley stepped forward. "How dare you…"

But I cut him off. "One more step and the whole folder goes in. Even if the pigs have to save some of it for tomorrow's breakfast. Let's see what else we have in here."

I turned some pages at random. Came to a chapter entitled: The Inferior Races.

I read: "The reason the white peoples of the earth are the most prosperous and most educated is because they have advanced furthest in evolution. It follows that black, brown and other races are inferior. Although slavery has now been abolished in most places, it is right that these inferior peoples should be constantly reminded of their lesser role on this earth."

I said: "So that's it - a world of oppressed and oppressors."

"It's how the world has always been."

"No, it's how it has always seemed to people who think they're better than everybody else. So I think we can do without this legacy."

I yanked the pages out of the folder.

"Here, piggies, more lunch," I said.

The porkers fell on the pages like it was their best meal ever. A fat sow snatched a mouthful of paper while two others tugged at the other end of it.

The Tango School Mystery

Maundsley screamed: "You're destroying my life's work."

I turned to another chapter: The Strong Leader.

I read: "Because almost all people are fearful and confused, they need a strong leader. The leader must understand the darkest recesses of his followers' souls. For it is in these places that he will find the fears and nightmares with which he can frighten his followers into obedience."

I said: "You know, I'm beginning to find this book a bit tedious. Not many laughs. And I don't even want to know whodunit. Because I know it's a ratbag like you. I think I know what we'll do with this."

I ripped the folder open and tossed it high over the pigsty. Maundsley rushed forward and tried to catch the pages as they fluttered earthwards. He snatched one out of the air.

The rest sprayed across the sty. The pigs went wild. They grunted. They oinked. They squealed. They raced around grabbing the pages. They cannoned into one another with wet squelching sounds. Pages ripped apart as they fought over them. The clever ones grabbed a mouthful and retreated to a corner to eat them quietly.

Maundsley's face was red with fury. His eyes had misted. He held a single sheet in his hand.

I said: "Which chapter have you rescued there?"

"No chapter," he said.

He handed me the sheet. There were just two words on it: The End.

"The end. It is for you," I said.

"And for you," a voice said behind me.

I spun round.

Captain Wellington Blunt stalked into the hut. He pushed Shirley in front of him. Her hands were bound with a red cord and he was pointing a gun at her head.

Chapter 25

Shirley turned on Blunt with a spark of fire in her eyes.

"Don't push me, whacker. I'd kick you in the balls - if you had any. It's my hands that are tied, not my feet."

I ran towards her. Took her in my arms and kissed her.

Blunt poked the gun into my shoulder and pushed me away.

"What happened?" I asked Shirley.

"I'm sorry, Colin. I went to the tango school after all. I was rootling around, looking for a way in when this bludger turned up. We had a rumble and I thought I'd beat him. But the fat basket has a weight advantage I couldn't top. He got me on the ground and tied my hands."

"Don't call me a fat basket," Blunt snapped.

"Got a sensitive nature have you, Blubberface?" Shirley said.

"I'm going to untie your hands," I said.

"If you do, I'll shoot her," Blunt said.

I gave him a look that would've melted a steel girder. But looks don't stop bullets.

I said: "I thought your normal method of execution was a cut throat. Just like you killed Derek Clapham."

Blunt smirked. "Clapham was no match for a trained soldier."

"Trained for what? Captain Bogbrush, they used to call you."

"That's enough," Maundsley said. "Who is this girl?"

He had stepped towards us. He was looking at Shirl like she was a serving wench who'd strayed into the master's quarters.

"I'm a woman, not a girl. So watch your mouth, Adolf."

Maundsley bridled. "Don't use that revered name as an insult," he said.

"That name is revered about as highly as kangaroo crap," Shirl said.

Maundsley stepped forward and raised his hand to slap Shirley's face. I moved fast, grabbed his arm, yanked it behind him, and forced it up his back. Maundsley yelled in pain. I clamped my left arm around his neck and held him tight.

I glared at Blunt. "Untie Shirley's hands or I'll break the *Führer's* arm," I said.

"I'll shoot you first," Blunt said.

"That will be second. You may have noticed I'm standing behind Maundsley. The bullet will perforate him before it reaches me."

I yanked Maundsley's arm a further inch up his back. He screamed in agony.

"Untie her," he yelled. "Just do it."

Blunt looked confused. His bewildered gaze travelled from Maundsley to his gun. From his gun to me. From me back to Shirley.

He shoved the gun roughly in his jacket pocket and went to work on the knots around Shirley's wrists. The red cord came free and fell to the ground.

Shirl's arm moved like a blur.

Slap!

She hit Blunt on the right cheek. He staggered back and reached for his gun.

I released Maundsley's arm and he moved towards Blunt.

"Leave that," he said. "You're an army officer."

"Retired," I said.

"And useless," Shirley added.

Maundsley snapped: "Report to your commanding officer."

Blunt looked around, confused as though he'd expected a stray field-marshal to have walked into the hut.

"I'm your commanding officer," Maundsley said. There was a note of exasperation in his voice. "Cover these two with your gun. If either of them tries to escape, shoot both of them."

"You're assuming he's loaded the gun with two bullets," I said.

Blunt fumbled the gun out of his pocket. He stood up

straighter. Snapped his feet together.

"Well, man, out with it," Maundsley said.

"I hid in a telephone box round the corner from Churchill's old school. I saw the old man arrive. I couldn't hear much inside the box so went to have a closer look. I thought I heard a rifle shot. But there were a couple of police officers outside the school and they thought it was a motorcycle back-firing. Anyway, Churchill was ushered safely inside the school."

"Nothing else?" Maundsley asked.

Blunt looked at the roof for a bit. Turned back to Maundsley. "Nothing else at the school. As we agreed, I went back to the tango school to rendezvous with Montez, but he didn't show up. Must've been detained elsewhere."

"He was detained in his sniper's apartment being dead," I said. "He shot himself."

"Why should he do that?" Blunt snapped.

"Remorse at his failure?" I suggested.

Maundsley strode towards me. "Be silent. Don't speak like that of a brave soldier." he snarled. He had lost his legacy, but regained his old arrogance.

"Nazi thug, more like," I said. "And you're a political has-been with a strong line in dodgy friends."

"I believe I'm being saved for greater work," he said loftily.

"Like cleaning out the pigs," Shirley said. "And they need it. This place pongs like the VIP suite at a farters' convention."

"Be quiet," Blunt snapped.

Shirley stuck out her tongue at him.

Maundsley said to me: "I don't understand how you found out about Montez."

"I'll tell you, if you answer one question for me."

"I don't see that can do any harm as you'll be dead in ten minutes' time."

Shirley shot me a worried glance. I took her hand and squeezed it gently. She forced a smile.

The Tango School Mystery

I turned back to Maundsley. "Who is Montez really?"

"Ah, you penetrated his guise as a tango teacher from Buenos Aires."

"A genuine Argentine tango teacher wouldn't think Al Costado scored a goal for Argentina in the last World Cup. Even after one lesson, I knew it meant 'move to the side'."

Maundsley cleared his throat like someone about to make an important announcement. "SS Stabsscharführer Conrad Schwarz was Germany's finest war-time sniper. He undertook several missions on the personal orders of Hitler. His speciality was removing individuals who'd become an embarrassment to the Reich. Naturally, as it became clear how the war would end, Schwarz realised his talents would not be appreciated by the advancing allies. He left for South America in April 1945 taking a large quantity of gold bullion with him. He lived on the money until last year, entertaining himself in Buenos Aires' casinos and bordellos."

"When, no doubt, the money ran out."

"And he discreetly passed the word, that he was available to use his skills on selected targets for an appropriate fee. As it happened, I had already decided that this would be the year when Churchill died."

"Why now?"

"Because it is forty years on from the date I first crossed swords with the arch-traitor."

"The 1924 general election - when Mr Churchill roundly defeated you in a democratic vote."

I should have known. Forty years on. It was like some kind of curse. Maundsley had been at Harrow school, just like Churchill. Yet Churchill had become a war winner while Maundsley was just a failed fascist. The truth would have gnawed at him like a rat at a ragbag. Killing Churchill wouldn't be enough for Maundsley. He'd need to do it in a symbolic way. A way that would convince Maundsley's twisted mind that the killing represented divine retribution.

Forty years on. It had caused me a lot of trouble.

I couldn't wait for forty-one and a quieter life.

"But Churchill has dodged your assassination attempt," I said.

"There will be another opportunity - next time successful. And I won't wait another forty years."

"And you had no shame about hiring a Nazi killer."

"The workman is worthy of his hire," Maundsley said complacently. "However, soon after Schwarz arrived in Britain, it was clear the dissolute lifestyle he'd enjoyed in South America had played havoc with his old skills. He needed practice and he needed confidence to shoot at an important target. It seemed the life-sized waxwork of Churchill would fit the bill. That's why I had it borrowed from Louis Tussaud's. I instructed that two other random waxworks should also be taken so that it would look like an ordinary robbery."

"I doubt they'll want the wax Winston back - not with the holes Montez left."

Maundsley waved his hand airily. "Collateral damage is always possible in affairs of this kind."

"So that's what Shirley and I are, is it? Collateral damage."

"I regret that is the case. But you can prolong your life by telling me what gave my plan away."

I said: "A hat box."

Maundsley's eyebrows drew together in a puzzled frown. "I don't understand. Whose hat box?"

"The one in the back of your car. We discovered it belonged to Françoise Dior. The French Nazi who you plan to marry secretly. And, by the way, where is Françoise? Shouldn't she be outside goose-stepping around the farm and singing the Horst Wessel?"

"Françoise has returned to Paris until this little difficulty has been resolved."

"So no wedding bells for you after all."

Maundsley's moustache twitched in irritation.

"If Derek Clapham hadn't suspected your wedding plans, he'd still be alive," I said. "At first, I thought Clapham had been killed by Gervase Pope. He had no reason to like Clapham or you - as you well know. But then I suspected Clapham was trying to blackmail you. He'd seen the same magazine picture of Françoise heading to England that I'd been shown by Shirley. He spotted the box with her wedding togs, as we'd done, and drew his own conclusions. He knew that if news broke that you were marrying a French Nazi, it wouldn't go down well with voters."

I pointed at Blunt. "The big boy here was your killer of choice for that execution."

"I was obeying orders," Blunt shouted.

"Shut up," Maundsley said.

"Blunt was still in the flat when I came in. No doubt he was searching for any evidence Clapham had of your plans to marry Dior secretly. But my arrival spoilt his search and he had to make a rapid exit through the kitchen window. Left a mess on the floor, too."

Maundsley scowled at Blunt. "Bungling idiot," he said.

"But that wasn't the end of the good Captain's duties, was it?" I said. "He also organised the heist of the waxworks. No doubt he thought he was a clever-clogs to nick glamour-pussies like Marilyn Monroe and Yuri Gagarin. After all, if they were among the stolen, who was going to bother about Churchill? But one person was suspicious. Gervase Pope. You had to deal with him before he could make trouble. And you turned to one of your old storm-troopers, Felix Delaunay, to handle that. Convenient, wasn't it, that Felix had his own reasons - the death of his sister - for wanting Gervase six feet under? In his case, it was water rather than earth. But just as well I turned up - although I can't say I really enjoyed taking his place."

"I don't know what you're talking about," Maundsley said.

"Too bad that you persuaded Unity Box-Hartley to supply the ducking stool that Felix used. If she hadn't I wouldn't have tracked down her warehouse and discovered the waxwork of poor old Winston riddled with bullet holes. After all that, it wasn't hard to tie Montez into the plot as your hired gun."

Maundsley nodded thoughtfully. Blunt waved his gun around a bit. He was getting nervous. After all, the old basket was only a soldier in name. Setting up a mobile latrine unit for six hundred beefy soldiers would be no picnic, but it wouldn't compare with going over the top with all guns blazing.

Finally Maundsley spoke. "So there have been errors in my organisation at every stage."

"You can't get the help these days," I said.

"Perhaps not," Maundsley said. "But I have got the help to kill you."

He turned to Blunt. "Put two bullets into each of them. One in the head, one in the heart."

Shirley threw her arms around me. "Colin…" she cried.

I gave Maundsley what I hoped was my most contemptuous look. "Do you want some of your legacy book back?"

"What? You fed it to the pigs."

"Not all of it. I'll tell you how to get some of it back in exchange for our lives."

"I won't bargain with you. Not after you destroyed my life's work."

"Suit yourself," I said.

But I knew he couldn't leave it there.

Maundsley looked at Blunt.

Blunt shrugged.

"I saw you throw my book in the air," Maundsley said.

"But you didn't see where it all landed," I said.

"What?"

Maundsley's head swung back and forth looking for the

remains of his book.

I pointed to the electricity duct that came into the room and carried the cable to the lights.

"Some of the pages became lodged on top of the duct," I said.

Maundsley looked up. He rushed to the wall at the edge of the pigsty and craned his neck.

"There must be thirty or forty pages up there. I think they're the pages about my Action Plan for Britain. We must save them. Blunt, climb up there and bring down those pages."

"I can't do that," Blunt said. "I'm covering these two with the gun. You've just ordered me to shoot them."

"I'm countermanding that order. For the time being. The new order is to rescue the pages."

"I don't like to go into the sty. Some of those pigs are feral. Besides, there's crap all over the floor."

"Why should that hold any fears for the former commander of a latrine unit?" Maundsley snapped. "Get in there and rescue those pages. History is depending on you. Use that ladder propped in the corner."

Blunt looked like a fat little boy who'd just been told he wouldn't be allowed any sweets for a week. He handed the gun to Maundsley and stomped off to the corner to get the ladder.

Maundsley watched him. I gave Shirl's hand a little tug and nodded towards the door. We edged down the wall. But Maundsley turned back to us.

"Stay where you are or I fire," he said.

We froze.

Shirley whispered: "What now, my hero?"

"Wait and watch."

Blunt collected the ladder. It was a heavy item and he slung it over his shoulder. He clumped over to the pigsty and pushed open the gate. He tiptoed through the enclosure avoiding the piles of pig poo. He propped the ladder up against the duct close to the wedged papers.

"Climb up," Maundsley ordered.

Blunt shot him a look like he wished a Tiger tank would roll over him. He grabbed both sides of the ladder and climbed. The ladder creaked and strained under his weight. Half way up, Blunt looked down.

"I don't like heights," he said to Maundsley.

"Just get up there and rescue my book - what's left of it."

Blunt climbed on like he was Sir Edmund Hillary making the final perilous steps to the summit of Everest.

Maundsley's eyes focused on Blunt. I nudged Shirl and nodded towards the pigsty. Blunt had left the gate open as I knew he'd have to when he carried the heavy ladder through. Already a couple of hefty porkers had come through and were making their bid for freedom.

Blunt arrived at the top of the ladder. He reached over and pulled the sheaf of papers from where it was wedged behind the duct.

Now he had to climb down holding the ladder with only one hand. He had the papers in the other one.

I whispered to Shirley: "When I shout, scream like you're in the back row of the flicks and a dirty old man in a mac has just sat down beside you and put his hand up your skirt."

"Kinky," Shirl whispered. But she grinned.

Blunt was half way down the ladder. He took one foot off and dangled it over the next rung down.

I glanced at the pigsty gate. Half a dozen sows had made their way through now.

I yelled: "Pigs at ten o'clock."

Shirl screamed.

"*Yeeeeoowwwww.*"

"Louder," I whispered.

"*Yeeeeeeeeeeeeeooowwwwwwwwwwwwww.*"

Blunt's head snapped in our direction. He let go of the ladder. His body twisted backwards through an arc Euclid would have been proud of. The papers in Blunt's hand flew out and scattered across the sty. He scrabbled for a hold on the ladder. And then he fell. Like a ten-ton bomb crashing to earth.

Squelch.

It was a soft landing. But not the kind he was hoping for.

Splodge.

"I'm in the shit," he screamed.

"Too right," I yelled.

Maundsley watched Blunt's fall. His eyes followed the scattering papers like a child's might follow snowflakes. He seemed frozen to the spot, too horrified by the sight to move.

But that didn't last for long.

Because when Blunt's body hit the ground, it sent the pigs into a panic.

Some squealed like a choir of off-pitch sopranos.

Some grunted like a taproom of saloon bar bores.

Some oinked like a street full of jammed motorbuses.

The noises filled the hut and echoed off the metal roof.

And then they rushed from the pigsty. They jammed together and fought one another to get through the gate.

Shirley and I pressed ourselves against the wall. But Maundsley rushed towards the sty to save his papers.

Big mistake.

The exodus of stampeding pigs hit him like a tidal wave of bacon on the hoof.

He fell backwards. The gun fired but the shot went wild and blew a hole in the roof. It sent the pigs into a fury.

And then the porkers were all over him.

They snuffled. They snaffled. They sniffled. They snivelled.

They chomped. And they chewed.

Bones crunched and flesh squelched.

Vital organs popped. Body fluids flushed across the floor.

The pigs foraged. And they ferreted.

Maundsley's body had disappeared beneath the starving

porkers.

But then an arm appeared. Stiff and erect above the pigs' surging bodies. Maundsley was giving his last Nazi salute. His hand flopped over, his elbow bent, and the arm sank from sight as more feasting pigs piled in.

The pigs' jaws opened and shut with wet slapping sounds as they fought for their share.

In the pigsty, Blunt had scrambled to his feet and climbed the ladder to escape the pigs that snuffled around him.

Shirley and I edged our way swiftly along the wall away from the horror. We reached the door. We opened it, slipped through and slammed it behind us.

Behind the door, we heard a long high-pitched scream.

Shirley threw her arms around me and I held her tight. She was shaking and I could feel her heart pounding like a distant aborigine's drum.

"Are we safe?" she asked.

"Yes," I said. "But I'll tell you one thing for certain."

"What's that?"

"I'll never eat another bacon sandwich again."

Frank Figgis lit up the first Woodbine since he'd given up extra strong peppermints.

He said: "I had to give up the mints on health grounds. They were making me fat."

I said: "If I could see through the smoke, I'd be happy to confirm that."

It was later that afternoon. We were in Figgis's office. First copies of the Night Final had just come up from the machine room. The splash headline read:

CHRONICLE FOILS CHURCHILL ASSASSIN

Further down the page another screamer read:

FASCIST LEADER EATEN BY PIGS

It described how, by the time the cops arrived, there wasn't enough of Maundsley left to make a decent sandwich. Blunt had escaped the ravenous porkers by clinging to the ladder. He'd had to be hosed down by the cops with cold water and industrial detergent before they could put handcuffs on him and load him into a black Maria.

Figgis said: "What gets my goat is that the nationals will have the story as well."

I said: "It could hardly be avoided after the cops arrived on the scene. We rang them from Maundsley's house. But only the *Chronicle* has my eye-witness account."

I'd written a separate piece for an inside page about Unity Box-Hartley. She'd been arrested and was being questioned about her connection with a number of crimes, including attempted murder.

Figgis said: "After that business with the pigs, I'll never be able to look a sausage in the face again."

"But at least you'll be able to hold your head up with His Holiness," I said. "Was he pleased to be reunited with his missing brother?"

"I don't know about pleased. He's taken the afternoon off to play golf."

"Rather than stay in the office to thank a reporter who saved his brother's life at a risk to his own."

"His Holiness said he wanted to improve on his handicap."

"Which handicap would that be? His failure to act like a normal human being? Has he explained why he disappeared like a phantom in the night when you told him we needed the name of the girl who died when Gervase was driving the car?"

"In a manner of speaking."

"I suppose that beats a manner of grunting."

"He told me he was worried that Delaunay might come after him as well - given that it was a fault in his car that caused the accident. His Holiness thought he'd better find somewhere safe to hide until Felix was out of the way."

"Felix is out of the way permanently now, thanks to brother Gervase whacking him with the ducking stool."

"Bad business," Figgis said.

"No contest there. But I think we'll have to let that matter rest. When Gervase is interviewed by the police, he'll just claim the ducking stool hit Felix by accident. They'd never get the evidence to convict, even with my testimony. I'd just be attacked by Gervase's brief as a journalist in search of a story."

Figgis sucked on his fag and blew out the smoke. He sighed contentedly.

He said: "We had a message an hour ago."

"What kind of message?"

"This kind of message."

He picked up a sheet of paper from his in-tray and handed it to me. I read it and looked at Figgis in astonishment.

"Well, I wasn't expecting that to happen," I said.

Chapter 26

The big door with the brass knocker was opened by a butler wearing a black tailcoat.

He looked closely at us and said: "Mr Crampton? Miss Goldsmith?"

We nodded.

It was exactly a week after I'd tussled with Montez as he'd tried to shoot Winston Churchill. A week since Figgis had handed me a piece of paper with a message - and an invitation.

The butler said: "Come this way. You are expected."

We stepped inside number 28 Hyde Park Gate, London. The hallway was an impressive room hung with paintings and lit by a crystal chandelier. It was furnished with an elaborate hat stand and a table which held a large pile of newspapers and letters.

The butler led us down a passage and opened a door. He held the door open and announced us as we walked in: "Mr Colin Crampton and Miss Shirley Goldsmith, Sir Winston."

Churchill was sitting in an armchair on the far side of the room. He had a cigar lodged in his left hand. He was wearing a blue velvet siren suit and had a pair of half-moon glasses balanced on the end of his nose. He'd been reading a copy of *The Times*.

He rested his cigar in an ashtray, flung off his glasses, and levered himself to his feet as we walked across the room.

His face broke into a beaming smile. He looked like a large baby who'd just had his tummy tickled.

He said: "I hope you will excuse my peremptory summons through a message to your newspaper, but I wanted to meet the second most intrepid journalist our great Empire has ever produced."

"The second most?" I said.

"With unbecoming modesty I am granting myself the first prize. I was a journalist, too, before I entered the rough and tempestuous world of politics. In pursuit of the story, as I believe you call it these days, I was shot at in Cuba and captured by enemy forces in South Africa."

"But you escaped with your life."

"As did you, I am delighted to see."

He turned to Shirley and offered his hand.

She shook it and said: "Jeez. Never thought I'd meet you. You're not as fat as I'd expected."

A scowl appeared on Churchill's face, but it disappeared and he grinned. It was like watching a cloud pass briefly across the sun.

"Everybody thinks I'm not as fat as they expected," he growled. "Including me."

He gestured towards a sofa and we sat down.

He said: "I'm told that you often take a modest refreshment of gin and tonic. It is a beverage which has cheered me more than once, but I believe this occasion calls for the finest champagne."

As if he'd heard the cue, the butler entered with a silver salver. It held an ice bucket with an opened bottle of *Pol Roger* and three champagne flutes. He put the salver on a table, poured three glasses, and handed two to Shirley and me.

"What shall we drink to?" Churchill asked.

"Death to our enemies?" I suggested.

"In a spirit of magnanimity, let us make it defeat," he said.

"Those old fascists didn't seem too magnanimous when they had us cornered and were seconds from finishing us off," Shirley said.

Churchill made a deep rumbling sound. It seemed to come from the depths of his chest. "In that case, I toast your courage and your continuing good health."

"And we yours," I said.

We hoisted our glasses and drank.

"And now I want you to tell me everything that happened," he said. "Clemmie loves me dearly but these days she allows me so little excitement."

And so we told him everything.

He sat in his chair, sipped his champagne, and puffed his cigar. Sometimes he smiled. Sometimes he frowned. Sometimes he growled as though recalling some hideous horror from the past.

At last we finished our story.

"Remarkable," he said. "And now I have something for you."

There was a bell on the table next to his chair and he rang it.

The door opened and the butler reappeared carrying a book. He crossed the room and handed the book to me.

It was a copy of *My Early Life*, the memoirs Churchill had written about his formative years.

"Thank you," I said.

Churchill said: "Open the book at the title page and you will see that it is a gift for both of you."

I opened the book. In what he used to call "my own paw", he'd written: "To Colin Crampton and Shirley Goldsmith. For Courage. 'None but the Brave deserve the Fair'."

Churchill grinned, but apprehensively. "I hope you both will not regard my use of a quotation from John Dryden as presumptuous."

"No, sir," we said together.

He turned to Shirley with a little bow of his head. "Mr Dryden neglected to mention that sometimes the fair are the brave."

"I expect the old codger had too much on his mind," Shirley said.

Churchill gave a throaty chuckle. "No doubt you're right."

He turned towards me. "Do you think you will ever write the memoirs of your own early life?"

"I haven't ever thought about that," I said.

"If you do, you will need some new stories with which to

embellish the old. Such as the one I am about to offer as a final parting gift and a thank you."

I smiled. "I understand the terms of trade. This is for my memoirs, not my newspaper."

Churchill grinned. "You have my point exactly, Mr Crampton. Very well, then. A few weeks ago, a gentleman came to see me. He is one of those men who work in the shadows and whose sombre duty it is to oversee the security of our nation. He told me that a known Nazi, one SS Stabsscharführer Conrad Schwarz, who'd been hiding in Buenos Aires since the end of the war, had smuggled himself into Britain. Naturally, this gentleman was puzzled that one of our enemies, a man who has never renounced the foul creed he served, should have risked his freedom and possibly his life to come to our shores."

"If this gentleman knew Schwarz was here, why didn't he have him arrested?" I asked.

Churchill blew on the end of his cigar to revive the tip. "For some time, this gentleman had been concerned that the forces of fascism had been organising underground in our country. We live in troubled times. The government has been undermined by scandals."

"Such as the Profumo affair."

"Yes, such as that… affair," Churchill said. "In such a febrile climate, public opinion is fickle. It seeks a strong man, even if that strong man's views are, judged against the touchstone of common humanity, repellent and repulsive. He believed that undercover forces were planning an event, an outrage, something that would crystallise the genuine unease of so many of our people about the way our affairs have been conducted of late."

"*A coup d'état?*" I asked

"Nothing so crude," Churchill said. "All that is needed is a terrible event, a cataclysm, which makes people fearful for the future. It is when fear strikes that ordinary decent folk are most susceptible to sacrifice their liberty."

"But as Benjamin Franklin noted, those who give up liberty to purchase temporary safety deserve neither," I said.

Churchill nodded and sucked at his cigar. "You are well read, young man. In any event, the gentleman believed that the fascists were planning an outrage that would turn public opinion towards them. He had in mind the example of the Reichstag fire in 1933, when I was warning the world about Nazis, but nobody would listen."

"Before my time," Shirley said.

"Hitler used the Reichstag fire as an excuse to clamp down on civil liberties in Germany," I said.

"You are correct," Churchill growled. "But he was not the first to use a manufactured outrage as a reason for persecution. In the fourth century the enemies of the Christians burnt the palace of the Roman emperor Diocletian. They blamed the fire on the Christians. Their persecution which followed was cruel and terrible. The gentleman believed the fascists had learnt their history too well and were planning a similar outrage. He had evidence which suggested they planned to assassinate me."

"I bet that bludger Maundsley was behind it all," Shirley said.

Churchill grinned. "The gentleman had information that several were involved in the plot and that Schwarz, a skilled sniper, would be the instrument of execution. But he believed more were involved and he had a plan to collect the evidence so that he could convict as many as possible - and cauterise the threat to our liberties for which we have fought so long and so hard. I was asked whether I would be prepared to play a part in this plan. Naturally, I agreed."

I leaned forward. "Are you saying that your visit to the Misses Thompson school was planned as a set-up?"

"A set-up. The Americans have such a colourful way with our language. I approve. But, to answer your question, yes. We seemingly fed information accidentally through the man Potter.

Of course, the main players were carefully monitored in the days leading up to the visit. The plan was to arrest all the participants at the critical moment. But it is always the unexpected which undermines even the best laid plans. We did not expect Schwarz to shoot Potter. After he'd done so, he went to ground. The watchers could not find him. The gentleman came back to me crestfallen. He said we would have to abandon the plan, but I insisted we continue. I said that Schwarz would show himself at the critical moment. Once he was arrested, the fascists' whole conspiracy would collapse like a house of cards and the security forces could arrest them at leisure."

"But it didn't work out like that," I said.

"No, it did not. There was an error in communication which meant the empty flat where Schwarz lurked with his rifle was not searched. But thanks to your timely intervention, my funeral will not yet take place. I am very much obliged to you, Mr Crampton. And to you, Miss Goldsmith."

Churchill shifted uncomfortably on his chair. He levered himself up.

"And now, I fear, it is time for my afternoon nap. Once again, my profound thanks to you both. I wish you a very good day."

The door opened and the butler came in. Churchill took his arm and walked slowly from the room.

Frank Figgis trotted across the newsroom and stopped by my desk.

It was nine o'clock on the day after my meeting with Churchill. The newsroom was gearing up for the first deadline of the day.

"Well?" Figgis said.

"Well, what?" I said.

"Well, what did Sir Winston say to you yesterday?"

"Just thanked me for my help."

"Is there a story in it?"

"I wouldn't think so. He was talking about Diocletian most

of the time."

"Who?"

"Nobody you know."

"So you haven't got any copy for me?" Figgis said.

"Not at the moment."

"Then it's just as well that I've got this for you."

He handed me a sheet of paper.

"Today's list at Hove Magistrates' Court," he said.

I glanced down it.

"The biggest thing here is the shoplifting of a pair of knickers from Debenham's."

"That's what I thought. But at least there won't be anything about stolen waxworks from Louis Tussaud's. They got back Marilyn Monroe and Winston Churchill with a few bullet holes in him, didn't they?"

"Yes, but the cops never traced Yuri Gagarin, the first man to circle the earth in space."

"I don't suppose you'll hear any more about that," Figgis said.

He turned and trotted back to his office.

But Figgis was wrong about the waxwork.

Epilogue

Shirley looped her arm through mine, cuddled closer, and said: "I just love these winter markets."

It was Christmas Eve, three months after our meeting with Winston Churchill. We were strolling around Brighton's London Road market. The air was crisp and cold. A few lazy snowflakes were falling. A busker with an accordion was playing *Frosty the Snowman*.

Shirley was wrapped up warm in a fake fur coat. Her blonde hair cascaded from a Cossack-style matching hat. The lights from the market stalls made her face seem luminous and her blue eyes shone with happiness. She looked more beautiful than I'd ever seen her.

I said: "If they ever got round to making a film of that book *Dr Zhivago*, you'd be great in the part of Lara Antipova."

She nudged me in the ribs. "You're crazy, reporter boy."

But I could tell she'd enjoyed the compliment.

I said: "This is the first time we'll have been able to spend the whole of Christmas together."

"Yeah! No more stories to cover until the New Year."

"Unless something big breaks."

"Don't even think about it."

I raised my hands in surrender. "I'm not, I promise."

We passed a stall loaded with turkeys and geese.

I said: "I wonder how Captain Wellington Blunt will enjoy his first Christmas in prison as a lifer."

"Not a lot, I hope," Shirley said. "And that Unity Box-Hartley won't have much fun in Holloway, either."

"They got what they deserved," I said. "But it's Dolores Esteban I feel sorry for. She was forced into helping Montez. He told her that her old Ma and Pa back in Buenos Aires could have a difficult time if she didn't play ball by giving him cover."

"As her partner in the Tango Academy?"

"She was scared witless by the Nazi - especially after she discovered his reputation. When the cops searched the office at the academy they found three sniper's rifles and enough ammunition to gun down a regiment. No wonder the office door was always locked."

Shirley said: "At least, now she can rebuild her business free from the monster."

I nodded. "Perhaps we should take some tango dancing lessons there."

Shirley's hair flicked from side to side as she shook her head. "Count me out, buster. I'm a twist girl. If it's a contest between Dolores and Chubby Checker, I'll choose Chubby every time."

I shrugged. "You win," I said.

"I usually do."

We passed a stall selling Christmas decorations. There were baubles and tinsel and streamers to hang from the Christmas tree. They sparkled in the lights.

Shirley said: "Seeing those decorations reminds me. I think we deserve some Christmas candles to put in the window. I think I saw a stall selling them on the other side of the market."

We jostled through the crowds. The stall was one I'd not seen before. It was run by a small man with a pencil moustache and a squint in his left eye. He was bundled up in an anorak and had a scarf wrapped around the lower part of his face. A light covering of snowflakes had gathered on the top of his flat cap.

I said: "He looks like he's dressed for robbing a bank rather than selling candles."

We threaded our way through shoppers towards the stall.

Shirley picked up one of the candles: "Hey, Colin, look at these. They're really cute. They're made in the shape of little space rockets."

I took a closer look. Shirl was right. The candle's wick came out of the rocket's nose cone.

The stall-holder sauntered towards us. "A tanner each," he said. "Or you can have three for one and threepence."

"We'll take three," Shirley said.

The stall-holder reached for a paper bag and put the candles inside it. He handed the bag to Shirley.

I said: "I've never seen these before. Where do they come from?"

The stall-holder squinted at me. "Couldn't say, guv'nor."

"You must have some idea."

"All I know is that my normal candle supplier told me he'd come into an unexpected supply of wax and could let me have them cheap."

"Well I think they're out of this world," Shirley said.

I thought about the Tussaud's waxwork of Yuri Gagarin. The cops hadn't recovered it. Now never would.

"Out of this world," I said. "Yes, I suppose that's not a bad way to describe them."

Read more Crampton of the Chronicle stories at:

www.colincrampton.com

Acknowledgements

Bringing out a book involves a lot of work by a lot of people. So, first, an enormous thank you to Barney Skinner who formatted the book for publication and designed the fantastic cover. Thanks also to Frank Duffy who brought to life the main characters from the Crampton of the Chronicle series in her illustrations. You can see them on the Colin Crampton website at www.colincrampton.com.

I'd like to say a very special thank you for the hard work of those members of the Crampton of the Chronicle Advanced Team who read the manuscript, and made helpful comments and corrections. So thanks to (in alphabetical order) Jaquie Fallon, Andrew Grand, Jenny Jones, Doc Kelley, Andy Mayes, Christopher Roden and Chris Youett. Any errors that remain are mine and mine alone!

Finally, a big thank you to all my readers for choosing to read Colin Crampton's adventures.

For more Crampton of the Chronicle adventures, visit www.colincrampton.com.

About Peter Bartram

Peter Bartram brings years of experience as a journalist to his Crampton of the Chronicle crime mystery series. His novels are fast-paced and humorous - the action is matched by the laughs. The books feature a host of colourful characters as befits stories set in Brighton, one of Britain's most trend-setting towns.

Peter began his career as a reporter on a local weekly newspaper before working as a newspaper and magazine editor in London and finally becoming freelance. He has done most things in journalism from door-stepping for quotes to writing serious editorials. He's pursued stories in locations as diverse as 700-feet down a coal mine and a courtier's chambers at Buckingham Palace. Peter wrote 21 non-fiction books, including five ghost-written, in areas such as biography, current affairs and how-to titles, before turning to crime – and penning the Crampton of the Chronicle series.

Follow Peter Bartram on Facebook at:
www.facebook.com/peterbartramauthor
Follow Peter Bartram on Twitter at:
@PeterFBartram

A message from Peter Bartram

Thank you for reading The Tango School Mystery. I hope you have enjoyed reading it as much as I enjoyed writing it. If you have a few moments to add a short review on Amazon, Goodreads or Apple iTunes Store, I would be very grateful. Reviews are important feedback for authors and I truly appreciate every one. If you would like news of further Crampton of the Chronicle stories, please visit my website.

More great books from Peter Bartram…

HEADLINE MURDER

When the owner of a miniature golf course goes missing, ace crime reporter Colin Crampton uncovers the dark secrets of a 22-year-old murder.

STOP PRESS MURDER

The murder of a night watchman and the theft of a saucy film of a nude woman bathing set Colin off on a madcap investigation with a stunning surprise ending.

FRONT PAGE MURDER

Archie Flowerdew is sentenced to hang for killing rival artist Percy Despart. Archie's niece Tammy believes he's innocent and convinces Colin to take up the case. Trouble is, the more Colin investigates, the more it looks like Archie is guilty…

MURDER FROM THE NEWSDESK

Seven short stories featuring Colin Crampton - download free from Amazon.